A JOURNEY TO WHOLENESS

Intimately involving God through prayer for resolution and healing

Richard D. Smith, PhD

A Journey to Wholeness:

Intimately involving God through prayer for resolution and healing.

Copyright © 2005 by Richard D. Smith

All rights reserved. Written permission must be secured from the author to use or reproduce any part of this booklet, except for brief quotations in critical reviews or articles.

Unless otherwise indicated, Scripture quotations are from the Holy Bible: New International Versions. Copyright 1973, 1978, 1984 by the International Bible Society. Scripture identified **GNB** are from the Good News Bible: The Bible in Today's English Version, copyright 1966, 1971, 1976 by the American Bible Society. Scripture identified **NAS** are from the New American Standard Bible. Copyright 1960, 1963, 1968, 1971, 1972, 1973, 1975, 1977 by The Lockman Foundation. Scripture identified **NKJV** are from The Holy Bible, New King James Version, copyright 1982, Thomas Nelson, Inc Nashville, Tennessee. Scripture identified **RSV** are from Revised Standard Version. Copyright 1946, 1952, 1971 by the National Council of the Churches of Christ in the United States of America.

The poem "Transformed" is used with the permission of the author and is from the book *From the Heart: Wounded and Healed* by D.E. Wiering (Bland VA: Cross Ministries, Inc., 2004).

In essence, the events related here are true. However, names have been changed and some details have been altered to protect the privacy of the persons involved.

Published by Cross Ministries, Inc.

Library of Congress Control Number: 2005902420

Smith, Richard D., 1938 –

A journey to Wholeness: Intimately involving God through prayer for resolution and healing / Richard D. Smith
Includes bibliographical references
   1. Prayer counseling – Christianity – Pastoral counseling.
   2. Prayer – Counseling – Therapy – Psychology.
   3. Prayer guidelines – Sin.
   4. Forgiveness – giving – receiving. I. Title.

ISBN 0-9673142-1-6

Printed in the United States of America by

Morris Publishing - 3212 East Highway 30 - Kearney, NE 68847

Acknowledgments

I am grateful for the comments and suggestions that people have made to improve this book. Tanja Poppek and Connie, my wife, had insightful comments, and suggestions. Together they reorganized the chapters in a way that better presents the material. Becca Johnson helped in the formatting.

Finally, my deepest gratitude goes to those many men and women who trusted Connie and me enough to share their lives. It is not easy to allow the stark light of reality to shine on one's life and expose the contents.

Naturally, any lack of clarity or confusion is purely my fault.

Table of Contents

Acknowledgements		*iii*
Poem: "Transformed"		*ix*
Forward - Dr. Gary Waller		*xi*
Preface		*xiii*
1	Rethinking the Birth of Counseling	*1*

PART ONE The Source of Resolution

2	Counseling: Past and Present	*13*
3	Effective Prayer	*38*
4	Counseling and/or Prayer	*51*

PART TWO The Basis of Resolution

5	Law & Grace	*70*
6	The Reality of Sin	*84*
7	Implications from the Law	*105*
8	Christ's Sacrifice	*115*

Table of Contents

PART THREE The Essentials for Resolution

9	The Father/Child Connection	*124*
10	Jesus and Holy Spirit's Participation	*139*
11	Satan's Opposition	*156*
12	The Priestly Role	*165*
13	Forgiveness: A Key	*183*

PART FOUR Hindrances to Resolution

14	Misconceptions About the Way	*210*
15	Misconceptions About God	*216*
16	Misconceptions About Forgiveness	*224*

PART FIVE The Procedure for Resolution

17	Counseling Considerations	*240*
18	General Checklist	*262*
19	Putting it all Together	*271*
20	Some Emotional Responses	*296*
21	After Resolution	*305*

22	Conclusion	*321*
	Bibliography	325

Transformed

I was worried and depressed
    Not acquainted with the reasons.
Into myself I had regressed
    Barely cognizant of the seasons.

Are you not a Christian? You ask.
    Yes, I have been all my life.
But at times we must take off the mask
    Which covers the chaos and strife.

As Christians we're not immune
    To the afflictions here on earth.
And it's not enough to just commune
    With Jesus after your rebirth.

To my Heavenly Father I went
    To inquire about the source of the pain.
Two counselors to guide me He sent
    Who led me from the gloom and the rain.

With my Heavenly Father's protection
    And my counselors to help me through
I had a right to make accusations
    For He was pointing His finger too.

After accusing came forgiveness
    Oh, what a cleansing release!
With prayer, guidance and assurance
    I now face life with so much ease.

                              D. Wiering

❧ Foreword ☙

JoAnn came into my office with a story not unlike that of many others. We chatted but I mostly listened. I listened as she unburdened her soul—as she told her story of pain and abuse and neglect and sorrow. Having been trained as a pastor and a counselor I was deeply committed to helping her. But this time I had a new tool—a new skill. This time I had the added benefit of prayer counseling.

This is a book about counseling, but it is more than that. It is a book that seeks to answer the question: What is God's role in the healing process? It is not only a text or a how-to book—it is a book that lives and breathes the life and commitment of Richard and Connie Smith. They spent years of their lives working in world areas, seeking to be instruments of healing in a dark, lonely, lost world. Out of that context they discovered that some of the "tried and true" methods didn't work. It was then that God led them to discover the power of prayer.

I first met Richard and Connie Smith while I was pastoring a small evangelical church in Western Washington. I had heard about them for months from one of the men in my accountability/growth group. He talked about how they had helped him and his family in many ways. He discussed with me a concept of prayer that was deeper than any I had encountered. I was intrigued; so when the Smiths came to town to present a *Prayer Counseling Seminar* I went to see what it was about. I was a bit skeptical as one might imagine, after all I had been very successful and God had used me for years. How could there be a revolutionary technique out

Foreword

there that I didn't know about? And after all, I was a Christian counselor and I did pray for my clients.

Immediately I found a kinship of spirit with Richard and Connie. Unlike many who teach "Christian Counseling" programs, they were not ready to throw all counseling techniques out the window. Rather, they added yet another level, a deeper level, a spiritual level.

As a pastor and later with my own counseling practice I had always used prayer as an entry point and a concluding point. I prayed for my clients in my own personal devotional time. But, I had never seen prayer as curative—as "the" counseling technique that could provide the healing needed. Richard believes that you cannot separate counseling and prayer into separate activities. "One cannot exist/function without the benefits of the other." The individual and the specific issues determine the approaches needed. Also, the way that prayers are structured is critical to the approach.

This resource goes beyond theory to practice. Richard and Connie are intensely practical. Never allowing issues to stay theoretical, they constantly weave theory and practice into the warp and woof of daily experience. The stories charm and inspire. The examples teach. Most of all huge human issues are dealt with in wise and sane ways.

Richard's intent is to call those in the helping professions to see the value of directed specific prayer in helping people overcome debilitating life issues. This book provides yet one more tool to help those who seek to be ministering agents of grace in a hurting and dying world. Richard and Connie Smith have added a significant volume to the Christian Counseling library. May its impact be widely felt.

Dr. Gary Waller, D Min
Northwest Nazarene University

❧ PREFACE ☙

Prayer that Touches Eternity

Why is there a need for yet another book on prayer or counseling? What will this book contribute that others have not already said?

Connie and I spent time in Prayer and Resolution Counseling with John, an actor and a graduate of Yale. John is an intellectual and needs to get to the heart of issues. His question was: What is Prayer and Resolution Counseling in the light of Christianity?

We can say that it is counseling people in the context of prayer but that is a simplistic answer. If we can talk about Christianity having perspectives, for example, Pietistic, Legalistic, Formalistic, then Prayer and Resolution Counseling is a form of "Transactional Christianity." By that, I mean that Prayer and Resolution Counseling emphasizes the legality of our prayers based on God's system.

Preface

Old Testament Christianity

New Testament Christianity rests on the foundation of the Old Testament where God dealt with Israel through a series of transactions. The entire system of sacrifice is an example of this. God gave detailed instructions and concise measurements for the temple and all that went into it. He also gave detailed instructions about who could be in the temple, their qualifications, their dress, behavior and limitations.

The system of sacrifice operated at three levels: (1) the Day of Atonement sacrifice that covered the sins of Israel for the past year; (2) the daily sacrifices that covered the daily sins of Israel and (3) the sacrifices required when individuals came to the temple for their personal needs— not always because of sin.

In the prayer of salvation, there is a general blanket of forgiveness given to us because Jesus became a curse for us so we do not carry that curse on ourselves. That is what SIN is about and that is what was foreshadowed in the sacrifice on the Day of Atonement.

Jesus also handled the daily sacrifices that were given. I John 1:9 refers to this daily sacrifice. His sacrifice is always available to cover our on-going sins. This is one reason why Christians can sin and yet still be saved. His sacrifice continues to cover us once we accept his death on our behalves.

There was a third system of sacrifice at work that Christ also handled: the sacrifice for individual needs. People went into the temple and approached the priest. They acknowledged their sin (or need for purification) and the priest saw that a proper sacrifice was made on their behalf.

A Journey to Wholeness

It is at these last two levels of "sin" that Prayer and Resolution Counseling is concerned. These are the sins, or their consequences, that cause us to live defeated lives.

Psychology or Prayer?

Psychological and spiritual reality are not that far apart when it comes to uncovering the surface issues. However, they are often far apart when it comes to understanding the deeper issues and the way to resolution.

Psychologically, after a man has raped a woman, she will feel dirty and often she will feel guilt. To a certain extent, she will feel owned by her attacker and there will be other harmful, long lasting, effects.

Spiritually, she will have been defiled and will be spiritually connected to her attacker as "one." Often she will carry the burden that somehow, she was at fault and usually, her rape will affect her relations with her husband if she is married.

Just a cognitive approach, to create awareness and understanding, is not enough to bring resolution and healing. We must involve God whenever strong negative or harmful emotions are involved. We help such a woman to accuse and forgive her attacker: that is a transaction. We must free her from the false guilt she has carried: that is a transaction. We must guide her in receiving cleansing from the spiritual defilement that happened through her rape: that is a transaction. Her attacker created unholy bonds of "oneness" with her and God must break that oneness between them: that is a transaction.

Preface

I have not seen general prayers handle such specific needs. When a general prayer is used, or when the woman has received cognitive counseling so that now she "knows and understands," then all she can hope for is life as a survivor and with the ability to cope.

After Christ came and died at the cross, did God suddenly shift from the specific to the general? Did he give us one picture in the Old Testament and another in this Age of Grace? I do not believe so.

To be the perfect sacrifice for us, all Christ needed to do was die and fulfill the Old Testament system. Instead, he also suffered physically, emotionally and psychologically. Why was this necessary? His death handled the sin issue but his further suffering covers the on-going effects of sin. For the woman, it was for her cleansing: Jesus knows what it feels like to have people look on our nakedness. She can now forgive: Jesus died and is willing to cover even her attacker's sin. (If that person repents and seeks forgiveness, otherwise, "*Vengeance is mine, I will repay says the Lord*" (Romans 12:19b RSV.))

I cannot separate counseling and prayer into separate activities. One cannot exist or function without the benefits of the other. The individual and the specific issues should determine our approach and our prayer structure. Depending on the issues, there are different kinds of prayer for resolution. One counseling approach may be more useful than another depending on the issues and the individual. Some reject most or all counseling methods and some reject prayer in counseling—except as a spiritual placebo—and accept only counseling approaches.

The answer is not either counseling or prayer but both. Otherwise, it is like having the equation A + B + C = D but never allowing us to have the 'C' and the 'D' (for

A Journey to Wholeness

you must have at least one of these filled in to get the answer).

When we put the "God factor" in, however, we must do it on God's terms. We must see the issues from his perspective and with awareness bring our requests to him in a way he can answer.

My purpose is to stimulate and expand our understanding of the factors in prayer that are significant. God deals in specifics, not generalities.

I am hitting the high spots of Prayer and Resolution Counseling in this book. I could not include all the details and ramifications that come when sexual sin occurs, when occult sins happens, when there is rebellion or harmful words of power.

I hope to impress on my readers that God through Christ has left nothing out. He told us that life should be a blessing and that means without the load of sin consequences that many Christians carry. If we want our prayers answered then we must present our prayers to God on his terms. On his terms means that we see things from a spiritual perspective and in the context of eternity.

1

Rethinking the Birth of Counseling

I know of one large church that will not allow the word "counseling" to be used in any approved sense. I find it hard to understand how a church can take such a stand when the scriptures give the name Counselor to the Messiah.

One young woman, helped through Prayer and Resolution Counseling, shared her experience with her fiancée. She asked him to read about Prayer and Resolution Counseling (the Cross Ministries' books) to understand better the wonderful things that had happened to her. Upon hearing the word "counseling," however, he refused to read the books on the basis that counseling was of the Kingdom of Darkness, and demanded she renounce what she had experienced in her healing. Fortunately, she recognized that she could not reject what her heavenly Father had done in her life—she could deny neither herself, her healing, nor her

Rethinking the Birth of Counseling

heavenly Father. Because of this, he broke off their engagement.

Some Christian authors say that we should use only the Bible as our source for counseling hurting people. The Bible has all the answers we need.

My background and training are in linguistics and Bible translation. I believe that the Bible is the inspired word of God. I accept the verbal, plenary inspiration of the scriptures. I do not accept, however, that the Bible contains all available truth. It was written to prepare us to receive the Messiah and to give us *general instructions* on how to live righteous lives. There is much that the scriptures do not talk about or go into detail about: There is little about the origins of demons or the war that took place in heaven except in general terms. There is almost nothing (except for some episodes in the Gospels and Acts) about exorcism and healing. Paul did not explain what he meant when he said some disciples had fallen away. The scriptures do not tell us anything about the background of Mary Magdalene; nor does it tell us why she had seven demons or how Jesus cast them out. The story of creation is an abbreviated account.

God created us with minds and with the ability to discover new things and increase our understanding. If we start on the right premise, from the correct perspective, then new truth comes out and increases our understanding about what the Bible says about old truths. For example, the book of Job talks about the stars singing. Now we know that colors (lights) create sound so that light and sound are connected. This brief comment in the scriptures we understand now in the light of discoveries in science. We needed more information from outside the scriptures to understand the scriptures better. Nothing in our expanding of truth will jeopardize the truths of scripture.

A Journey to Wholeness

There is little in the Bible about our human make-up. The scriptures do not explain the function of dreams (except for historical examples in the Old and New Testaments). There are no details on what happens when we sin (why there are power and consequences of sin). God does not explain how generational sins can pass from one generation to another. Nor does he explain why certain sins can take a long time to dissipate. Why four generations for one sin to dissipate? Why ten generations for another sin to dissipate?

We cannot throw out anthropology, sociology and psychology. If we do so, we throw away valuable tools that can help us understand ourselves, our cultures and our relationships with God and man. Much of the time such tools help us to recognize the distortions that we have that are counter to God's character and standards.

We live in a world that has shaped us from the time we were born and before we were born, according to psychological studies. The world we are in governs our behavior to a certain extent. Unfortunately, often we are unaware of the forces that drive us. Therefore, when we operate unconsciously in less-than-righteous ways, we cannot allow the Holy Spirit access to those parts of our lives. We need tools to help us understand ourselves and we find those tools in anthropology, sociology and psychology.

Now that I have elevated these disciplines to respectability, I must add a warning. These behavioral sciences are models created and shaped by humans. These have distortions but that does not mean we must toss out the baby with the bath water. Many anthropologists do not consider God anything more than a force, if at all. Nor do most anthropologists consider that there is a universal standard of right and wrong.

Sociology has given us the concept of group dynamics. We understand better how space affects human interaction. We value and use statistics to explain project growth and real and potential conflict, just to name a few items. Sociological applications have helped explain church growth or lack of it. Yet again, normally, sociology does not have the relationship between God and man in focus. In the world of politics, the science of sociology can manipulate people. Victory and results are more considerations than right and wrong.

Psychology (psychiatric treatment and counseling included here) has an even more troubled past and this past is what has created the backlash by Christians. Yet again, psychology has given us tools that we must not toss aside because some premise is faulty.

Whenever people think of psychology, they think of Freud. He had some good insights but unfortunately founded on a wrong foundation. We cannot take God out of the picture, as Freud did, and still arrive at undistorted truth.

Sigmund Freud

Sigmund Freud (1856-1939) was a medical doctor trained at the University of Vienna and specialized in neurology (embryology of the nervous system). He is the father of psychology and psychiatry and established the grounds for dream analysis and psychoanalysis. He had a great influence on the development of anthropology and education.[1]

His foundation was faulty from the start since he said there was no God. He felt that religion had evolved as a natural outgrowth of animism. To him, our religious

---

[1] Sigmund Freud, *A General Introduction to Psychoanalysis* (New York: Liveright, 1920).

experiences were nothing more than illusions of the mind. What I find sad about Freud is that his beliefs did not give him much of a foundation for living. Freud had a phobia about death and dying. He was frightened of corpses and could not attend a funeral. He had a mild form of agoraphobia, was a self-proclaimed neurotic and had frequent blackouts.[2]

Despite this, he had some helpful insights. For example, he concluded that many people suffering from nervous disorders were suffering from mental conflicts and neurotic states. The mind could affect the body and this could result in outward physical symptoms of fatigue, insomnia, rash, and so on. (The scriptures mention this tie between the spirit and body but do not elaborate.) As Freud sought to understand more of this connection between the body and the mind, he approached the problem as a materialist. Yet, contrary to this, he got his material via hypnosis and altered states of consciousness. Unfortunately, he also used cocaine for himself and for his patients to enhance their hypnotic states. He used hypnosis to uncover and analyze the early lives of patients. He recognized that the past could affect the present. His therapeutic technique was to have them relive traumatic experiences and they appeared to improve. Often their symptoms resurfaced, however, in different forms.

Later Freud used free association and dream analysis (besides continuing to use hypnosis). To create the right conditions, Freud had the patient comfortably reclining on a couch, in a submissive position, and encouraged the client to share whatever came to mind. He felt that when a person was free to speak freely about anything that his defenses were down.

---

[2] Robert Epstein, "Why Shrinks have so Many Problems," in *Psychology Today* (July/August, 1997), p. 76.

Rethinking the Birth of Counseling

It was through the patient's recall of the emotional experiences which had ultimately been repressed and through the release of dammed-up tensions that the conflict could be resolved and the patient's mental health restored.[3]

Freud did does not consider sin an issue, nor forgiveness or forgiving others. Guilt was recognized but reasoned away when possible. Since God does not exist, there is no standard to violate.

Using free association did not always solve the problems. "*Sometimes the elimination of a symptom was followed by the appearance of new symptoms.*"[4] Because of this, Freud tried dream interpretation as a way into the unconscious and the unconscious mental processes of people. He felt that "*traditionally, the rational side had been overemphasized in accounting for human behavior.*"[5]

We in the church have emphasized the rational, cognitive side, and failed to appreciate the place of the underlying (unconscious) beliefs, emotions and feelings of people. Freud went to dreams as his "gateway to the unconscious" but we have the Holy Spirit to reveal our hidden thoughts and sins:

Search me, O God, and know my heart; test me and know my anxious thoughts. See if there is

---

[3] Louis P. Thorp & Barney Katz, *The Psychology of Abnormal Behavior: A Dynamic Approach* (New York: The Ronald Press, 1948), p. 739.
[4] Ibid
[5] James P. Chaplin & T. S. Krawiec, *Systems and Theories of Psychology* (New York: Holt, Rinehart and Winston, 1960), p. 65.

any offensive way in me, and lead me in the way everlasting (Psalm 139:23-24).

Still, Freud had good insight when he pointed out that we bring up issues in dreams, in symbolism, that we are unwilling to face consciously. Also that slips of the tongue were indications of hidden motives.

Freud gave us the terms id, ego and superego as symbolic processes of thought. While there are no biblical counterparts here, he created a useful frame of reference in understanding the why of our behavior.

Id: It is the biological part of the personality. The id is concerned with body wants and, according to Freud, has no notion of right or wrong but is amoral and without a value system. The "pleasure principle" dominates the id. That means that pleasure and its fulfillment are id's aims. He considered the id to be a mass of blind instincts, without any logical organization and with inherent contradictions. Possibly the closest biblical term here would be the "flesh."

Ego: It is the psychological part of the personality. The ego is the part of the id modified by contact with the world. It is logical and ordered. The "reality principle" rules the ego and knows right from wrong. We might say that conscience is here, though Freud would not.

Superego: It is the social part of the personality. The superego is autonomous and detached. The superego is the closest thing to a "conscience" in Freud system.

According to Freud, the Id and superego are in constant conflict with ego. That is not a bad picture of the war between our "wanting to do the good" and our "doing the bad instead" that Paul talks about in the Epistle to the Romans.

He also gave us the concept of "behavioristic determinism:" People are victims of inner forces that have a certain amount of control over them. He also felt that people forget as a way of protection: repressing to keep the memory from reaching the conscious.

Many in secular and Christian counseling, tend to accept in practice Freud's statement,

> *that through recognition of the infantile nature of his trends the patient would automatically realize that they were not adequate for adult life and that he would thus master them.*[6]

Though some Christians reject Freud and his teachings, they endorse what he is saying. They believe that if we bring information to the conscious level, or if we receive teaching, then understanding brings control and release. This is only partly true.

Carl Jung

I mention Carl Jung (1875-1961) here because many Christians refer to him and his teachings. When I first read references to Jung, I thought he must be a Christian but far from it, as we will see. Carl Jung was a medical doctor and pupil of Freud. He is the founder of modern psychology, "Analytical Psychology," in sense of the study of the mind and psyche.

Jung introduced the terms "extroversion" and "introversion" into psychology. He also used the term "complex" to refer to the unconscious feelings and memories that come out of traumatic experiences. These can conflict with conscious ideas and affect thought and behavior.

---

[6] Thorpe & Katz, *The Psychology of Abnormal Behavior*, p. 767.

A Journey to Wholeness

Jung disagreed with Freud on the nature of the unconscious. He felt there were two levels of unconscious: (1) individual (repressed) and (2) collective (inherited). He felt there was a "limitless potential of the unconscious" and that there was a shared knowledge that we all have, a collective unconscious, available from the cosmos. We can tap into this collective unconscious through meditation, hypnosis and channeling.

He created the concept of archetypes of collective unconscious impulses to action with emotion and feeling. Therefore, a Jungian therapist helps "the patient explore the collective unconscious in order to achieve a sense of oneness with the entire human race."[7] The goal or cure is to "integrate and harmonize the personal and collective unconscious . . ."[8]

Conventionally, Jung used dream analysis and psychoanalysis but he had a fascination with the dead and the spirit world. He used the *Tibetan Book of the Dead* and preached to the dead (corpses). He believed in reincarnation and studied the mind for the potential existence of past lives. The proof he looked for was information that people could not have gotten on their own or in their own life experience.

Jung also practiced necromancy (contact with the dead), which included visits with his dead father and grandfather. He had a spirit guide named Philemon, a "wise old man" with a lame foot and "horns and wings."[9] This guide supervised and inspired *Seven Sermons to the Dead*. Jung wrote the book, *Psychology and the Occult*. He used the Ouija board, I Ching and (1911) astrology:

---

[7] Chaplin & Krawiec, Systems and Theories of Psychology, p. 389.
[8] Ibid.
[9] Paul J. Stern, C.G. Jung, *The Haunted Prophet* (New York: Dell, 1976), pp. 122-123.

Rethinking the Birth of Counseling

"My evenings are taken up very largely with astrology . . . to find a clue to the core of psychological truth."[10]

Peter Kramer, M.D. tells of Jung's first patient, Sabina Spielrein, whom Jung diagnosed as schizophrenic and then seduced. He asked his wife to take in Sabina and permitted her to worship him as if he were some sort of guru.

Both Freud and Jung were less-than-perfect in their lives and behavior. Nevertheless, they have had a tremendous influence in the development of psychotherapy, of which there are now more than 250 methods. Freud and Jung have some useful insights but their thinking and perspectives are flawed. Freud because he rejected the spiritual side of man and the existence of God; Jung because he accepted the spiritual side of man and the existence of God but shifted to the "dark side" of the spiritual realm. That still does not mean that we must reject all that they say.

Probably more than any others, these two men laid the foundation for modern psychology and practical counseling. The foundation is faulty but we should not throw away every stone in the foundation. Christian psychology and counseling have patterned themselves after the secular psychology that these men pioneered and, while they have rejected the occult side of Jungian thought and recognized that man is a spiritual being yet they have tended to treat man apart from God as Freud has done. They hold that reason and understanding,

---

[10] Carl G. Jung, *Psychology and the Occult*, translated by R. F. C. Hull (Princeton: Princeton University Press, 1977), p. ix.

A Journey to Wholeness

gotten in various ways, is all that we need to cure people. We do not need God to intervene because, like some *Star Trek* movie, once we know the problem we can fix it. Man has the power within himself to bring lasting change. It just takes determination and will power.

As we will see in the next chapter, Freud and Jung have influenced Christian counselors and helped create the chasm that exists between counseling and God.

Part One

THE SOURCE OF RESOLUTION

    I just thought I'd share this with you as further confirmation of your ministry. I felt that the enemy was trying to discourage you and that you needed some encouragement about now.

    Psychology has its place, no doubt, and has helped people but until God does a work of healing you can talk till you're blue in the face and it won't do any good. We perhaps need to understand where our hurts come from and deal with them, but until God does a supernatural work of grace, I don't believe there's much accomplished.

    All this to say that we believe wholeheartedly in what you're doing and ask that out of His glorious unlimited resources, God will give you the mighty inner strengthening of His Holy Spirit.

- DH & DH

2

Counseling: Past and Present

The Reality

A great chasm exists between practical Christianity and counseling. One Christian counselor said that we were not doing counseling; we were doing pastoral work. As I understand it, when we bring God in, we are pastors. When we leave God out, or on the fringe, we are Christian counselors. Yet, how are guilt, false or otherwise, and the violation of God's standards handled? How can we leave God out as we deal with wrongs against us or our wrongs against others? How can we leave God out and effectively bring anything to resolution?

The premise that Prayer and Resolution Counseling rests on is this: *Unless God intervenes, we cannot hope for lasting resolution of most problems.* If God does not intervene then we are relying on our understanding and determination to change as the power source for change. When we rely only on ourselves, instead of being healed and renewed people, we will have to cope with life and survive. We learn how to live despite the burden we carry, rather than live without the burden. Christ died, however, so we could live without the burden. He was not deceiving us when he said his yoke was easy and his burden light.

Counseling Perspectives

Before we can consider the different perspectives in counseling, we need to consider if sin is an issue at all. A few Christians might consider themselves without sin, but for the rest of us, sin is a constant concern with which we must deal. Christian or non-Christian, when we carry around a burden of anger or unresolved sin long enough, it affects us. In time, we will have emotional, spiritual and physical consequences. Carried around long enough, and we will have a room at the Ritz Psychiatric.

Secular and Christian counseling has shifted in the past years from a solution-oriented process to a coping-oriented process. Often after counseling, all people have are labels and coping techniques to use for day-to-day living, or a prescription for medication or both.

Counseling comes at human problems from different perspectives. Both secular and Christian counseling accept the cognitive approach that says that what we perceive depends on our past experience. Chicken Little, the hen, is a good example. A leaf falls on her head and she reacts and assumes that the sky is falling. Then she rushes around warning all the animals of the impending doom. We process information based on our perception of the world. Unfortunately, these perceptions are not always accurate but have shaped both secular and Christian counseling.

A Journey to Wholeness

Secular Counseling

Both psychoanalytical and behavioral approaches tell us that forces outside our own control determine our behavior. In the psychoanalytical approach, our inner psychic forces control us; in the behavioral approach, outside environmental forces control us. Both approaches may lessen or explain away our responsibility for our actions.

Cognitive Behavior Modification: We see this influence when the legal system excuses people for terrible crimes on the basis that they were not responsible for their actions because of abuse or poverty. This is in keeping with Behaviorism, the approach developed by B. F. Skinner, which focuses on *stimulus-response* psychology.[11] Man is a product of his environment and these outside forces affect him. If man reacts in a less desirable way then, as we change the reward, we can change the behavior so it is more acceptable. This creates the distorted notion that when society does not provide a healthy environment for good then it cannot condemn a man for wrongdoing.

Non-Christian counseling evaluates hurting people in terms of themselves and the world, without taking into account any active participation by God. It is humanistic in focus, considering that people can effect and change their own destiny through understanding and determination. Since God's standard is not recognized, people do not need to deal with violating God's standard. Therefore, such an approach considers guilt *feelings* but not guilt, since sin is relative. It may explain away wrongs

---

[11] B. F. Skinner, *About Behaviorism* (New York: Knopf, 1974).

committed against people or by people toward others as a product of environment.

Reality Therapy: Secular counseling can have a standard. Mower created a "Moral Model" of responsebility that says that a patient's problems are moral, not medical.[12] When the patient stops blaming others and takes responsibility, healing begins. William Glasser in *Reality Therapy* clarifies values for people and evaluates their present behavior in relationship to these values.[13] People come to recognize the consequences of their actions when these violate their value systems. When they accept responsibility for their actions on moral grounds, this creates the basis for mental health.

Reality Therapy does not consider the past particularly significant in understanding behavior in the present, nor is the value system viewed in the light of God's standard. While understanding often brings acceptance of responsibility and even release from guilt, it does not provide the grounds for forgiveness. Nor does it provide the real grounds for forgiving others that is a necessary ingredient for receiving forgiveness.

Psychoanalytical approach: Developed by Sigmund Freud, this stands on the premise that thoughts, fears and wishes govern our unconscious and affects our outward behavior. We are unaware of these forces within us. Through talk, the patient brings the unconscious to the conscious level and this can affect change. Freud talks about warring members within our unconscious:

---

[12] Hobart O. Mowrer, *The Crisis in Psychiatry and Religion* (Princton: Van Nostrand , 1961).
[13] William Glasser, *Reality Therapy: A New Approach to Psychiatry* (New York: Harper and Row, 1965).

A Journey to Wholeness

the Id, Ego and Superego.[14] The Id has instinctive drives that the Superego restricts and controls. Ego acts as the referee with self-interest in mind.

Transactional Analysis: Thomas Harris popularized the therapeutic approach developed by Eric Berne. The goal is to become aware of the intent behind our communication and see our behavior for what it really is.[15] The underlying theme is that, basically, we are good. We are sufficient within ourselves to affect change. God is more an impersonal force than a being.

Harris refers to the Child, Parent and Adult, in us. To a degree, these parallel Freud's Id, Ego, and Superego. A "felt concept of life" shapes the Child and feelings motivate it. A "taught concept of life" shapes the Parent and is a kind of conscience. The Adult is the "thought concept of life" and is a kind of self, motivated by the rational. This means that while our Adult is trying to live a certain way, our Parent might be restraining and controlling and our Child might be afraid or governed by other emotions.

Maloney, a psychotherapist, explains how he uses this approach,

> In Transactional Analysis terms, I stay as close to my Free Child as possible. I am confident, as was Berne, that there is within the child part of me an area of primitive intuition (often termed the Little Professor) that can be trusted. I implicitly count on

---

[14] Sigmund Freud, *New Introductory Lectures on Psychoanalysis* (New York: Norton, 1933).
[15] Thomas A. Harris, *I'm Ok - You're Ok* (London: Pan Books, 1969).

this part of my psyche to guide me in making judgments and in making interventions.[16]

Gestalt: Another form of psychotherapy, Gestalt therapy, developed by Max Wertheimer, believes that when people can integrate the parts of their personalities into healthy wholes that psychological disturbances will cease.[17] The therapist seeks to make us aware of our "whole personality" and to walk us through unresolved conflicts and bring them to greater awareness. Being fully aware of the feelings and behavior that come from the exposure of an issue is the emphasis. This is partly done through our acting out as a way to increase awareness.

Rational-Emotive Psychotherapy: Developed by Albert Ellis seeks to change harmful beliefs and thinking since irrational beliefs cause neurosis.[18] It seeks to rid us of irrational ideas. As we are more rational, we are more in control of our emotions. In other words, cognitive change creates emotional change.

Client-Centered Therapy: Carl Rogers left Union Theological Seminar and his ministry goal and developed what he called "Client-Centered Therapy," a non-directive approach.[19] We are autonomous beings so the solutions

---

[16] Gary Collins, *Psychology and Theology: Prospects for Integration* (Nashville: Abingdon, 1981), p. 112
[17] Max Wertheimer, *Productive Thinking* (New York: Harper & Row, 1959).
[18] Albert Ellis and Catharine MacLaren, *Rational Emotive Behavior Therapy: A Therapist's Guide* (Practical Therapist Series) (Atascadero, CA: Impact Publishers, 1998).
[19] Carl R. Rogers, *Client-centered Therapy: Its Current Practice, Implications, and Theory*. (Boston: Houghton Mifflin, 1951).

A Journey to Wholeness

to our problems are within us. Thus, we bounce ideas and questions off the counselor. The counselor rephrases, clarifies what he hears and seeks to create the grounds that permit us to come up with answers.

Primal Therapy: This is an approach developed by Arthur Janov.[20] He seeks to lead patients back to the first major "primal scene" to experience the emotions of that time and to suffer "primal pain." This unblocks and releases the pain that causes neurosis. Release is encouraged and can come via screams, sobbing, weeping, gagging, and so on.

Humanistic Approach: The humanistic approach focuses on subjective experience, in other words, on our own perception and interpretation of events. Since we have free will, we cause change within ourselves. An underlying premise is that we naturally strive toward growth and our full potential. Therefore, encounter groups and consciousness expanding can help us realize and move toward our desirable goals.

Notice how naturally this slides along the Divine-Human Continuum with its two opposite poles: God on one side, Man on the other. The humanistic approach moves us from the Human side of the continuum, past the middle, to the Divine side. The predictable conclusion is that we are gods or that god is in us.

Hypnotherapy: Therapists use hypnosis as an analytical tool and therapy approach. Straight Hypnotherapy seeks to relieve symptoms, through hypnosis or

---

[20] Arthur Janov, *The Primal Scream* (New York: Dell Publishing 1970).

self-hypnosis, by setting reality aside and using imagery. Using hypnosis or self-hypnosis, this method seeks to change or modify a person's symptoms through suggestion and displacement. This approach is not solution oriented in that its goal is to strengthen a person's ability to cope with life. When the issues are clearer, this removes doubt and lessens conflict. The New Age movement uses this approach, hypnosis, as a means for searching for past lives.

Jungian: The psychoanalytical approach of Carl Jung considers God awareness an essential ingredient to wholeness for the individual. His psychological therapy involves four stages:[21]

1. The therapist helps the individual gain awareness of his unique psychic structure as it relates to the personal and collective unconscious. By "collective consciousness" Jung considers that we are all connected at a certain level of the subconscious.

2. Integration or individuation can only come through involvement. He considers the ability to give and receive love are forms of this and essential to come to wholeness.

3. The healing of a personality is not automatic. The individual must be trained and disciplined to bring the conscious will into harmony with the unconscious.

---

[21] Morton T. Kelsey, *Healing and Christianity* (New York: Harper & Row, 1973), pp. 300-304.

A Journey to Wholeness

4. Understanding, the will, and consciousness can bring wholeness but only over time and with persistence. He calls the final product the "constellation of the Self."

Jung, like the humanistic approach, believes that we have an "instinctive drive toward wholeness." He considers that we cannot be whole until we have accepted the reality of God in our lives. This position sets him apart from the other approaches and is the closest thing to a merger of psychology and religion.

An Observation

With many approaches to choose from, one would think that a particular approach would stand out and have consistent results for its patients but that is not so. How do therapists use these approaches in their own lives?

> *If therapists really have special tools for helping people, shouldn't they be able to use their techniques on themselves? . . . University of Scranton psychologist John Norcross, Ph.D. and his colleagues have studied this issue. . . . 'When therapists treat patients, they follow the prescripttions of their theoretical orientation. But the amazing thing is that when the therapists treat themselves, they become very pragmatic.' In other words, when battling their own problems, therapists dispense with the psychobabble and fall back on everyday, commonsense techniques—*

chats with friends, meditation, hot baths, and so on.[22]

Though I consider hypnosis suspect, many of these approaches are effective to a point. They help us get to the facts that are an essential part of understanding and determining a continuing procedure. Nevertheless, far as they do go, they do not go far enough. This is probably why many therapists do not follow their own methods in getting personal help. No approach goes far enough if we leave God out.

In general, psychology treats people apart from and in isolation from God. Psychoanalysis says that the answer is within us and that we should trust the psychoanalyst to help us draw it out—instead of trusting the Holy Spirit to reveal it. Dream analysis and hypnotherapy both encourage unhealthy introspection as we go deeper into our "inner selves." Such activities can open the door to occult involvement. Despite this, the church finds most of these acceptable approaches and often refers believers to such practitioners.

The problem is that secular counseling deals with issues with which the church should be dealing. Only recognizing Gods' standards and intervention can adequately handle such issues as anxiety, feelings of personal unworthiness, insecurity, lack of self acceptance, uncontrolled appetites, guilt, resentment, selfishness, and wrong priorities and reasons for living, just to name a few.

The church should be the first stop for a hurting person, not the last resort. Unfortunately, the church has given its role as healer over to the (Christian and

---

[22] Robert Epstein, "Why Shrinks Have so Many Problems" in *Psychology Today* (July/August 1997), p. 76.

secular) school of psychology. This is because the church does not understand how to bring God in to handle such problems.

Christian Counseling

Christian counselors recognize the need to conform to and deal with God's standards. Normally the issues are discussed, clarified and understood but there is still an emphasis on pulling one up by one's own bootstraps. When counselors assume that when we change our minds we also change our behavior then such thinking pushes aside the need for God's intervening power.

Larry Crabb: This is true, for example, when Larry Crabb presents the seven stages that comprise his deeper (Level III) counseling:[23]

1. The counselor empathizes with the hurting one.

2. The sinful behavior is identified (with emphasis on the client's behavior, not the others involved).

3. The counselor identifies the wrong thinking the client has.

4. The counselor shows or gets the client to acknowledge what the truth is.

5. The counselor gets the client to commit to behaving according to the truth.

---

[23] Larry Crabb, *Effective Biblical Counseling* (Grand Rapids: Zondervan, 1977), p. 183.

6. Together counselor and client plan behavior changes that are according to that truth.

7. Steps 1-6 results in the client having feelings of love, joy and peace.

Crabb places tremendous emphasis on the power of actions and understanding to effect lasting change. His solution for one woman was to "behave in faith on the *conscious understanding* that her needs are met in the Lord . . ."[24] Implied is that we can handle this when we understand and believe the truth. As we change our mindset, we get release and future control.

This is partly true. The fallacy here is that just reading and accepting the truths of the scriptures have the power to change a life. (One I held for many years.) If the person has right perception, that is true. If they have wrong perceptions, however, about themselves or God, then that is false. The rational mind does not overcome inner beliefs and feelings just because it accepts truth. Instead, the person creates two systems, one for himself and one for others. God loves others, for example, no matter what they do but he does not love me unless I perform. I can read the scriptures, see the truth and even teach it to others, but not accept it for myself.

Jay Adams: This approach creates a "nouthetic confrontation." He considers man as primarily a sinner and acts accordingly. There are three stages:

---

[24] Ibid., p. 184

A Journey to Wholeness

1. The counselor teaches the hurting one so that the real issues are recognized. This is "to effect personality and behavioral change."[25]

2. The problem is solved noutherically through a "person-to-person verbal confrontation." This is to "effect a characterological and behavioral change. . . ."[26]

3. The counselor's job is to "meet obstacles head on and overcome them verbally, not in order to punish but to help him."[27]

Notice that heavy emphasis is on our ability to understand, admit an issue and then control our future behavior. In its own way, this is a humanistic approach.

Jesus said,

> *Don't you see that whatever enters the mouth goes into the stomach and then out of the body? But the things that come out of the mouth come from the heart, and these make a man 'unclean.' For out of the heart come evil thoughts, murder, adultery, sexual immorality, theft, false testimony, slander. These are what make a man 'unclean'; but eating with unwashed hands does not make him 'un-clean.' (Matthew 15:17-20)*

According to Jesus, our behavior comes out of our heart, the seat of our emotions, not from our minds, the seat of our intellect. Our rational center does not control

---

[25] Jay E Adams, *Competent to Counsel* (Grand Rapids: Baker Book House, 1970), p. 45.
[26] Ibid., p. 46
[27] Ibid., p. 50

us. Our feelings and deep beliefs do. Mental assent is not enough to change behavior or alter our deep-seated beliefs and feelings of what is right and wrong or what is reality.

Paul considered our belief system to be in the heart when he said,

> *That if you confess with your mouth, 'Jesus is Lord,' and believe in your heart that God raised him from the dead, you will be saved. For it is with your heart that you believe and are justified, and it is with your mouth that you confess and are saved* (Romans 10:9-10).

According to Adams, the counselor advocates the accepting of responsibility and blame by the wrong doers. The counselor gets us to admit guilt, confess it and receive forgiveness. The counselor puts little emphasis, however, on the part others play in sinning, only our response. "In nouthetic counseling the stress falls upon the 'what' rather than the 'why' because the 'why' is already known. . . ."[28] As he puts it, "The question 'Why' may lead to speculation and blame-shifting. . . ."[29] So we become the center of the universe in the session when the counselor should include others—but does not. Therefore, it is "our problem" oriented rather than including how others affect us and our problem.

It is often a fact, because of circumstances, that we are victims. Naturally, we do not want this to be our life style or identity, but facts are facts. Even in the midst of our own sin, we can realize what others have done to us

---

[28] Ibid., p. 48.
[29] Ibid., pp. 48-49

A Journey to Wholeness

and react in anger. One Christian counselor says that anger is out of place in repentance. I disagree.

Bobgan says,

> . . . the biblical counselor has to be careful about encouraging the victim role . . . Whenever the conversation focuses on what the other person is doing rather than upon the counselee's actions and reactions, the counselee may remain in the stance of victim . . .[30]

The issue is not holding on to the victim role or blame shifting but recognizing the part others have played in aiding, abetting or conditioning us to sin. Such awareness can generate anger in us. It should. Knowing the parts others have played (the greater circle of participants) allows us to forgive. It also makes us more responsible for our own actions in aiding, abetting and conditioning a whole set of other people to sin.

Cathy has a right to be angry in the midst of her repentance. Her mother used drugs and was sexually promiscuous even in front of Cathy. In addition, she was a member of a coven and brought Cathy into it. The members abused her physically, sexually, and emotionally.

Cathy went on to live a throw away life of drugs and sex, following the model of her mother, until she became a Christian. Even after becoming a believer, she continued to commit sexual sin.

---

[30] Martin & Deidre Bobgan, *Psychoheresy: The Psychological Seduction of Christianity* (Santa Barbara, CA: Eastgate Publishers, 1987), pp. 218-219.

In understanding the reasons behind her own actions, Cathy had to admit that her mother modeled to her harmful patterns for living. Her mother encouraged her throw-away life style, and taught her to do evil. She got angry thinking about what her mother had done to her.

Cathy is still responsible for her actions but considering her as only a sinner is unreasonable. She was also as a victim. Her mother, the coven members, Cathy's sexual partners and circumstances (among others, victimized in Satanic rites) are all necessary ingredients to consider as she seeks God's intervention. Cathy can only ask for and receive forgiveness for her part and cannot do that until she has the perspective that comes from the whole picture.

Neil Anderson: The approach by Neil Anderson is refreshingly different, yet still not enough.[31] I agree with Ellenberger when he says, "The truth encounter methodology uses a highly cognitive approach."[32] Anderson's use of creeds is useful and has its place. His approach brings structure and direction but this approach is holistic and mixes our relationships. This blurs the important lines between the believer as a servant and the believer as a child of God.

William Backus: Misbelief Therapy says that,

When we inject the truth into our every thought, taking a therapeutic broom and sweeping away

---

[31] Neil Anderson, *The Bondage Breaker* (Eugene, OR: Harvest House Publishers, 1990).
[32] C. Peter Wagner & F. Douglas Pennoyer, Eds., *Wrestling with Dark Powers* (Ventura, CA: Regal Books, 1990), p. 165.

> *the lies and misbeliefs which have enslaved us, we find our lives radically changed for the happier better.*[33]

Interestingly, he maintains the gap between prayer and counseling when he says,

> *Counseling is only one of many ways to become whole. Prayer, deliverance, study of the Scriptures, changing one's circumstances, medication, and wisdom gained through experience can bring healing too. Counseling is dialogue intended to heal.*[34]

Backus states that his approach is a form of cognitive psychology. It is a talk between the patient and the counselor and involves a three-step process: (1) Find and understand your misbeliefs or lies, (2) Argue against them and remove them and (3) Replace your misbeliefs by stating the truth. "When he learned to see the truth about himself, he also learned to argue and get rid of the lies which would have destroyed him."[35]

As does Anderson, Backus' approach is a highly cognitive one. Counseling, both Christian and secular, has considered that a rational, cognitive approach to problem solving is equivalent to a spiritual approach. If we understand the problem then we can solve it. Such an approach leaves God out of the picture or involves him only marginally. A cognitive approach is a necessary

---

[33] William Backus & Marie Chapian., *Telling Yourself the Truth* (Minneapolis: Bethany House, 1980), p. 10.
[34] William Backus, *Telling the Truth to Troubled People* (Minneapolis: Bethany House, 1985), p. 22.
[35] Backus & Chapian, *Telling Yourself the Truth*, p. 15.

step in the process of healing but not the end. The solution to a spiritual problem is not a cognitive answer but a God answer. If God is involved then the only way I know to involve God is through prayer.

Prayer and Resolution Counseling

There are four distinct stages in the Prayer and Resolution Counseling process: (1) Search, (2) Discovery, (3) Understanding and (4) Petition. Both Christian and secular counseling tend to stop at stage three and assume that the hurting one knows what to do after understanding. All four stages differ in Prayer and Resolution Counseling from most of the other models. As we discuss the particulars of Prayer and Resolution Counseling recognize that we are talking about ideals. Having all the time needed and the perfect conditions are not always possible.

Search

A person comes with issues that concern her. These issues are not always the central ones. Searching for the important issues of life comes in the context of all of life. We start by getting a chronological time-line of the person's life. We do this in person. We do not want her history written ahead of time because such a process allows her to decide what is significant and what is insignificant. It is brief and abbreviated. A chronological time-line gives us points of reference, control and the ability to recognize recurring destructive patterns.

A Journey to Wholeness

Discovery

The issues become clearer as we highlight a person's life and see patterns in the context of all of life. Patterns start in the past and grow. That means that the past is important. The ministry of the Holy Spirit is an important factor at this time as he brings to mind significant events and issues. The discovery stage allows us to map out the Prayer and Resolution Counseling plan of action. If sexual sins are an issue, we start with these, going from the earliest times to the present and staying as much as possible with that one topic.

Understanding

The person must understand what has been going on with a particular sin or event. The Prayer and Resolution Counseling team (ideally a man and a woman) helps the person gain perspective in how God views the issues and events: she needs to see things from God's viewpoint. The person also needs to recognize the "greater circle" of participants involved: this creates the grounds for forgiving others with awareness, and for asking forgiveness with awareness, if personal sin is an issue. Notice that we need the cognitive process but also we need the Holy Spirit's ministry. Until we understand, there is no way we can effectively pray.

Petition

The Prayer and Resolution Counseling team guides the person in prayer in the sense that they make sure she prays with awareness and completeness. The type of sin committed determines the particulars of prayer. For example, in sexual sins there is a need for spiritual cleansing. In occult sins, there is a need for renouncements. In sins involving words of power, an unwise vow may need to be confessed and release given by God, and so on.

Part of the resolution process involves seeing and understanding what sin is, what sin does, the effects of sin in time and the effects of sin over time. In this way, she sees the greater picture as God sees it—including the greater circle of people involved, for good or evil.

Notice that in Search, Discovery and Understanding that Prayer and Resolution Counseling differs from the way most counselors operate. Nevertheless, most models of counseling have their uses. To use a more extreme example (from my point of view), in Psychodrama, developed by psychiatrist J. L. Moreno, the techniques the therapist uses to bring people to awareness (search and discovery) have their uses. Granted, God is not involved and should be, but the beginning of a solution in any counseling is finding the real issues.

Psychodrama recreates the setting and emotional reactions to a trauma and out of that re-living comes insights. Nevertheless, people getting an "outlet" through an explosion of emotion may think they have been cured when, in fact, such therapy only provides temporary release and relief. Psychodrama does not consider the most important elements: forgiving and receiving forgiveness (the God factor).

Prayer and Resolution Counseling is not a substitute for other models but other models should incorporate "the God factor" by adding it or making the God factor more central to their model. Christian counseling may open and close a session in prayer but that is not bringing God into the session in an active way. Counseling people without including God's intervention is like trying to make cement without water. It does not work.

Non-Applied Christianity

Overall, Christian counseling has not integrated counseling and theology in practical ways. Some Christians reject all forms of psychology, as brought out in the book *Psychoheresy: The Psychological Seduction of Christianity*.[36] The focus is on us as sinners, never victims. Others want to rely only on the Bible as the source for help; any other source is suspect. On the other hand, such secular approaches as the book *I'm Ok -You're Ok* of Transactional Analysis have displaced theology.

Does there have to be an either-or solution? I believe in the verbal plenary inspiration of the scriptures but that only means I trust the scriptures and I will not accept anything that contradicts them. Using the Bible as the only source for truth sounds pious but the notion is wrong. For one thing, God never intended to present *all truth* in the scriptures. God gave us the scriptures to provide us a standard, prepare us for a savior and equip us for righteous living through some general guidelines and principles.

Truth is out there that is not in the Bible. If there is not, then God has done a disservice to his human creation, created in his image. Because that image includes a mind and the ability to reason, process and discover. We must often choose between right and

---

[36] Martin & Deidre Bobgan, *Psychoheresy: The Psychological Seduction of Christianity*.

wrongs without clear guidelines. We do not need to fear truth, for truth will never violate any of the principles of the Bible nor the character of God himself.

God intends for us to do our part in partnership with him and to make right choices, based on his character and as his children. He wants us to act apart from his *absolute direction* so that we perform freely and yet please him. He wants us to come into fellowship with him as equals: in the sense that fellowship with him is as our father and we as his children. It is not the same as worship (God–man), nor is it the same as obedience (master–servant). It is friendship and kinship (heavenly Father–children).

Even when the Christian receives both counseling and theological training, often he cannot integrate the two into a unified package. For example, one counselor, trained at a Christian university in psychology and at a seminary in theology, worked with a woman for many months. She had been a victim of molestation and, even after treatment, she told her counselor that she felt dirty. She had been baptized three times and, after each baptism, she felt clean for a time until she felt a need for another baptism.

What is the problem here? Is this just a spiritual woman? With molestation comes spiritual defilement. Showers, baths or baptisms will not provide the spiritual cleansing necessary. Unfortunately, her Christian counselor did not recognize the notion of spiritual cleansing. His response to her need was to tell her not to worry: the feelings would go away someday. How sad. For in the spiritual realm time has little meaning; such a spiritual condition does not dissipate over time. *Time is not the issue. Spiritual cleansing by God is.*

A non-Christian psychologist reported a case of obsessive-compulsive behavior that manifested itself in the person taking many showers a day. The patient was a victim of gang rape. An absolute requirement for her healing will be to receive spiritual cleansing yet how will this be possible unless we merge the spiritual and the secular? Unfortunately, even the Christian counselor often does not recognize the spiritual dimension or is unwilling to assume the priestly role necessary.

One young couple went to their pastor before marriage to confess their sins of fornication. His response was for them to "take it to the Lord in prayer." This sounded good but how? If this couple had known how to deal in prayer with their sins, they would have done so. They prayed ineffective prayers and entered marriage under a cloud.

A pastor must learn to pray effectively for and with people. Being a pastor is not just teaching and preaching. Gary Collins says that, "counselors free pastors and other church leaders for the overall work of the ministry."[37] Yet how relevant are pastors' ministries if they are out of touch with the day-to-day issues and concerns of their people? Many sermons do not address the real issues and concerns of today. Working with people may not come naturally, but pastors can learn and must learn how to guide people in prayer for resolution because hurting people are part of the normal package that comes with a ministry.

If the pastor cannot help people come into wholeness because of his or her disinterest or inability, then that pastor must either get the tools or find another job. Having someone else around to do this for the pastor is not acceptable—except to help share the load.

---

[37] Gary Collins, "Christian Counseling and the Church" in *Christian Counseling Today* (Vol 7, No. 2, 1999), p. 15.

In or out of the church, resolution involves God and includes the difficult task of forgiving the offender. Often, instead of specific prayer for healing, prayer opens the session in the counseling session. At most, someone voices a general presentation of the problem and makes a general prayer for God's help. Inferred is that if we just "give the problem to God," even in a vague way, then God is actively involved and he will somehow handle it. Such blind and ignorant faith does not work.

Resolution also involves recognizing the existence of categories of sin and accepting the fact that certain types of sin create stronger forces than others do. The forces of some sins, once committed, live on past the salvation experience. How is this possible? We will look into this in Chapter 6.

Counseling is not an either-or proposition. We must consider the spiritual nature of people as we help them resolve issues. Leaving God out ignores that essential part of humankind that sets us apart from animals.

Secular counselors need to revise their approaches if they have not considered the spiritual side of people. We can criticize secular counselors for being so blind to this need but Christian counselors are no better off. They talk the talk but have done little to address the spiritual nature of people. The theme of one article I read: how to add "spirituality" to the counseling session because people were beginning to expect that. Christian counseling should not have to add "spirituality;" it should be there as a normal part of the session.

A Journey to Wholeness

As we will seen in the coming chapters, whenever we counsel another and there are strong emotions involved, then we will have to put on the robes of the priest, whether we want to or not, and actively bring God into the session.

3

Effective Prayer

Science Enters the Stone Age

When Connie and I first entered the Amazon jungle tribe, our priority was to analyze the language and understand the culture in preparation for Bible translation. When we arrived, the medical system in place centered on the shaman. When Indians were sick, they went to the shaman and asked for healing. Through his power, he chanted and blew on them and brought healing—more often than we liked to admit. When the shaman failed, there was no other medical help available until we came. There were many who would have died without our medical intervention, even with something as simple as aspirin. With our presence and our medicine, we brought change. Though the shaman did continue to operate, in part we replaced him with pills and injections. *Science had entered the Stone Age.*

Our organization trained us well and gave us both linguistic and cross-cultural discovery tools. Both of us had a good Biblical foundation. In addition, we had some

A Journey to Wholeness

training in basic medicine and had access by radio to an experienced doctor. We came academically prepared but spiritually naïve.

Notice what we did. Indians came to the shaman because they recognized that in him resided a spiritual power that could heal. They came to us because they recognized that we had medicine that could heal. We introduced the power of medicine but left out the power of the spiritual when we could have brought in both. Indeed, we substituted science for the spiritual. It was not until later, when faced with a dying child, and in desperation, that we turned directly to the spiritual and really prayed.

When the Indians brought seven-year-old Helena to us, she was already comatose and did not respond to pain. We talked by radio to the center doctor but nothing he suggested helped as she sank deeper toward death. We had to leave the tribe the next day for several weeks. Since we could not take Helena out with us, we assumed that the child would be dead when we returned.

The night before we left, Connie took Helena in her arms and paced up and down praying. She did not pray in faith; she prayed in anger and frustration. The next morning the plane landed and we left.

Weeks later, we returned. When we climbed out of the plane the usual crowd of Indians was waiting for us by the side of the airstrip but one stood out from the others. There was this smiling little girl, Helena, alive and well.

One day Helena was in our house—a hut is a better word for our bark-walled, thatch-covered dwelling—and Ernesto, the local shaman, was there visiting. He pointed to Helena and said to me, "You know, she belongs to Jesus." I did not understand what he meant so I asked him why. Ernesto answered, "Because Jesus healed her (caused-her-to-live) she belongs to him."

God can heal us physically and he can heal the emotional traumas of our lives. There was no excuse for our failing but we were a product of our church and our Western orientation. Until that special time, God lived up to our expectations. Better said, God did not work as much as he wanted because we did not expect him to and because we did not ask him.

It took an apparently hopeless case of a child near death for us to approach God for healing. Indians, with a spiritual orientation before we came, became less spiritually aware after we arrived. We had come to bring them the Gospel and brought them a Gospel that was for a future heaven instead of a present life.

Science Enters the Church Age

The church has done much the same when it comes to spiritual and emotional issues. We have replaced God's power with rational understanding; instead of God's power. A totally rational approach says that knowledge heals the mind, spirit and soul. Often this means assigning a label to the hurting one as the solution. When we understand the problem, we have the power to change it or we have an excuse as to why we are powerless to change it.

In psychology, it has been helpful to label a bundle of behavioral symptoms. However, labeling all alcoholism, egomania, pedophilia, nymphomania, and so on, as *diseases* takes away our responsibility for such behavior. "We caught it," like some disease, says we did not cause it or do it. We are powerless against its force so we are

A Journey to Wholeness

not at fault or responsible for our actions. We are just victims.

A pill often replaces resolution and a label releases us from responsibility:

"I have ADD."

"I have a bipolar disorder."

"I am addicted to sex (or alcohol, shopping, stealing, pornography)."

"I am a survivor of incest (or rape or molestation)."

"I can learn to cope with life and survive. And, even if I don't, I am not really responsible for my behavior."

Even Christians accept such reasoning.

God does not intend that we handle our problems without him, nor does he intend that we cope with life and survive. The blessing of a righteous life is long life. That shows that life is to be a yoke, according to Jesus, that is easy and light. He wants us to walk in fellowship with him and come to him when we need help and guidance. The way we come to him is through prayer.

Prayer has several important functions: worship, intercession and petition, to name a few, and each have its own protocol. The function or purpose determines the style and items in a prayer. In other words, function determines form. We have gotten quite adept at conversational prayer, formal prayer, prayer and praise, prayer and worship. There are many books out on these forms of prayer. Interestingly, the form we know the least about is the prayer of confession. When we shift to this form of prayer, we are vague, without a direction or even apparent purpose other than "forgive me." Yet the prayer of confession is the cornerstone of our Christian walk. Until we handle the sins committed against us (accuse and forgive) and the sins in our lives (confess and ask forgiveness), we are not fully free to worship or praise God. Nor can we come to God and feel that he hears us.

James says, *"You ask and do not receive, because you ask with wrong motives, so that you may spend it on your pleasures"* (James 4:3 NASB). We pray amiss whenever we try to sidestep God's way by shortcutting the process of accusing and forgiving, confessing and receiving forgiveness. A glib prayer is praying amiss. We tend to think that James is alluding to big houses and fancy cars as praying amiss. I believe that there is more to it than that. We pray amiss when we pray without understanding the issues involved. We need to know what God's standard is and what he thinks. We must remember the high price God himself, through Jesus Christ, paid so he could answer our prayers.

James also tells us that, *"The effective prayer of a righteous man can accomplish much"* (James 5:16b NASB). This and the previous verse are two sides of the same coin. We can have our prayers answered when we pray *for the right things and in the right way.* Effective means that we do things in a way that works. We think that the shortest and fastest method is the best. When it comes to effective prayer, however, the long, hard narrow road may take longer but we reach our destination whole and healed.

Prayer is an active way of having a talk with God. God says,

> *"Come now, and let us reason together,"* says the Lord, *"Though your sins are as scarlet, they will be as white as snow; though they are red like crimson, they will be like wool"* (Isaiah 1:18 NASB).

Reasoning together is a two-way conversation. Hard to imagine that the mighty God actually wants to talk with us but it is true. It takes effort to pray with focus and understanding but God created us with minds and he expects us to use them.

One friend asked, "Doesn't God just fill in the blanks when we pray?" I have not seen him do so. I have heard sermons on why God answers when he does not. Silence is God's way of saying, "Be patient." However, Jesus said,

Ask, and it shall be given to you; seek, and you shall find; knock, and it shall be opened to you. For everyone who asks receives, and he who seeks finds, and to him who knocks it shall be opened. Or what man is there among you, when his son shall ask him for a loaf, will give him a stone? (Matthew 7:7-9 NAS)

The verbs he uses are *proactive verbs*—not passive ones such as "hang around and hope that God notices," or "wander around and hope you stumble on it," or "stand by the door and hope someone goes out, so you can get in before the door closes." Determination, purpose and direction, these are the fuels for prayer.

Prayer in Practice

We can help neither Christians nor non-Christians when they deny the presence of sin. People must confront sin and evil, with their causes and effects, as a necessary step in the healing of their minds, emotions and souls.

The humanistic approach to healing sees evil as merely an imperfection in the human psyche. Sin is a culturally relative value that does not provide a point of reference. Sin is relevant only as it hurts another. Even when we recognize sin, it has ceased to be a personal thing. Instead, we blame the environment, culture, parents or the weather.

With such views, we have no avenue to attack evil as a real living force. If evil is nothing more than the absence of good then there is no battle, just a meeting of the minds. Since a consensus is the best way to deal with the issues then we do not need God and his powers. When we hold such a position then evil can operate at the unconscious level, unrecognized, autonomous and unopposed. Eventually, it will rein supreme because, without God, we have no way to combat it.

If sin is a relative thing, we only violate our personal standard. We have no absolute standard to arrive at, or to miss, and life becomes even more uncertain than it already is. If we need to forgive, only we are involved which means that we must suffer the injustice because, if God is out of the picture, he cannot satisfy justice for us. When we bring God into the picture, we must also include evil and acknowledge sin. God's presence brings a standard and forces a confrontation, a judgment and the defeat of sin and its power. When God enters the room, Satan steps out of the shadows to do battle as the Evil One and the Prince of this world.

The American Association of Christian Counselors has begun to talk about "adding spirituality" to counseling sessions because people are expecting this. Prayer in a counseling time is not an extra that we tack on because people want it.

Anytime a person is angry or hurt because of another's actions, there will be a focus on the one who caused it, rightly or wrongly. When that happens, there is a need to accuse and extend forgiveness and, much of the time, confess and receive forgiveness. Just talk does not do that, prayer does. The more traumatic the event, the more involved the person is, the more he will need the validation (or invalidation), insight and perspective of "safe others." Safe others stand with and guide the person in prayer. Just counsel is not enough. Just counsel does not automatically include God in the process of healing. Prayer and Resolution Counseling does.

One Christian psychologist, after listening to the principles of Prayer and Resolution Counseling, was not interested. He commented that any system worked if people believed in it enough. If people believed in prayer and it helped them then that was great. However, is Prayer and Resolution Counseling just another method of helping people or is it a way of working in harmony with God as he brings healing and wholeness?

Prayer and Resolution Counseling

Prayer counseling is a term widely used in the Christian world today. There are over ten-thousand sites on the internet under prayer counseling but it means different things to different people. For some, it means opening a session in prayer and talking about an issue before closing the time in prayer. For others, it means bringing up an issue and then the Christian counselor, pastor or priest prays for the person. In some sessions, the Christian shares her feelings with the counselor or with a group. Some sessions try to get the believer to feel her emotions and "let them out."

For others, it means "claiming victory" over an issue through Jesus. Some are cognitive based; others faith believing based; still others are interventions by one or more Christians. Some focus heavily on the work of the Holy Spirit; others on Jesus. Not all prayer counseling is the same.

I have used the phrase *Prayer and Resolution Counseling* because it is counseling in the traditional sense we have come to know—one individual being helped by talking with and being advised by others. However, it also incorporates the act of prayer from beginning to end. Prayer is not the "bookends" to start and end a session, as if to sanctify what comes between. It is the active means of inviting the Spirit of God to guide so forgiveness, healing, freedom from the power of sin and cleansing can take place.

Prayer and Resolution Counseling incorporates many of the insights and methods of both secular and Christian counseling but there are perspectives that are constant throughout. Here are distinctions that, taken together, set apart Prayer and Resolution Counseling from any other prayer counseling we know of to date.

• Prayer and Resolution Counseling recognizes that, while understanding is both useful and needed, only God can deal with the issues involved.

• We must deal with what others have done against us, but this does not lessen our own responsibility for wrongdoing.

A Journey to Wholeness

- There must be *resolution*. Resolution comes only when God acts on the believer's behalf to complete a heavenly transaction that influences current living. Implied is that "Only God can handle this."

- Only when we present our needs to God with focus, presenting specifics, can he answer in specifics.

- Through Christ, Prayer and Resolution Counseling is solution oriented. We must appropriate Christ's sacrifice.

- Prayer is the vehicle for God to resolve those issues that hinder a person from an effective and satisfying life.

- God is our Father and we are his children but all the Godhead is involved in resolution. So, our prayers are to the Father, through Jesus the Son and under the direction of the Holy Spirit.

- Prayer and Resolution Counseling is resolution based. There is a need to define the issues, know and understand them, but without resolution, there is no lasting effect.

- Only God's intervention and power can break the on-going force and power of sins.

- God provided through Christ's death and resurrection all we need to have an abundant and victorious life.

- Prayer and Resolution Counseling is dependent on the Holy Spirit to guide, to reveal the issues to be handled during a session and to bring long-buried issues to light.

- Forgiveness means that we trust God enough to believe that he will see that justice is done on our behalf to the extent that even our sense of justice will be satisfied. Forgiveness is a central issue: forgiveness of others without excusing their actions and confession of one's sins without excusing them.

- The Prayer and Resolution Counseling team consists (ideally) of a man and a woman. Except for extremely sensitive issues, there are two counselors with one hurting person.

- The team prays with, not for, the hurting one. The team guides the hurting one but she is the one who does the praying to her heavenly Father.

- The team prays in agreement with and as witnesses to the prayer of the hurting one—adding the power, authority and assurance of answered prayer that Christ promised.

- Prayer and Resolution Counseling deals with one topic at a time: sexual, occult, words of power, and so on, and the related issues that come with the topic.

- Initially, sin is the focus but the goal is to get rid of sin so that truth and righteousness become focal. In Prayer and Resolution Counseling the grounds and roots for sin are recognized and God's intervention is sought.

- In Prayer and Resolution Counseling, there is a need to be as specific as possible; details are important. There is a lot of discussion before the person prays, so the person is fully aware of what she is asking God, as her Father, to do.

- Prayer and Resolution Counseling requires signifycant time blocks—three to four hour sessions with a break. Most people finish in thirty hours or less.

- There is much teaching that takes place during the sessions as issues come up due to distortions about God, sin, forgiveness, and others.

- The Prayer and Resolution Counseling sessions can be quite intense with grief, tears, anger, even rage as the person begins to see the issues with more understanding and from God's perspective.

Prayer and Resolution Counseling is a supplement to, not a replacement for, other approaches. It is not in competition with other counseling techniques. Whatever techniques or schools of thought are used, we need the tools of Prayer and Resolution Counseling to bring resolution.

We have been able to go to the moon and have steadily progressed in our knowledge of the physical world but continue to be in the Dark Ages when it comes to understanding the dynamics of spiritual change.

When people have experienced harm or given harm to others, it will take time to bring resolution and healing but normally it is hours and weeks, not months and years. The past does not have to be a present reality. When God is involved, we have his power to affect change and bring healing.

In the next chapter, we will look at what happens if we leave God out or include God in the Session.

4

Counseling and/or Prayer

Though my background is in Bible, linguistics and cross-cultural education, I do not apologize for writing a book on prayer and counseling. All of these disciplines have helped as I have attempted to understand God's role in the prayer and counseling process. I have written this book on Prayer and Resolution Counseling to put my findings down on paper. Neither secular nor Christian counseling actively involves God in the healing process as much as they should. Involving God gets in the way of schedules and predetermined methods. Involving God can bring the unpredictable into a session.

The five-month training program we ran overseas was quite intense. We put people into unpredictable and stressful situations. Over the years, a number of participants struggling under these conditions came to us for help. Most of the time the help they needed did not relate directly to the training program except that their inner turmoil interfered with their training. Thus, Prayer and Resolution Counseling came out of necessity.

Two Realms

When we began to close down the program, I wrote to my agency and explained to them what Connie and I had been doing in counseling. We focused on people forgiving others and receiving forgiveness. The issues were sexual, occult or authority violations by or against those we guided in prayer. Although we did our counseling on the side, often in the evenings and weekends, the way God worked amazed us as we prayed with and for people. After I described what we were doing, I asked the agency to permit us to get some education in counseling and get our credentials, then we could join the counseling department and continue what we were doing in utilizing prayer in our counseling.

The head of the counseling department wrote back with an unexpected response. The director told us that we were not doing counseling. We were doing pastoral work. We should contact the pastoral department.

That surprised me. Even now, I cannot understand how Christian counselors can leave out either God or prayer in counseling. It seems like an unworkable system for counselors to try to help people without involving God.

It appears that we have two realms of influence: the realm of counseling and the realm of God. If these realms are distinct and separate, like on different sides of the Grand Canyon, then we can make some assumptions.

The Realm of Counseling

No matter what approach we use in counseling others, God must be totally either in or out of the process. (Either he is in the realm of counseling or he is on the other side of the canyon rim.)

- If God is merely a passive bystander, then he is out of the process of counseling. This also means that a cross or picture of Jesus on the wall does not mean that God is involved. He is just an abstract presence.

- If God is not involved in the counseling process then all we can expect is a reactive approach to problem solving and surface solutions to help us strive, cope with life and survive.

- When God is not involved then counseling means that someone shares our burdens for a time. They allow us to express ourselves and receive advice or clarification. They stimulate us toward solutions within us or from others.

- Leaving God out infers that there is a standard for right and wrong apart from him, or a standard does not matter, or we make our own standard.

- If God is not involved then we are sufficient within ourselves to direct and control our destinies. (I call this approach "the *Star Trek* Approach.") This also implies that our reasoning powers are sufficient apart from God.

- If God is not involved, we must pull ourselves up by our own bootstraps through our determination and will.

The Realm of Prayer

On the other hand, if we merge the realms, do we want the realm of counseling with God in it? Or, do we want the realm of God with counseling in it? Counseling should be a tool that helps us as we approach God in prayer. If we accept this then we can make the following assumptions:

- If God is involved in counseling then he can effect change. The counselors are actively engaged in seeking his solutions for us. These changes, such as healing, renewing and destroying destructive patterns and forces, will be long lasting and deep.

- When God is involved, he is an active participant, not a passive bystander.

- God gave us new natures and the ability to make right choices but he never intended for us to be independent of him. However, God does not usually impose his will on us.

- God wants to work with us in partnership because he respects and values us, both as his creation and as his children. He wants to be in our lives but not take over and control every aspect of our lives.

- As we conform to the image of Jesus Christ, we do not disappear, nor are we absorbed. That is Hinduism.

- We have unique personalities and identities. God relates to us as we are.

- Our reason, belief system and feelings are not sufficient in themselves as reliable guides. This means that we are dependent on the guidance of the Holy Spirit.

- Christ's death and resurrection are essential but he alone is not focal. The heavenly Father is our focus with Christ as High Priest and the Holy Spirit as the Guide and the one who reveals. *Once redeemed, our primary relationship with God is as his children and him as our Father.*

- If God is involved in the counseling process then our primary method for involving God is through prayer.

- If God is involved in an active way, then such prayers are dynamic and life changing.

God wants us to live responsible and righteous lives. He created us with the ability to judge, evaluate, reason and decide courses of action. He wants fellowship with us because we chose to do so, not because he forces us.

If this is true, we can expect God to do everything within his power to help us as we seek to be like him. His only limitations are keeping within the boundaries of his holiness and justice.

I used to act with the unconscious belief that God was around, just busy doing other things, far off in a corner somewhere. I have changed my thinking. I was not persuaded by logic or clever arguments. I saw God working through prayer done on his terms. *Many approaches used in counseling are useful but no approach in counseling replaces or substitutes for God's intervention.* I am not suggesting that we throw out the useful approaches, but that we bring God into the process so true resolution takes place.

The Problem of the Past

After many years in linguistics and Bible translation, I began the study abroad program referred to earlier, training Christians to live and work overseas. I used Europe and North Africa as the classroom setting for the entry program I directed. Two universities endorsed the program. I began to recognize that, if Christian workers arrived with emotional or spiritual cracks, the cracks only got wider in a cross-cultural entry program.

If Christian workers had had life styles of sexual promiscuity before they were Christians then feelings of guilt or unworthiness plagued them or lustful thoughts assailed them.

If they came from families that practiced the occult, or if they had been involved directly or indirectly, even if this took place before they were Christians, Satan would attack them with vigor in the new setting.

If they came from dysfunctional homes and, as a result, they had rejected their parents or authority then this showed in their attitudes and actions toward me, as the director.

Words of power, perhaps spoken over them as children, put great stress on their attitudes and behavior today.

The Past versus the New Birth

I noticed a pattern. The only destructive forces at work were those fed by sins ranked in the Old Testament

A Journey to Wholeness

as "power or death sins." When the person committed one of these sins, the sacrificial system did not cover him. He himself had to die or, in the case of a vow, he had to fulfill it.

Other "minor" sins did come up but only attached to one of these four categories. This seemed contrary to my Bible School and church teaching. Then I realized that the sins were not in focus as much as the ongoing consequences. Jesus handled SIN at the Cross but the consequences of certain sins, the power and death sins, continue to have power and can spill over from the old life into the new.

Since the force of these sins comes from the past into the present then we need to deal with the past. If our past includes holding an *ought* against another then how does that effect our present state of being reborn? Continuing to hold a grudge against another after we accept Christ may not hinder our salvation but it does allow the past to live in the present.

Tracy hated her father because he had treated her unjustly. This happened more than ten years ago yet Tracy still felt the rage against him. He was on her mind constantly because of what he had done. It happened long ago but, experientially, it was still happening every day for Tracy. Until she forgave her father, this part of her past continued to live and fester inside her, robbing her of a part of her life in the NOW.

Where do the scriptures say that, when we sin or someone sins against us, the sin disappears after ten years? Or that God forgives after ten years, even if we do nothing? That is not so. We must deal with sin, once committed. It does not go away by default. Justice must be satisfied. The penalty for sin has no time limit. We have only one way to handle the temporal effects of sin: We must forgive and that, in turn, releases forgiveness for us. Only God can put finish on it for us and free us from the past. Otherwise, we carry all the accumulated effects of these power sins until the day we die. Even as Christians, unresolved sin pays us a daily wage of death that affects us physically, emotionally and spiritually.

Some Christians not only discourage us from looking at the past but say it is wrong to do so because we are new creatures in Christ. They base their conclusion on II Corinthians 5:17. *The Good News Bible* puts it this way, "*When anyone is joined to Christ, he is a new being; the old are gone, the new have come.*" Therefore, the teaching surmises, it is wrong to bring up the past. However, if we look at the context we will come to a different conclusion:

> *Therefore, if anyone is in Christ, he is a new creation; the old has gone, the new has come! All this is from God, who reconciled us to himself through Christ and gave us the ministry of reconciliation: that God was reconciling the world to himself in Christ, not counting men's sins against them. And he has committed to us the message of reconciliation. We are therefore Christ's ambassadors, as though God were making his appeal through us. We implore you on Christ's behalf: Be reconciled to God. God made him who had no sin to be sin for us, so that in him we might become the righteousness of* God (II Corinthians 5:17-21).

The old being referred to here concerns *reconciliation. The past* is not the focus but rather *a change of relationship*. When Christ became sin for us, he provided the way for us to be acceptable to God so we were no longer enemies but friends. In this passage, *a relationship is in focus, not the presence or absence of the forces of sin or of the past*.

A Journey to Wholeness

People using this verse deny comfort to those troubled by past sins. They have ignored the Apostle Paul's teaching. He also emphasized our relationship when he said, *"Now that we have been put right with God through faith, we have peace with God through our Lord Jesus Christ"* (Romans 5:1 GNB). Paul goes on to tell of the struggle between the old and the new nature. In Romans, chapter 6, he implies that sin still has a force and that we should think of ourselves *"as dead, so far as sin is concerned"* (5:11 GNB). He does not say sin is dead but that we need *to think* as if it were.

Later Paul talks of the conflict of natures but the freedom that can be ours in Christ (Romans 8:1-2). He adds in 8:12 *"So then, my brothers, we have an obligation . . . if by the Spirit you put to death your sinful actions, you will live"* (8:12-13 GNB). Obligation refers to our wills. Paul is not talking here about salvation as a point in time (the new birth) but salvation as an ongoing process that includes our getting rid of the old!

> *But now you also, put them all aside: anger, wrath, malice, slander, and abusive speech from your mouth. Do not lie to one another, since you laid aside the old self with its evil practices* (Colossians 3:8-9 NAS).

Not only are we urged to forgive those who wrong us but also we are commanded to do so. The assurance of our own forgiveness hinges on our willingness to forgive others. For those who refuse to look to the past, forgiveness is an impossible task, because forgiveness is for deeds done in the past. One cannot forgive for either the present or the future. Forgiveness is only for what has been done already, whether done minutes ago or years ago.

When we read the epistles, which were written to the Christian, we find words and phrases like "put them all aside," "get rid of," "take on," "no longer do . . . but do . . ." Saved, yes. Nevertheless, there can be, and often are, ongoing consequences because the power of the past still affects the present.

Dealing with the Past

Connie and I were available at all hours to talk and the participants did come to us. The overseas training program that we ran demanded that, at times, we all live together or nearby and have many of our meals together. These circumstances created strong trust bonds and the participants felt it safe to come and share. Often they felt the ongoing power of sin in their lives and assumed that they were exceptions to the rule: after all, Christians are supposed to be victorious. Naturally, they did not share about the power of sin in their lives until these became overwhelming.

The participants were from every denominational orientation, age and level of education yet the forces of sin were there in their lives. If Christian workers, pastors and missionaries have these issues, then it must be true for most believers.

Directing this program, we traveled around North Africa living with local people and visiting local market places. One section of M___ has a street that specializes in the black arts. People can buy charms, dried lizards, etc. to drive away the spirits, cast spells and heal. Several in every group of participants I directed had nightmares or felt uneasy after we had visited such a place. Significantly, only those with unresolved occult backgrounds reacted in these ways.

I saw that the past had power in the lives of trained people who came from long established Christian backgrounds and cultures. New believers from pagan, Muslim, Hindu and other non-Christian backgrounds will be hindered in their new Christian walk unless we recognize and address these issues.

In much of Africa, a shaman attends the birth of a baby and calls the ancestors as witnesses. He or she keeps the evil spirits away or calls friendly spirits for protection or direction in naming the child. In parts of Muslim Africa, the child is dedicated to Mohammed and Islam before the midwife cuts the umbilical cord.

Ideally, discipleship methods should include the recognition and means to deal with the power of the occult sin, sexual sin and authority violations. It should also handle the obligations new believers are under because of past vows or declarations.

As I traveled around Europe, North Africa and the Middle East, I shared what I was learning with Christian workers. It surprised me to see eighty-percent of the listeners coming up afterward and sharing with me. The power of past sins were a problem for them and could I help?

Out of times like this, Prayer and Resolution Counseling as a model began to take shape—as a means of dealing with the forces of the past. It also tested my theological orientation. This Prayer and Resolution Counseling model came about through circumstances, not inclination; through need, not to prove a theory and it drove me to the scriptures to find out *why* these forces were at work. Not *if* they were at work, for I knew these people were not marginal, misfits or mentally ill, but rather were dedicated Christian workers

The Hypothesis

My working hypothesis came out of my linguistic background, not out of my Bible education. As a linguist, I gathered language data, for example, nouns and how they pluralized. After I elicited many examples from native speakers, I saw patterns emerge and formed a hypothesis on how the language worked at that level. I assumed that a noun started singular and that I added an affix to make it plural. After a time I formalized this and created formulas and charts that showed how the language worked.

After I had this neat set of formulas and charts, the problems showed up. I found a few nouns that did not fit the pattern. Did I throw away these misfit examples? No, of course not. My theories should not *dictate how* people speak the language, but rather *account for how* people speak the language in real life. In the same way, our theology, our hypotheses concerning God, is supposed to be true to scripture and reflect real life.

These new nouns and the ways they formed plurals forced me to a new perspective: some nouns began as plurals and rarely are singular, for example, wasps, bees and gnats. (My context was the Amazon jungle.) My original assumptions were close but not good enough to handle all the nouns in the language.

This way of working, I carried over into Prayer and Resolution Counseling. Real life is not at odds with scripture. Notice, I am not saying that the scriptures are wrong but rather my perceptions and assumptions color my interpretation and application of the scriptures. My premise is that:

> *If the data (what people are experiencing in real life) does not fit the model (my theological training and*

A Journey to Wholeness

doctrine), then the model might be faulty (my perspective might be off). Therefore, I need to review, change or adapt my model (so it consistently works).

The people I was involved with were not marginal types who could be suspect and who, as Christians, earned the burdens they carried. Most were missionaries, pastors and Christian workers. Many had college degrees and some had trained in anthropology, counseling and psychology. Many were lay Christians with Bible school training or at least years of teaching within the church. A few have been new believers with sordid pasts but, regardless, all these people had the same dilemma: they carried burdens because of the consequences of past sins.

If this is true of missionaries and pastors, with their training and screening, screening that sometimes required traditional counseling, then it was true of other believers. I know of one church that assumes that if their members are constantly struggling in life and burdened then they are not Christians at all. Such an assumption only increases the weight people carry instead of lightening the load. Their burdens and struggles are real, not imaginary. We, as prayer counselors, burden bearers, brothers and sisters in Christ, must be in a position to give them hope and provide answers and resolution.

The Christian walk is not a helpless hopeless journey into darkness. God, through Christ, has provided all that we need to live an abundant and victorious life.

The effects of Christ's sacrifice and resurrection are available to us now. His sacrifice was for more than just salvation. His death and resurrection created an account, an ATM, so to speak, from which we can draw daily. We cannot successfully use the ATM when we fail to see the issues from God's perspective, when we do not

Counseling and/or Prayer

approach the issues or him on his terms. When we approach God on his terms, however, then resolution is not only possible, it is expected. Often when there are problems in dealing with issues in people's lives, the problems center on how to present these to God. How to pray according to his will and in a way he can answer. The assumption here is that there is a way and he wants to answer.

Are there in fact two realms of counseling that exist, side by side, and coexist without touching each other? Can we have "pastoral counseling" (with God) on one side and "real counseling" (without God) on the other side? Sometimes, maybe so; most of the time, no. Some secular counselors have recognized that counselors are priests of a sort while Christian counselors have been unaware or unwilling to take on that role. Carl Jung (whom I do not consider a Christian) said,

> *Religions are systems of healing for psychic illness. . . . That is why patients force the psychotherapist into the role of a priest, and expect and demand of him that he free them from their distress. That is why we psychotherapists must occupy ourselves with problems which, strictly speaking, belong to the theologian.*[38]

---

[38] Carl G. Jung, "Psychotherapists or the clergy," in *Modern Man in Search of a Soul* (New York: Harcourt, Brace, 1933), pp. 240-241.

I would rather say, "which, strictly speaking, belong to the *priesthood of believers*." Conventional psychiatric and psychological approaches have their uses and we should not reject any approach that helps if that approach is not a violation of biblical principles. Nevertheless, these approaches cannot leave God out if true resolution is to take place.

We must involve God any time we have strong emotional responses, anger or grudges over what someone else has done to us or guilt over what we have done. Whenever guilt, anger, pain or hurt occurs then forgive-ness is an issue. If forgiveness is an issue then God must be in the session because he provides the grounds for us to forgive. He will see that justice is ultimately satisfied.

Christian counselors often assume that once we understand the reason for our anger then we can leave their offices and bring the issue to the Lord by ourselves. However, often that is not true. True forgiveness is hard to give if we understand the terrible nature of the wrong. We cannot be detached for we need clear perspective as we forgive. We normally need the help of others to gain such a perspective.

Counselors must either explain away sin and its consequences or deal with it. Counselors, Christian or otherwise, may not want the job of a priest but like it or not they have it anyway.

We must utilize all the approaches needed to bring the past to God for final and complete resolution. The force of the past in our lives now will be because of any or all of the following: sexual sin, rebellion, participation in the occult and/or unwise vows, declarations and lies that shape us.

Looking back at the past is not an option. It is a necessity. The past, be it a one-minute past or a forty-year past, must be resolved if we are to walk in freedom and victory in the present. Once we handle it God's way, we never again have to deal with the effects of those past sins by us or to us. God takes both the sin and the force behind it and separates us from it. The past is no longer an issue. No longer does the past have power in the NOW. No longer can the past create harmful reactions.

Satan can no longer bring these things before God to accuse us. Nor can he any longer use these things to condemn us. However, unconfessed sin or holding onto a grudge is like leaving the window open at night in a crime-ridden city. Satan will use the window to get in and use our unresolved past as a way of temptation, condemnation or confusion.

Whenever I have shared the principles of Prayer and Resolution Counseling, as a factor in spiritual warfare, in marriage encounters, as discipleship materials, or as a counseling tool, the Christian workers themselves have asked for help. They asked because they found that past sins and life patterns were continuing forces in their lives and were interfering with their relationships and the effectiveness of their ministries.

In the next few chapters, we will see that we need both the realm of counseling and the realm of prayer, to bring the full resolution that leads to freedom and victory.

❧ Part Two ❦

The Basis for Healing

I wanted to share with you immediately all that happened especially in the following two weeks after it [prayer and resolution counseling]. No only did my Heavenly Father handle my anger, but Satan tried to test it to the fullest. It was quite interesting to see how he tried to make me fall! However, the healing I received was certainly definite, because I have grown in more peace than I have experienced for years.

After I left the retreat, each day has been a future to look forward to, albeit some days were not a bright as others. I have felt healthier and more alive. The depression has lifted considerably, and when it does come, it is fleeting. I am more in touch with myself (the Holy Spirit within me), and that has made me come alive.

As for the testing, to see if I had indeed given my Heavenly Father the pain of the past with regard to M___, was remarkable. Also *immediately, I was confronted with issues that had created painful memories, or walked into a situation unexpectedly which brought me up against the past pain. In each situation I was filled with peace instead of pain and when it happened, I was able to say to myself, "amazing, the pain is gone!" I know I truly gave M___ to God and He has taken care of her. I don't mean punitively, but taken care of her as his child also. When I gave up my hold on the pain I was experiencing and asked Him to take it for me, I knew He truly had done so. I was amazed myself how much pain I had actually held on to and was not aware of until our session at the retreat. I did not realize how poisonous that pain had been to me. You were right, the hatred for Dr. K___ dissipated with the pain of the entire situation with Mary. I do not think of them except in fleeting moments of memory which I have no need to bring to mind by my will, but which will still come in connection with another memory. I do not hate Dr. K___. I don't have to because he has no hold over me any longer. . . .*

* * * * *

My therapist, J____, was as excited as I was when I shared this experience with her. God worked through me for her also. She has asked me questions about discipleship, the spirit with me, etc. since then. She was quite taken back with the truly therapeutic experience the retreat turned out to be. . . . She seemed to feel that she had not done enough herself to help me. I told her that there was no way she would have known the amount of pain still there, as I had not really expressed it to her. I told her that only God would have known the depth of the pain and only He could have handled that pain for me. No man has the power to do what He did in this situation. He brought me to the retreat, and he led me there through people who had been a part of my life during that pain and she [the therapist] was one of those people. God works his miracles today through people.

Since the tremendous release of this pain, I have been able to walk into gift shops again; see, hear, remember experiences that were directly connected to memories of M___ without pain (in fact, the memories have taken on a pleasant instead of painful feeling); I even saw M___ briefly one day as she was in a parking lot entering her car. I had wondered if the prayer asking for detachment from her would be tested, and it was as I had not seen her for almost three years. I had no loss/pain feeling. Only one of sadness. I had been living in fear that I might meet her one day and often fantasized what I would do if it happened. Sometimes the fantasy was filled with anger and retribution and other times it was a "see I told you so" situation. Neither of these were very healthy, so when it finally did happen (although she did not see me), I was detached from her and felt comfortable with the feeling. I felt a peace from the anxiety I had produced for myself by not letting go and letting God . . .

5

Law & Grace

Through Christ's sacrifice, God has provided all the necessary ingredients to live a victorious life. Jesus said his yoke was easy and his burden light. When he said this, his listeners had a clear mental picture of what a burden and a yoke were like. They saw a burden that was heavy but they also saw a yoke that would harness two animals to it. We only fill one side of the yoke. God the Holy Spirit fills the other side

If instead, our walk is hard and our burden is heavy then the problem is not with God but with us. When God is out of the picture then we live as if the other side of the yoke were empty. We not only carry the burden ourselves but the weight of the yoke as well. We are fully responsible for leading the way. Living in such an off-balanced way can only lead to frustration and despair.

If we want God to intervene with his power in our lives then it must be on his terms. We must know and adjust our standards and perspectives to his. God never intended for us to solve the issues of life without his help or the help of other Christians. He never intended for us to cope with life or to survive as a life style.

A Point of Reference

We cannot fully receive or claim the benefits of forgiveness if we ourselves have not forgiven others. In addition, certain sins create ongoing consequences. (I will explain this in the next chapter). The only way to break the power and ongoing influences of such sins is through God's intervention.

We must deal with sin by judging it according to God's standards. We cannot fully receive forgiveness until we have given forgiveness to others. By focusing on sin for a time, we can stop the consequences of sin but sin should not be a preoccupation for the Christian. Nevertheless, by-products of Prayer and Resolution Counseling should be an increased awareness of the effects of sin, why it pays to avoid sin and a better understanding of the balance between law and grace.

Sin has always been a focal point in Christianity. Christ had to die because sin created a barrier between God and us. With sin came a penalty that we had to pay. Instead, Christ chose to make that payment for each of us. However, has sin or its effects ever been the issue?

When Adam and Eve sinned, payment came eventually in death. However, the most important daily consequence was that they had to leave the Garden and God's presence.

When we sin, there are consequences. Some consequences are short-lived. Others continue. Steal something minor and neither you nor the person you stole from loses sleep over it a month later. Rape someone and both you and the victim will carry it to your graves unless God stops the ongoing consequences.

The consequences are what make sins have greater or lesser weight. It is wrong to say that, since God is holy, all sins are the same to him. This is not true. Sins differ because they affect the people involved differently. Not all sins are the same because we know that God demands a stricter penalty for some.

We cannot approach God for help until we clearly understand what sin is and its consequences are. Saved by faith, by his grace, does not mean that sin is a dead issue. The Law is a part of this Age of Grace because, within the Law, there are principles that we cannot violate without serious consequences. When we talk about the wages of sin being death, we view this as a salvation issue. Someday we will face sin and death, or life in Christ. Nevertheless, even as Christians, we receive the wages daily in small doses of death until we appropriate what God has provided in Christ for forgiveness and release. Otherwise, we live with the consequences as sinners or victims of sinners.

Johnson and Van Vondreven answered the question: Why did God give the Law? Their response is interesting: (1) "We could see that we have sinned." (2) "to convince us that we are helpless, through our own efforts, to hit the mark. . . . imprisons and defines us . . ." (3) "to bring us into a grace-full relationship with God . . ."[39]

The authors fail to see that God gave us the Law as a standard (principles) for living.[40] The Law is a schoolmaster helping us understand the concerns, character and personality of God. He gave the Law as a blessing, not a burden to weight us down.

---

[39] David Johnson and Jeff Van Vonderven, *The Subtle Power of Spiritual Abuse* (Minneapolis: Bethany House, 1991), p. 84.
[40] An excellent book on the practicality of the Law is Laura Schlessinger and Rabbi Stewart Vogel, *The Ten Commandments: The Significance of God's Law in Everyday Life* (New York: First Cliff Street Books, 1999).

A Journey to Wholeness

Some see the God of the Old Testament as a God of harshness and discipline; he demands we do it his way or else. They see him in the New Testament as a God of love and understanding. He is the same God, however, in both sections of the Bible. He has not evolved, as time went on, into a God of love. God gave us the Law as an act of love. The principles for living that the Law provides are still good for us today. They give us a standard for behavior as we relate to God and as we relate to those around us. When we obey the principles of the Law there is blessing and long life. When we violate its principles it results in broken relationships and physical, emotional and spiritual harm.

If we step off a two-story building then we are going to get hurt. We cannot violate a natural law without suffering the consequences. The same is true when we violate a spiritual law; we cannot do so without suffering the spiritual, emotional and physical consequences. God knows this and wants to keep us from suffering the natural consequences of violating his principles for living. For when we do so, we sin or suffer the effects of what others do when they sin.

Sin is sin. True. No sin is an unimportant one but there are major sins and minor sins as far as consequences go. To a holy God any sin can stand between him and us but certain sins, once committed, set in motion a series of events far out of proportion to the act itself. Peter lied and denied the Lord but repented and lived. Ananias lied about some money and died for it. A father molests his daughter and both pay for it: one as the perpetrator and one as the victim.

The World Standard

Peck rightfully points out that what is normal is not necessarily right. "On the basis of cultural norms, we usually assume that if everyone is thinking this or doing that, it must be normal and correct."[41] The way we can tell if such behavior is, in fact, a "negative norm" is if it discourages growth. Unless we have a secure frame of reference, how can we know what is normal and correct versus what seems normal and correct because everyone is doing it? As we live in society and experience life, our exposure to life around us shapes our thinking and becomes our norm or standard. Custom is familiar and feels comfortable. The problem is that we cannot trust our feelings of what is right or wrong.

Our task is to judge others and ourselves rightly and we can only do so using the standards that God has given us. When we do not evaluate our behavior, or other's behaviors, in the light of rightness then we dishonor ourselves as God's creation.

We honor ourselves when we hold ourselves responsible and competent to stand on our own two feet and account for our actions. God gave us the ability to make choices and, whatever our relationship, we must answer for our actions, good or bad. We want to show this same honor to others as well.

Hurting believers are often reluctant to hold people accountable if those people have a special relationship,

---

[41] M. Scott Peck, *The Road Less Traveled and Beyond: Spiritual Growth in the Age of Anxiety* (New York: Simon & Schuster, 1997), p. 32.

for examples, a parent, pastor or friend. Yet holding people accountable for their misdeeds is *an act of honor.*

We should respect others and give them their due. They can stand on their own two feet and answer for their wrongdoing because God will someday ask from them an accounting for their actions. If justice is impartial and God holds all to the same standard then all are responsible for their actions no matter who they are.

Thus we show honor to our parents when we hold them responsible for their behavior. We do not dishonor the position of father when we accuse him and hold him responsible before God for right behavior. It does dishonor the position of father when we condone his poor performance as acceptable behavior, or the best he could do. To condone is to accept his performance as a right definition of what father is! When we do so, then we naturally project that same expectation unto God as a father. Therefore, we cannot trust him. God is waiting to smack us down. God does not care. He is far away.

We cannot come to God and say someone else made us do it. Nor can we say, "My mother was a poor model and so my behavior is not my fault." We are responsible for our own actions.

In American society and the justice system, the standard says that I am not responsible for my actions. I grew up in a terrible environment. I never had a chance.

Rush to Diagnosis

> *A Nov. 29 Letter writer responding to the page-one story on bullies claimed that Douglas Milteer's bullying behavior "suggests quite strongly that he had a serious behavioral disorder." She implied that such disorders are mental illnesses.*
>
> *I think the writer has fallen victim to a common pattern of reasoning within the mental health industry: Put a "mental illness" label on a set of unwanted behaviors, then claim that the mental illness is what causes the behaviors in question. While such circular reasoning may attract a lot of business for the writer's early diagnosis and treatment center, parents should be a bit more skeptical about mental illness labels.*
>
> *Common sense provides effective ways to deal with bullies, and none of them involve medications or therapy sessions.*
>
> Michael J Reznicek, M.D.
Psychiatrist
Lewiston, Idaho

---

[42] Letters in *Wall Street Journal*, December 3, 2002.

A Journey to Wholeness

A few years ago, a wife helped her husband rape and murder a woman. Nevertheless, she was not as responsible because she was afraid of the man and in his power.

God's system of reckoning is different. God, according to the standard he put into the Law, says that all involved, to whatever degree of involvement, are as guilty as the actual perpetrator. Knowing what is happening and helping a little is the same as full participation. Knowing a crime is being committed and doing nothing to stop it is actual participation.

People may feel that they have good reasons for sinning but there is no excuse for sinning. We want to have the same standard that God does. Not just because it is God's standard but because it is for our own well-being to accept and want that standard for our lives and the lives of others.

Any justification for wrong behavior disappears when we look at normal secular life around us. David grew up under Jack, a brutal father and abusive husband. David, as a man, later married and was brutal to his children and to his wife. David did not know better, or did he? He experienced abuse and knew what it felt like. This made him doubly responsible when he abused others in the same way.

Another boy, Nat, had a brutal father, Tom who was an abusive husband and father. Nat became a man, married and became brutal? No, he was gentle and caring to both his children and wife. David and Nat had the same backgrounds but they reacted differently to what they experienced.

Psychology has given us three ways to view behavior: (1) There is responsible behavior (sane) where we know right from wrong and do what is right. (2) There is irresponsible behavior where we do not understand or know right from wrong (insane) so we did not mean to do what we did and (3) There is diminished capacity where it was not our fault; we could not help ourselves. Most people, claiming insanity (temporary or otherwise) or diminished capacity as the excuse for their behavior, *understand enough to hide or hide what they have done.* Our reactions to our misdeeds show that we know what we have done both before the act and afterwards.

Let us come back to living out the wrong modeling of our parents. What happens in the homes of Jack and Tom whenever others people drop by? While others are around, both fathers are less brutal. Such wrongdoers keep their behavior hidden or altered when others are around. They judge themselves as guilty and acknowledge by their altered actions, or lack of them, that they do know what they are doing. They choose to act as they do and are not helpless victims of society. *When people can turn it off and on, it shows they have the power to choice.*

There is no difference in the standard for the Christian and the non-Christian. We cannot excuse sin because a person is unsaved. God holds all equally accountable and judges all by the same standard. Even the non-Christian world knows right from wrong. It does not always do right but it knows what is right. When we as Christians or non-Christians shift to *ideal behavior*, it is an indication that another system exists and is available for us to use. While all have consciences, Christians have additional accountability because they also have the Holy Spirit but, even without the spiritual dimension that Christ brings, all humans have a system of right and wrong and use it.

If Jack and Tom, the two fathers mentioned above, had been Christians and had sought help in the church, the church would have given them little help. The church has approached the results of Christ's sacrifice in a simplistic manner. Christ's sacrifice is for salvation in

A Journey to Wholeness

the bye and bye, not for today. Jack and Tom would be encouraged to, "Wait until you get to heaven and you will understand." Or, "Pray and read your Bible more each day. Your problems will go away." Or, "Just give this to Jesus." Jack and Tom would need guidance, however, that led them toward confession and forgiveness. This is prayer that deals with real life issues and concerns. Jack and Tom would need healing that can only come from God himself.

The Scriptures talk about sowing and reaping, about cause and effect. When we disobey the principles of the Law, we reap the natural consequences of sowing sin. Some sins, once set in motion, not only affect us but our children and our children's children . . . to the tenth generation.

In forgiving another, or when asking forgiveness for ourselves, we must accept that a standard has been violated or broken. This standard is not relative, nor is it culturally determined. God has established it. This means that when we forgive another we are holding them accountable for sinning against us *according to God's standard*. If so, then we need to understand the principles involved and the very mind of God.

I say principles because we do not want to judge others based on their surface behavior that we can misunderstand. But, judge we must for "we cannot lead decent lives without making judgments in general and moral judgments in particular."[43] Peck rightfully says, "The issue, then, is not whether to judge . . . The question is how and when to judge wisely."[44] Therefore, if we must judge, our frame of reference should be the

---

[43] M. Scott Peck, *People of the Lie: The Hope for Healing Human Evil* (New York: Simon & Schuster, 1983), p. 256.
[44] Ibid., p. 257

underlying principles upon which God's Law rests. God gave the Law as a guide to righteous living. It is to help us avoid the consequences of living otherwise.

God's Standard

We can view God's standards as a series of dos or don'ts. When we obey, we receive blessing; when we disobey, we receive consequences. This is true, but the Law provides a point of reference and principles that allow us to understand the issues involved. We must never assume that because everyone is doing it that such actions are acceptable. We must always compare the standards of the world to God's standards in the Law. God's standards always overrule those of the world.

Many see God as the big bully forcing us to do it his way. He is God and can do anything he wants. He can make us to do it his way just because he is bigger. Instead of showing love, they see God as pulling rank. This is not true. God gave the Law so we would know how to live his way. His way is voluntary but his way leads to long life and blessing. His way helps us avoid many pitfalls that come in life.

The Law also reveals the character of God. In the Law, we see that God is firm but fair, considerate and impartial, compassionate and caring. He has a special concern for orphans, widows and even strangers and foreigners who do not know him. His Law helps us find the right road in life.

When we fail to follow his principles then natural consequences come into play: shortened life, disease, insanity, to name a few. God would rather we did it his way and avoid all these tragedies. Though he is God, he will not force us to do it his way. God is not a bully. God

A Journey to Wholeness

is a God of love. He wants us to follow him willingly and live his way because this is best for us.

We lived with an Amazon tribe for several years. The tribe had no laws except taboo-type restrictions. One day Jose came to us upset because a woman had stolen his beads. He was going into the jungle to "cool off" since being "an angry one" was not acceptable. The woman stole his beads and he was at fault because he got angry!

The tribe had no definite laws as standards for behavior or for governing relations between themselves. Peer pressure was the norm to control society. But those Indians who were "thick skinned" could violate the norms and cause dissatisfaction with the rest. The only recourse was to talk to the offenders and try to make them "hearing ones" (obedient). If that did not work, then the members of the communal house would poison them or drive them out of the community by withholding food. When driven out, the offenders would go to another communal house and continue their offensive behavior.

Except for peer pressure, this tribe did not have rules of law. Therefore, they did not have a clear concept of sin, its penalty, justice, guilt or any means to make things right except in a vengeful way. Long ago, this tribe had forgotten the existence of God. When God is not in the picture, neither are his rules for living righteously.[45]

Having no standards of right and wrong voids any basis for accusations or judgments. No one needs payment for wrong because nothing is wrong. Society is redefining right and wrong. Right is whatever does not hurt another. Right is whatever people choose to do

---

[45] After an Indian became a Christian, he or she had no trouble knowing what sin was and acknowledging it. The concept of sin was there, just under the surface but not overtly a part of that society.

because they are free agents. Right is doing whatever seems or feels right to do. Right is what everyone else is doing. By condoning the behavior, society has endorsed it.

Even when people do evil by society's standards, they are not at fault. Their environment was faulty. They had poor parental models. Their fathers abused them. They did not have a chance. Helen was afraid of her boyfriend and that is why she helped him kill the girl. Jake was mentally challenged and so did not know right from wrong. (Whatever the excuses, people like Jake usually know enough to attempt to pretend it did not happen, hide it, hide themselves or run away. Those actions show knowledge of right and wrong.)

As God's children, we want to judge people in the light of God's standard, not society's standard. Jesus said, *"For in the way you judge, you will be judged; and by your standard of measure, it will be measured to you"* (Matthew 7:2 NAS). He does not say, do not judge. However, we do not judge by our own standards; we judge using God's Law and standard. If we use our own standard—even if it is unfair standard—God will use that same standard against us!

God's standard, the law, forms the reference point for evaluating right and wrong. The same standard applies to both the Christian and the non-Christian. God will judge us all in the end by that standard. We will satisfy his justice system by making a payment ourselves or by having our payment placed on Jesus Christ at the Cross. Either way, justice must be served.

God's standard is his basis for rewarding us as well. Both his right to judge and his right to reward is recognition that we can make choices. With right choices come accountability, blessings and reward; with bad choices come accountability and negative consequences.

A Journey to Wholeness

As his children, we want to accept the fact that we can make choices. We want to hold ourselves, and others, accountable for these choices, both the good and the bad.

❧ ☙

Law and Grace work together in harmony. If we live only under the Law then it will burdened us down with its message and potential judgment. *"I found that the very commandment that was intended to bring life, actually brought death"* (Romans 7: 10). If we live by grace, without the Law to establish our boundaries of behavior, then we will live without direction, dependent only on our con-sciences to guide us.

What shall we say, then? Is the law sin? Certainly not! Indeed I would no have known what sin was except through the law (Romans 7: 7a).

What shall we say, then? Shall we go on sinning that grace may increase? By no means! We died to sin; how can we live in it any longer? (Romans 6:1-2)

6

The Reality of Sin

More and more, sin is an unpopular word. The word mistake is taking its place but, semantically, there is a difference. Mistake implies a desire to do it right and making a mistake. Often we never intended to do it right in the first place.

We now see the guilty at their sentencing saying they are sorry for what they did. Sorry when they did it? No. Sorry now that they are caught? Yes. Did they make a mistake when they shot the desk clerk or did they sin with premeditation?

Sin has a life of its own once we commit wrongdoing. While we cannot see or measure sin, we know it exists because we see its effects in our lives. There are various categories of sin as we have seen and certain sins have greater power in our lives than others. There are sins of commission and sins of omission (in some cases, mistakes); sins with premeditation and sins through ignorance (in some cases, mistakes). Regardless, we must place all sin at the foot of the cross or we must personally pay what is due.

While Christ's sacrifice fully handled general sins at salvation, others continue to have a life of their own until we personally have a hand in killing them. As we will see later, Christ's sacrifice is available to handle all sin.

Consider the following examples:

Long Term Sins

A child born out of wedlock:

No bastard shall enter the assembly of the Lord; even to the tenth generation none of his descendants shall enter the assembly of the Lord (Deuteronomy 23:2 RSV).

Ammonites and Moabites:

No Ammonite or Moabite or any of his descendants may enter the assembly of the LORD, even down to the tenth generation (Deuteronomy 23:3).

Prostitution:

Do not degrade your daughter by making her a prostitute, or the land will turn to prostitution and be filled with wickedness (Leviticus 19:29).

The Death Sins

Jesus said of Judas who betrayed him, "*It would have been good for that man if he had not been born*" (Matthew 26:24 NAS). Some acts deserve more punishment than others do. If there are degrees of sin, then this explains why certain sins have more force and power than others do. It explains why certain sins might need special treatment to void their effects.

In the Old Testament, the daily sacrifices did not cover certain categories of sinners and neither did the atonement sacrifice.[46] Instead, the guilty person's penalty was personal death. Examples of these special crimes were murder, adultery and occult activities. These *death and power sins* of the Old Testament function even today. Once committed, these sins release forces and ongoing consequences that operate even after conversion until we deal with them specifically before God.

These fall into four categories: (1) sins against God, such as the practice of the occult; (2) sins against the body, such as violation of sexual norms; (3) sins against the established order, such as rejection of and rebellion against authority; and (4) the only one without the death penalty attached to it, sins involving words of power, such as making vows and failing to fulfill them.

Sins against God

Blasphemy:

Say to the Israelites: 'If anyone curses his God, he will be held responsible; anyone who blasphemes the name of the LORD must be put to death. The entire assembly must stone him. Whether an alien or native-born, when he blasphemes the Name, he must be put to death' (Leviticus 24:15-16).

---

[46] Once a year the High Priest entered the Holy of Holies and presented a blood sacrifices for the past sins of Israel.

The Reality of Sin

False prophecies:

But a prophet who presumes to speak in my name anything I have not commanded him to say, or a prophet who speaks in the name of other gods, must be put to death (Deuteronomy 18:20).

Idolatry:

The LORD said to Moses, "Say to the Israelites: 'Any Israelite or any alien living in Israel who gives any of his children to Molech must be put to death. The people of the community are to stone him.'" (Leviticus 20:1-2).

If a man or woman living among you in one of the towns the LORD gives you is found doing evil in the eyes of the LORD your God in violation of his covenant, and contrary to my command has worshiped other gods, bowing down to them or to the sun or the moon or the stars of the sky, and this has been brought to your attention, then you must investigate it thoroughly. If it is true and it has been proved that this detestable thing has been done in Israel, take the man or woman who has done this evil deed to your city gate and stone that person to death (Deuteronomy 17:2-5).

Sabbath profaning:

Observe the Sabbath, because it is holy to you. Anyone who desecrates it must be put to death;

whoever does any work on that day must be cut off from his people (Exodus 31:14).

Sorcery:

Do not allow a sorceress to live (Exodus 22:18).

Sins against the Body

Adultery:

If a man commits adultery with another man's wife—with the wife of his neighbor—both the adulterer and the adulteress must be put to death (Leviticus 20:10).

If a man is found sleeping with another man's wife, both the man who slept with her and the woman must die. You must purge the evil from Israel (Deuteronomy 22:22).

Animal Cohabitation:

If a man has sexual relations with an animal, he must be put to death, and you must kill the animal. If a woman approaches an animal to have sexual relations with it, kill both the woman and the animal. They must be put to death; their blood will be on their own heads (Leviticus 20:15-16).

The Reality of Sin

Incestuous relationships:

If a man sleeps with his father's wife, he has dishonored his father. Both the man and the woman must be put to death; their blood will be on their own heads. If a man sleeps with his daughter-in-law, both of them must be put to death. What they have done is a perversion; their blood will be on their own heads. If a man marries both a woman and her mother, it is wicked. Both he and they must be burned in the fire, so that no wickedness will be among you (Leviticus 20:11-12, 14).

Kidnapping:

If a man is caught kidnapping one of his brother Israelites and treats him as a slave or sells him, the kidnapper must die. You must purge the evil from among you (Deuteronomy 24:7).

Anyone who kidnaps another and either sells him or still has him when he is caught must be put to death (Exodus 21:16).

Murder:

But if a man hates his neighbor and lies in wait for him, assaults and kills him, and then flees to one of these cities, the elders of his town shall send for him, bring him back from the city, and hand him over to the avenger of blood to die. Show him no pity. You must purge from Israel the guilt of shedding innocent blood, so that it may go well with you (Deuteronomy 19:11-13).

Manslaughter:

If a bull gores a man or a woman to death, the bull must be stoned to death, and its meat must not be eaten. But the owner of the bull will not be held responsible. If, however, the bull has had the habit of goring and the owner has been warned but has not kept it penned up and it kills a man or woman, the bull must be stoned and the owner also must be put to death. However, if payment is demanded of him, he may redeem his life by paying whatever is demanded (Exodus 21:28-29).

Rape:

If a man happens to meet in a town a virgin pledged to be married and he sleeps with her, you shall take both of them to the gate of that town and stone them to death—the girl because she was in a town and did not scream for help, and the man because he violated another man's wife. You must purge the evil from among you.

But if out in the country a man happens to meet a girl pledged to be married and rapes her, only the man who has done this shall die. Do nothing to the girl; she has committed no sin deserving death. This case is like that of someone who attacks and murders his neighbor, for the man found the girl out in the country, and though the betrothed girl screamed, there was no one to rescue her (Deuteronomy 22:23-27).

Sodomy:

If a man lies with a man as one lies with a woman, both of them have done what is detestable. They must be put to death; their blood will be on their own heads (Leviticus 20:13).

Sins against Established Order (Rebellion)

Hitting or cursing a parent:

Anyone who attacks his father or his mother must be put to death (Exodus 21:15).

Anyone who curses his father or mother must be put to death (Exodus 21:17).

*If a man has a stubborn and rebellious son who does not obey his father and mother and will not listen to them when they discipline him, his father and mother shall take hold of him and bring him to the elders at the gate of his town. They shall say to the elders, "This son of ours is stubborn and rebellious. He will not obey us. He is a profligate and a drunkard." Then all the men of his town shall stone him to death. You must purge the evil from among you. All Israel will hear of it and be afraid (*Deuteronomy 21:18-21*).*

The Power Sins

Breaking or failing to fulfill a vow:

If you make a vow to the LORD your God, do not be slow to pay it, for the LORD your God will certainly demand it of you and you will be guilty of sin. But if you refrain from making a vow, you will not be guilty. Whatever your lips utter you must be sure to do, because you made your vow freely to the LORD your God with your own mouth (Deuteronomy 23: 21-23).

Cursing a brother:

You have heard that it was said to the people long ago,"Do not murder, and anyone who murders will be subject to judgment." But I tell you that anyone who is angry with his brother will be subject to judgment. Again, anyone who says to his brother, "Raca," is answerable to the Sanhedrin. But anyone who says, "You fool!" will be in danger of the fire of hell (Matthew 5:21-22).

Good and Evil Declarations:

From the fruit of his mouth a man's stomach is filled; with the harvest from his lips he is satisfied. The tongue has the power of life and death, and those who love it will eat its fruit (Proverbs 18:20-21).

For these first three categories, the death of the wrongdoer was the only satisfaction that the Law permitted. The normal Old Testament sacrifice did not apply to those people who committed these death sins. Nor did the daily sacrifice release someone from the effects of words of power. If this is true in the Old Testament, what about the New Testament? Might we need to treat these sins in a special and specific way before God? Salvation is not the issue here. Christ paid for these sins but he had to go "the extra mile" to do so. Why? Because these cases required that the wrongdoer be sacrificed – his or her death was the only payment.

The Power of Sin

The issue is not sin, but the consequences of sin. When we commit one of these special sins then the results carry over to other people and continue in us as a destructive force until broken at the cross. When Greta's father committed incest, his sin affected her. It also affected his wife. It affected his son who also violated Greta. It affected Greta's view of herself and possibly the fact that she is unmarried today. It affected her later work as a missionary.

Certain sins create a tsunami-like effect, a tidal wave that starts out small and increases in size as it travels on and affects life after life in destructive ways. God's answer in the Old Testament was to take the life of the perpetrator to break the cycle at it source. Death was the price for sexual sin. Death was the price for witchcraft. Death was the price for rebellion. Death was the price for committing murder. The focus was on protecting society by eliminating the source (the offender) and affirming the right standards.

A Journey to Wholeness

Not all sin has the same weight in its effects on others. For example, the price for stealing was not death but repayment plus additional restitution.

While Christ's sacrifice does handle all sin, we must present these special classes of sin specifically to God to obtain all that we need: forgiveness, cleansing, and release—and the accompanying breaking of the power that these particular types of sin have in our lives.

This is not about the loss of salvation or being unsaved. But, until the forces of these special sins are eliminated, they will continue to nurture the old man and allow Satan to touch the believer's life.

I have worked with missionaries who had practiced the occult arts before they were Christians. Satan continued to have a claim on a part of their lives as a result. During the training program I directed, I would take the participants through an area of an ancient city where storekeepers sold magic wares. Afterwards some participants reported nightmares and feelings of unease. Always the ones with unresolved occult issues reacted. Never, to my knowledge, were the others affected. Sins against God have extra power released when we commit such acts.

While I am referring to mild forms of demonic influence, Ensign and Howe state:

> *We have been reared in a tradition that taught that demons could not invade or control people and certainly not Christians. Severe questioning and review of the whole matter of the deliverance work were continued for several months as we tested every conceivable theory of explanation for what was happening. The only explanation that was systematically consistent and in harmony*

with the Word of God was that our brothers and sisters had been invaded by evil spirits.[47]

These authors also confirm what I have seen: often before people have trusted in Christ, they gave opportunity for a certain degree of demonic influence through acts of sin and this relationship with the Kingdom of Darkness carried over into their Christian lives.[48]

Pastors promiscuous before or after salvation continued to be troubled. They seldom continued in outright physical sin but shifted to pornography or fantasizing and masturbation. Sexual sin releases a special force that does not automatically go away with time.

Missionaries who have rejected parental controls also rejected other authorities. They appeared to submit to authority but were always reluctant or distrustful of their leaders. Most focused on Jesus only and found it hard to address God as father. Rebellion in various forms affected their relationships with people over them and with God.

I have worked with a few pastors and missionaries dedicated to God's service by a parent. Many were ungifted and unhappy in service but they felt compelled to serve. Others have been in secular work, often successful, yet unsettled because they had once dedicated their lives to God's service. Words of power create obligations that do not disappear just because we want to will them away.

These examples are not exceptions to the rule. They are the norms for people who have committed what I

---

[47] Ensign, Grayson H. and Howe, Edward. *Bothered? Bewildered? Bewitched?* (Cincinnati: Recovery, 1984) p. 136.
[48] Ibid.

have termed the death and power sins of the Old Testament.

The Law in Operation

Death   Sin

It has helped me to view our lives as a scale that sin can weigh down on one side: Every time we sin, the scale is out of balance. When that happens, we must bring the scale back to zero by adding a counter weight. Only two counter weights are available: one weight means that we pay for that sin and carry the consequences, the other weight means that Christ pays for that sin through his sacrifice. Either way, death is the payment due.

Only one of those two counterweights will put the scale back to zero. There is no other way in the universe to handle sin or stop its consequences. As Christ said,

> *For truly I say to you, until heaven and earth pass away, not the smallest letter or stroke shall pass*

away from the Law, until all is accomplished (Matthew 5:18 NAS).

That includes the Law's demand for retribution.

We talk of the consequence (wages) of sin as death. Christ's sacrifice handles this death when we come to him at salvation. Nevertheless, sin creates ongoing living consequences that are as important and Christ's sacrifice also provided for these. If not dealt with, these ongoing consequences plague us, hold us down or chain us so we are the slaves of sin. Christ handled these consequences also but we often consider these as the cross we bear. We are mistaken. Christ's sacrifice covered all sin and all the power, forces and consequences of sin when he died on the cross. Yet sometimes we must ask God to apply this sacrifice for us in specific ways.

We have viewed the Cross and resurrection only in the light of Christ making it possible for us to receive forgiveness and be in God's family. His sacrifice did more than that. The Lord said that he came to fulfill all the Law. If that is true, then we find issues in the Law that we need to reconsider, issues we have assumed no longer matter in the New Testament.

The Ongoing Consequences of Sin

When sin occurs, there can be lasting effects. Once we accept that, we can appreciate the need for the church to operate at a different level than it has up to now. The Law dealt with all areas of life. So did Christ when he died at the Cross, rose again from the dead and now sits on the right hand of the Father. Christ gave us the power to apply what he did at the Cross to purify both us and the land. Much of what the sacrificial system covered in the Old Testament should have carried over into the New Testament, into this Age of Grace. For example, are any of these relevant today?

The Need for Cleansing

> *The LORD said to Moses, "Say to the Israelites: `A woman who becomes pregnant and gives birth to a son will be ceremonially unclean for seven days, just as she is unclean during her monthly period. On the eighth day the boy is to be circumcised. Then the woman must wait thirty-three days to be purified from her bleeding. She must not touch anything sacred or go to the sanctuary until the days of her purification are over. If she gives birth to a daughter, for two weeks the woman will be unclean, as during her period. Then she must wait sixty-six days to be purified from her bleeding.*
>
> *When the days of her purification for a son or daughter are over, she is to bring to the priest at the entrance to the Tent of Meeting a year-old lamb for a burnt offering and a young pigeon or a dove for a sin offering. He shall offer them before the LORD to make atonement for her, and then she will be ceremonially clean from her flow of blood.*
>
> *These are the regulations for the woman who gives birth to a boy or a girl. If she cannot afford a lamb, she is to bring two doves or two young pigeons, one for a burnt offering and the other for*

a sin offering. In this way the priest will make atonement for her, and she will be clean'" (Leviticus 12:1-8).

The Need to Purify the Land

If a man is found slain, lying in a field in the land the LORD your God is giving you to possess, and it is not known who killed him, your elders and judges shall go out and measure the distance from the body to the neighboring towns. Then the elders of the town nearest the body shall take a heifer . . . and lead her . . . where there is a flowing stream. . . . they are to break the heifer's neck. The priests . . . shall step forward . . . to pronounce blessings in the name of the LORD and to decide all cases of dispute and assault. Then all the elders of the town nearest the body shall wash their hands over the heifer whose neck was broken in the valley, and they shall declare: "Our hands did not shed this blood, nor did our eyes see it done. Accept this atonement for your people Israel, whom you have redeemed, O LORD, and do not hold your people guilty of the blood of an innocent man." And the bloodshed will be atoned for. So you will purge from yourselves the guilt of shedding innocent blood . . . (Deuteronomy 21:1-9).

The Need to Avoid Defiling the Land

If a man guilty of a capital offense is put to death and his body is hung on a tree, you must not leave his body on the tree overnight. Be sure to bury him that same day, because anyone who is hung on a tree is under God's curse. You must not desecrate the land the LORD your God is giving you as an inheritance. (Deuteronomy 21:22-23).

The Need to Purify Defiled Things

Gold, silver, bronze, iron, tin, lead and anything else that can withstand fire must be put through the fire, and then it will be clean. But it must also be purified with the water of cleansing. And whatever cannot withstand fire must be put through that water (Numbers 31:22-23).

The Need to Purify Areas of Occult Activities

Speak to the Israelites and say to them: "When you cross the Jordan into Canaan, drive out all the inhabitants of the land before you. Destroy all their carved images and their cast idols, and demolish all their high places" (Numbers 33:51-52).

The Need to Avoid Unholy Objects

> *The images of their gods you are to burn in the fire. Do not covet the silver and gold on them, and do not take it for yourselves, or you will be ensnared by it, for it is detestable to the LORD your God. Do not bring a detestable thing into your house or you, like it, will be set apart for destruction. Utterly abhor and detest it, for it is set apart for destruction* (Deuteronomy 7:25-26).

Christ's sacrifice has covered all of our sins, at salvation and after salivation. Nevertheless, we must appropriate his sacrifice when we sin as Christians. That is what I John 1:9 is all about. When we do not appropriate what Christ accomplished, it is not a question of salvation, but of empowering sin within us. When we sin, either his sacrifice covers it or, in some way, we pay – but not at the cost of our salvation.

We must keep God's moral laws or pay the consequences. The system is inflexible. Christ died so we would not be condemned, but not at the cost of sacrificing the Law. The penalty of breaking the Law must be satisfied through us or through Christ. The choice is ours.

Sandford is correct when he says, "This is a legal universe."[49] This legal system even extends to the land and things. These begin as "neutral" but take on the characteristics of holy (Numbers 16:35-38) by being presented on the altar, or profane through, for example, murder, sex sin or visitation by Satan through idol worship.

---

[49] John & Paula Sandford, *The Transformation of the Inner Man* (South Plainfield, NJ: Bridge Publishing, 1982) 75.

A Journey to Wholeness

Christ's death as sacrifice on the cross provides the grounds for the forgiveness of our sins, for our redemption, justification and atonement; his resurrection gave us new life. For restoration and new life we need more than forgiveness, we need to have the power of God to break the ongoing consequences of those sins.

Christ has paid our sin payment at the cross. This is an automatic part of our salvation experience. This includes the special death sins but their power and consequences continue until we present them to God in a focused way, acknowledging the particular awfulness of them to gain full release, and restoration. This usually requires forgiveness as well, since the ongoing forces at work produce more sin and more consequences.

God forgiving and pardoning us is not enough if we still live defeated lives. Justified says that in Christ our debt is paid. Redeemed says that we are freed. What we need in our lives, and what God has provided, is the means for living free from the ongoing power of sin. Whether the consequences are great or small depends on the sin committed. But, whatever the sin, the Cross must balance the consequences in life, caused by sin's weight.

This is the spiritual cause and effect that the Bible calls sowing and reaping. "*Do not be deceived, God is not mocked; whatever a man sows, this he will also reap*" (Galatians 6:7 NAS). What we sow depends on us and, in part, on those who have shaped and influenced our lives. Nevertheless, we have the final decision and must bear responsibility for our choices. What we ourselves sow determines what we reap and how much.

When we come to Christ, we often find that though God has lifted the burden of sin, the consequences of sin are still there. We continue to carry the scars and habits of living in a sinful culture and in the patterns formed by the past.

While the law of sowing and reaping is designed to bless, it can curse instead,

> *The one who sows to please his sinful nature, from that nature will reap destruction; the one who sows to please the Spirit, from the Spirit will reap eternal life* (Galatians 6:8).

The Law is impartial: we break the law, we pay the consequences. It matters not if we break the Law knowingly and with premeditation. It matters not that we act in ignorance or because we do not like the Law or think it is impractical or silly. Nor does it matter, according to the Law, if we are believers or unbelievers. No matter what, we are still under its force and consequences.

When we break the law, according to Sandford and Sandford, we set in motion irrevocable forces.[50] They point out a paradox.

> *[In] this most humble and obedient age, relative to natural science, we have become arrogant and deluded concerning laws which govern our hearts and spirits!*[51]

The Law covered all aspects of life, including forgiveness of sin and cleansing but break that Law and there is no escape or exception. Either Christ pays or we must pay. Both our good and our bad deeds shape and empower our lives. We will reap what we sow, unless God intervenes.

---

[50] Ibid., 72.
[51] Ibid., 74.

So how does this effect the way we do Prayer and Resolution Counseling? For one thing, we have points of reference. As we write down the brief details of people's lives in a chronological order, we look for these four categories of sin:

1. Sexual sins
2. Sins of rebellion
3. Sins concerning words of power
4. Occult sins

Other (less major sins) sins will group around these categories.

In a world that is becoming increasingly vague when it comes to a moral or ethical model, the Law is our point of reference for determining good and evil. Remember though that the Law deals in principles, not rigid form. We see this in the way Christ applied the law: not just adultery but looking at another with lust; not just murder but hatred toward another.

As important is that the Law helps us understand the character of God and his concerns as we relate to him and to one another. God gave us the Law to bless us and to give us long life.

7

Implications from the Law

Ministry Considerations

The Law contains principles that create an eternal standard for behavior. The Law also presents us with implications that can affect the ministry: needs that we may not have considered for the present time. We need to ask ourselves the question, where in the New Testament does it say that the details of the Law are no longer important?

God's Law gives us the principles for righteous living regardless of whether we are of the house of Israel or not. The principles of the Law carry past cultures and over time. The Law does not just emphasize behavior; it also emphasizes the consequences of violation. Do the consequences of sin no longer matter?

If they do matter today, then we must know how to nullify their effects. God will give us what we ask for in breaking the ongoing consequences of sin.

Identified by Ethnic Origin

The Statement: The Scriptures say that certain people, because of the actions of their forebears, cannot receive God's blessing. They specifically mention two peoples: "*No Ammonite or Moabite or any of his descendants may enter the assembly of the Lord, even down to the tenth generation*" (Deuteronomy 23:3). The effects of the sins of the forebears did not run out, so to speak, for ten generations.

The Edomites and Egyptians had a similar restriction but only running for three generations:

Do not abhor an Edomite, for he is your brother. Do not abhor an Egyptian, because you lived as an alien in his country. The third generation of children born to them may enter the assembly of the Lord (Deuteronomy 23:7-8).

The Implications: The offspring of people today may be under a curse because of what their forebears did. For example, the Germans attempted the genocide of the Jews, Slavs, Gypsies and others during World War II. The Turks attempted the genocide of the Armenians. When Turkish people become believers might it be necessary for them to confess the sins of their fathers and ask God to release them from the consequences of their fathers' sins?

Remaining in Adana is difficult for missionaries. Adana is a city in Turkey where many atrocities were committed. Does that location and its people still bear the stain of what happened in the early part of the Twentieth Century?

If our families profited from the unjust internment of American Japanese during World War II, then what is our response? Not all Americans shared in the betrayals of and atrocities against the American Indians but, if our ancestors were involved, then how do their crimes affect us now?

Identified Through Family

The Statement: In much of the world, especially in the West, illegitimacy is on the rise. The debate is not over illegitimacy but over whether a child needs one parent or two. The Scriptures say that the issues are spiritual, not environmental. They say,

> *No bastard shall enter the assembly of the Lord, even to the tenth generation none of his descendants shall enter the assembly of the LORD* (Deuteronomy 23:2 RSV).

Notice that the parents are not the focus here, the child and its offspring are, and that the effects or consequences do not dissipate for ten generations.

The Implications: What shows that the spiritual, psychological and social consequences have changed for today? My friend married a lovely young woman who was an illegitimate child. This young woman became a believer in her early teens and went regularly to a good church. When she was seventeen, like her mother, she had an illegitimate child. As I looked at this newly married couple and their wonderful five-year-old daughter, whom my friend accepted as if she were his own, I wondered about her future.

Might this illegitimate child need special prayer for cleansing and for release from the consequences of her grandmother and mother's sin (and of the unknown father's sin) both for herself and her future offspring? We can bless children but some children need both a blessing and a lifting of the consequences of sin placed upon them by others.

Identified Through Association

The Statement: God warned the people of Israel,

Do not bring a detestable thing into your house or you, like it, will be set apart for destruction. Utterly abhor and detest it, for it is set apart for destruction (Deuteronomy 7:26).

Notice here that it does not mention worshiping an idol. The issue here is that it is cursed and having it around will bring the curse on the person.

The Implications: Is there anything in the New Testament that nullifies this command and its consequences? Does it matter if we have a statue of the Buddha as a decoration?

When we were in Colombia at our agency center, the neighbors had a baby sitter in to watch their children. They normally lived and worked with a jungle tribe and had several artifacts displayed in their center home. The children were asleep in the next room. The baby sitter was alone in the living room. She was frightened when she saw faces and figures appearing in a corner of the room. Later she learned that the artifacts in that corner were used in a service of worship by the Indians.

If an object can have a spiritual force within it, or if an object can provide residence for a spiritual force, is it wise to have it as a house decoration? Do we need to destroy such items? Can they give entrance to the forces of Satan? Can they be a barrier to receiving God's blessing?

Identified Through Participation

The Statement: Witches and warlocks are on the World Wide Web. The New Heavens and New Earth computer magazine often has articles on spirit guides, channeling and increasing the inner consciousness. The Scriptures are straight forward,

> *A man or woman who is a medium or spiritist among you must be put to death. You are to stone them; their blood will be on their own heads* (Leviticus 20:27).

Authorities, counselors and pastors often do not believe satanic ritual abuse (SRA) victims when they report the ordeals they have experienced, including the birth and sacrifice of their babies. Are such activities possible? We do know from Scripture that such things did happen and, in fact, was a major cause of God's driving the Canaanite peoples from their land,

> *Let no one be found among you who sacrifices his son or daughter in the fire, who practices divination or sorcery, interprets omens, engages in witchcraft, or casts spells, or who is a medium or spiritist or who consults the dead. Anyone who does these things is detestable to the Lord, and because of these detestable practices the Lord*

your God will drive out those nations before you. (Deuteronomy 18:10-12)

God warned Israel, "*Do not turn to mediums or seek out spiritists, for you will be defiled by them. I am the Lord your God*" (Leviticus 19:31). The penalty for using the black arts was death: for both the practitioner and the seeker.

The Implications: A new believer may still be under a curse if he or she has used or participated in the occult. This includes using crystals, Ouija boards, crystal balls, taro cards, charms and participating in séances or sacrifices, to name a few occult activities.

I have seen missionaries open a door of invitation to Satan. This has happened because they have not specifically dealt with their occult pasts. Despite their activities being pre-Christian or post-Christian, and despite Bible training, Satan has a pseudo-claim on them. Because of this, they experience nightmares and psychic phenomenon that people without such pasts do not.

The effects of such a past do not disappear over time or with Bible study. People must deal with the occult issues. Their prayers must include renouncements of Satan and his kingdom and declarations for God and his kingdom, just to name a few issues.

Identified Through Words of Power

Excepting the illegitimate child, all the sins mentioned above have had the death penalty attached according to Old Testament Law. In working with people, I have seen that these sins set in motion forces that are powerful and ongoing in the lives of even believers. People must bring these things specifically to God in prayer. Only he can release them from the power and the ongoing consequences within themselves and often within their offspring.

The Statement: Words of power differ. No death penalty is involved. Nevertheless, when words of power are in operation the people involved are obligated to fulfill the vow. God clearly says,

When you make a vow to God, do not delay in fulfilling it. He has no pleasure in fools; fulfill your vow. It is better not to vow than to make a vow and not fulfill it (Ecclesiastes 5:4-5).

The Implications: When we make a vow, we put ourselves under its obligation until we fulfill it or confess our sin and ask for release.

Mary grew up in an Asian culture. She dated an American who tried to seduce her but she resisted him. Even so, he aroused her and she vowed that she would never allow herself to react like that again. A few years later Mary met and married. She found that she could not respond to her husband and asked for our help.

When we prayed the Holy Spirit brought to Mary's memory the vow she had made. She asked forgiveness for making such a foolish vow—foolish in that it was too all-inclusive—and asked God to release from that vow.

In New Mexico, I was looking at properties with a young woman. She had been a nun and had left her Catholic order. I did not know at first about her background but she stood out from other women. When a priest or nun, missionary or pastor decides to leave the ministry, does it matter that they have made a vow before the church and God to serve him?

When an authority has laid hands on our heads and blessed us and committed us to God's service does it matter? Can we go on into business or education and live a normal life without the call of God hanging over us? Is there a need for release from the vows we have taken? According to my Bible, I see that certain words have significance both here and in heaven.

Identified Through Rite of Passage

The Statement: When we go through a ceremony with one identity and come out with another, or an added identity, then we have gone through a rite of passage. For example, a man and woman go through the ceremony called marriage and come out as a husband and wife. Jesus quoted the Old Testament but also added more when he said,

> *For this reason a man shall leave his father and mother and be joined to his wife, and the two shall become one flesh.' So they are no longer two but one flesh. What therefore God has joined together, let not man put asunder* (Mark 10: 7-9).

"Flesh" is misleading. They become one. Notice that, according to Jesus, marriage is not just an earth transaction, it is a heaven transaction.

The Implications: If God joins us in marriage then does a legal divorce nullify what he has created? If a man and woman become one in marriage then when does that oneness cease? I have found that a former spouse still feels the oneness of his or her spouse from a previous marriage.

Connie and I prayed with a couple in Cyprus. They had both been married before. Both still felt tied to their previous spouses. We led them in a prayer asking God to break the oneness of spirit that their first marriages had created. We asked for spiritual divorces so they could be truly joined in their present marriage. (My point is not to condone divorce. Once someone has remarried, however, there is no going back. The best we can do is to free the spouses from their former relationships, bring God's blessing and create a good foundation for the present marriage.)

As we look at the Law as principles for living, we can see the implications behind the surface statements. Lust is adultery; hatred is murder. The purity and wholeness of the extended family prohibit sexual license. Consideration for others is a constant theme. Alms giving is not in focus as much as helping the needy help themselves through leaving portions of the harvest field untouched. Theft requires repayment. There are definitions of some types of perversion. Certain sins act like a cancer on society and the surest way to nullify its effects is to nullify the perpetrator with death. The emphasis is not on the individual and his or her welfare (life) but on society's welfare. The Law clearly states that sin affects us and those around us.

The authors of the New Testament wrote with the Old Testament Law as the backdrop. Leave it out and we leave out the context of life in which the authors lived

Implications from the Law

and wrote. The Law cannot give us life but it can give us blessing. It should not be a weight but a light to help us live according to God's standards and to provide us with a standard for determining right from wrong.

8

Christ's Sacrifice

The Perspective

From the very beginning, sacrifice has been the means of appeasing God. Even the heathen nations performed acts of sacrifice. God established three kinds for sacrifice for Israel: (1) there were to be daily sacrifices made for sins, (2) there were provisions for individuals to bring a sacrifice to the temple when they realized they had sinned and (3) there was a special once-a-year sacrifice to cover the sins of Israel for the past year.

In addition, there were sacrifices for purification after childbirth, a sacrifice to cleanse a house, even a sacrifice to handle the defilement of an unsolved murder and a murder scene, and so on. The sacrificial system covered many areas of life for Israel that we have condensed into one: the sacrifice pictured in the Day of Atonement.

Once a year, on the Day of Atonement, the high priest would enter the Holy of Holies and give a special sacrifice to cover the sins of Israel for the past year. This generic sacrifice gave a blanket covering for Israel. In God's timing, Christ's sacrifice replaced that special once-a-year sacrifice with a once-for-all-time sacrifice. We receive this general covering for our sins when we accept Christ as our sacrifice. Through his sacrifice, sin is no longer a barrier between God and us. Christ paid the sin debt. His sacrifice provided the means for our salvation and was necessary only once.

In focusing on salvation, we have neglected to see the parallel system also at work that gives forgiveness on a daily basis. The Day of Atonement sacrifice was a shadow of the salvation that came with Christ's death on the cross. The daily sacrifices built up to that day but also provided release from the effects of daily sin. These daily sacrifices are what John was referring to when he said, *If we confess our sins, he is faithful and just and will forgive us our sins and purify us from all unrighteousness* (I John 1:9).

I disagree with Paul Enns who says,

> *Forgiveness [by God] forever solves the problem of sin in the believer's life—all sins past, present and future* (Colossians 2:13). *This is distinct from the daily cleansing from sin that is necessary to maintain fellowship with God* (I John 1:9).[52]

Sin and forgiveness are issues for believers after salvation; the issue is not just cleansing but sin. We use this verse (I John 1:9) as part of our presentation of the Gospel to unbelievers but the context clearly refers to believers and clearly refers to sin. When we confess our sins, he does forgive. God is faithful in the sense that he is predictable. We can count of God being consistent in his response to our prayers.

God is just in the sense that while justice must be satisfied he will put that payment on Jesus rather than

---

[52] Paul Enns, *The Moody Handbook of Theology* (Chicago: Moody Press, 1989), p. 325.

us. He will not arbitrarily cover some sins through Christ while demanding that we pay for others.

Satisfied with our salvation, we have neglected to appropriate, or make use of, the means to have daily victory over sin and the means to break the power of sin. The old nature may be there until we die but it does not have to sit in the front room.

Christ's sacrifice created the grounds for our redemption, forgiveness and adoption. We can dwell so much on the redemption that we forget the adoption. His death and resurrection provided the means for daily release from sin and its power, including the ongoing consequences of sin. We are not to try harder, but to live in Christ and let Christ live in and through us.

The Dual Aspects of Christ's Sacrifice

Two distinct events happened when Christ died and rose again: First, he fulfilled the sacrifice system foreshadowed by the Day of Atonement, that blanket sacrifice that covered God's people for the past year. That is what is in focus when the scriptures say, "*He made you alive together with Him, having forgiven us all our transgressions*" (Colossians 2:13b NAS).

Second, he fulfilled the daily sacrificial system that took care of the individual sins that his people committed. In Hebrews (7:25) both sacrificial systems are in focus when it says, *Hence, also, He [Jesus] is able to save forever those who draw near to God through Him, since He always lives to make intercession for them.* (NAS)

The first sacrifice redeems us. It allows us entrance by adoption into the family of God once we have forgiveness and cleansing. The second sacrifice system allows us forgiveness and cleansing when we sin even as his children. This is the provision that John mentions when he says, *If we confess our sins, he is faithful and just and will forgive us our sins and purify us from all unrighteousness* (I John 1:9).

Christ's sacrifice occurred once for all time and was sufficient to cover all the sins humankind has committed past, present and future. It is available for all humankind, not just for those destined to be his children. His sacrifice has never been lacking but people throughout the centuries have chosen not to accept his sacrifice.

The sacrifice

Eternal.

Once and for all.

Satisfied and fulfilled the Law.

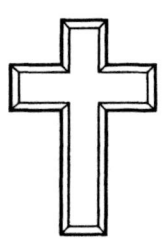

Jesus, Our Great High Priest

The Intercessor

When we approach God as our heavenly Father, we want to recognize that our Lord is also there before God as our Great High Priest. As such, he continually intercedes on our behalf.

The dictionary defines intercession as, "entreaty in favor of another" and intercede as, "to plead on another's behalf."[53] A priest is a mediator between God and humankind and performs the proper sacrifices to God for himself and others. Christ, on the other hand, was both the sacrifice and the priest; in this case the High Priest.

Christ, in his incarnated being as a man, was the sacrifice. This fact is important because it means that Christ intercedes for us out of knowledge of what it is to be human. According to Hebrews, Jesus was tempted in all ways as we are so, as intercessor, he understands us and the life issues we bring in prayer.

> *Since then we have a great high priest who has passed through the heavens, Jesus the Son of God, let us hold fast our confession. For we do not have a high priest who cannot sympathize with our weaknesses, but One who has been tempted in all things as we are, yet without sin* (Hebrews 4:14-15 NASB).

Christ intercedes in his role as Great High Priest and in his role as the eternal sacrifice for us. One is position and authority; the other is provision and mercy.

His Experiencing for Us

The sacrificial system foreshadowed the sacrifice of Christ that was to come. In the Old Testament, they

---

[53] *The American Heritage Dictionary of the English Language* (Dell).

Christ's Sacrifice

brought to the priest the animal and he killed and sacrificed it on the altar. There were clear standards and procedures in presenting an animal for sacrifice and it prohibited excessive suffering. So why does Christ experience the physical and emotional suffering and humiliation, in addition to his death, that we see in the Gospels?

John the Baptist called Jesus the Lamb of God. Before John the Baptist, Isaiah described the coming messiah in graphic terms:

> *He was despised and forsaken of men, a man of sorrows, and acquainted with grief . . .* (3a)
>
> *. . . our griefs He Himself bore, And our sorrows He carried; yet we ourselves esteemed Him stricken, smitten of God, and afflicted* (4) *. . . He was pierced through for our transgressions, He was crushed for our iniquities; the chastening for our well-being fell upon Him, and by His scourging we are healed (5). The LORD has caused the iniquity of us all to fall on Him* (6b).
>
> *He was oppressed and He was afflicted, yet He did not open His mouth; like a lamb that is led to slaughter . . .* (7).
>
> *But the LORD was pleased to crush Him, putting Him to grief; if He would render Himself as a guilt offering (*10a*). . . . will justify the many, as He will bear their iniquities (*11*). . . . He poured out Himself to death, and was numbered with the transgressors; yet He Himself bore the sin of many, And interceded for the transgressors (*12*).*
> (Isaiah 53:2-12 NASB)

Jesus did more than die. He suffered, was whipped, humiliated and exposed naked in front of his friends and enemies on the cross. He was thirsty, and his bones were all out of joint. Christ suffered a great deal as part of his death yet the sacrificial animals of the Old Testament did not. Why was it necessary for Christ to experience all these physical and emotional traumas?

His Identification with Us

Christ's suffering included more than death and payment; his sacrifice covered both sins and their consequences. Christ suffered humiliation so he can now take ours upon himself. Because his friends rejected and betrayed Christ, both before and during his suffering, he can now take on himself our sense of rejection and betrayal. Jesus knows what it feels like to humiliated and naked.

Because of his experience he can intercede with understanding and take on himself the horrible feelings a girl has who has been gang raped. Jesus is the perfect intercessor and Great High Priest. In his suffering, death and resurrection, he provided for every situation where sin occurs and took it all on himself.

ò€ €ó

The prophet Isaiah did not say that by Christ's death we are healed but *by his stripes we are healed* (Isaiah 53:5). Christ's suffering accomplished something different from his death. His death brought us salvation and satisfied the law's requirement for justice. His suffering provided the grounds for our healing. This healing is sometimes physically but most often is emotionally and spiritually because sin damages us in these areas.

The position of a high priest created a direct link between God and man. This link was an imperfect one until Christ took that place. In the Old Testament, priests had two primary functions: one was to stand between God and humankind, the other was to offer sacrifice. Priests carried out the rules surrounding the presentation of sacrifices.

In the New Testament, we can come directly to God through Jesus Christ, our Great High Priest. So he is not only the link, he has created direct access for us to God. As Great High Priest, Christ has his own sacrifice to point to so there is no need for another.

However, as we will see in Chapter 12, priests still have their uses.

❧ Part Three ❧

The Essentials for Healing

Well Richard, you said you were praying that I would have an opportunity to put my newfound knowledge and skills into practice right away, and the Lord has surely answered your prayers.

There was a couple I was already doing "pre-marital" counseling with when I came to visit you, and when I returned . . . I turned the course of the counseling toward prayer counseling for each of them before proceeding on to the typical pre-marital stuff (communication, etc.).

The young woman has been the first to go through the process and I am seeing tremendous results! She has been married before, divorcing because of a great deal of physical and emotional abuse, as well as an affair her husband had. He was her "first love" and she was wounded in her spirit and body because of the way her total trust in this person was violently thrown back in her face. As we've gone through the earlier events in her life where she has received great wounding (prior to her marriage) I have noticed an increased degree of "softening" going on in her personality, and a growing sense of humility and teachability in her attitude.

— **CG**

9

The Father/Child Connection

God's Way

We need the proper setting and perspective when we come into God's presence. The proper setting includes involving all of the Godhead and the right perspective includes a proper respect for sin, its powers and consequences, and the cost involved in dealing with sin. Prayer and Resolution Counseling is not a game. It is approaching the Throne of God knowing what we are doing when we ask him to give us a piece of the cross, so to speak, to bring us healing.

Our prayers touch eternity. After we pray and God answers, it is as if there is a page in a book of our life in heaven with writing on it but someone has blacked out sections of it. Parts resemble some kind of censored CIA document that is no longer readable. There are things that, once resolved, God will never refer to again, throughout eternity. If we want this result, then we must do it God's way.

God does not automatically hear or answer our prayers unless we can ask according to his will. More often, we ask with wrong motives and try to approach God on our terms, not his.

A Journey to Wholeness

The Lord says: "These people come near to me with their mouth and honor me with their lips, but their hearts are far from me. Their worship of me is made up only of rules taught by men" (Isaiah 29:13).

Our own sin, if unconfessed and with unrepentant spirits, can stand in the way.

When you spread out your hands in prayer, I will hide my eyes from you; even if you offer many prayers, I will not listen. Your hands are full of blood . . . (Isaiah 1:15).

On the other hand, God does hear our prayers and, while often we must live with the consequences, he can restore what we have lost:

They will fill the threshing floors with grain; the vats will overflow with new wine and oil.

I will repay you for the years the locusts have an eaten-the great locust and the young locust, the other locusts and the locust swarm–my great army that I sent among you (Joel 2:23, 25).

Prayer and Resolution Counseling is a legal way of approaching God in that we must consider his standards and use right procedures if the prayer system is to work.

God the Father is our focus. The hurting person must be a believer before or shortly after the sessions begin because he must appropriate the results of the death and resurrection of Christ for full resolution. Prayer and Resolution Counseling creates the grounds for God to intervene and bring resolution on a personal

Faith

Before Connie and I married, we applied for and received a license, paid a fee and took blood tests. We arranged with our pastor for a wedding ceremony. After the ceremony, we all signed the necessary paperwork. Once that happened, it did not matter if I felt married or not. In addition, it did not matter if I changed my mind. I was still married.

The State of California and the pastor involved in this had the authority to marry us. When I went through the procedure, on their terms, their authority created my marriage. I did my part; they did theirs and together we created a marriage. My attitude or depth of faith in the system did not matter, the system worked anyway.

That is the way it is with God. When we approach him on his terms and standards and present our case, he does answer. We are not talking about cars, riches and houses here; we are talking about breaking chains, forgiving and seeking forgiveness, cleansing and breaking bonds. These are issues affecting our walk and relationship with God and man. What is faith? It is nothing more than recognizing God's system and *assuming* it works. Matthew gives the best illustration to us of this type of faith (8:5-13).

A centurion asked Jesus for help, *"Lord,"* he said, *"my servant lies at home paralyzed and in terrible suffering."* Then he stopped Jesus from going with him with these words,

> *Lord, I do not deserve to have you come under my roof. But just say the word, and my servant will*

> be healed. For I myself am a man under authority, with soldiers under me. I tell this one, "Go," and he goes; and that one, "Come," and he comes. I say to my servant, "Do this," and he does it.

Matthew records that these words astonished Jesus and he said,

> "I tell you the truth, I have not found anyone in Israel with such great faith." Then he told the centurion, "Go! It will be done just as you believed it would." And his servant was healed at that very hour.

In addition, he endorsed the Centurion's definition of faith. The centurion *did not act as much in faith as in assumption.* He worked within an authority structure that worked. Soldiers could receive stiff penalties for disobeying an officer in the Roman Legion. You could trust the Roman army's system to work. The centurion naturally assumed the same consistency and predictability in Jesus' system. He was less a religious thinker and more a rationalist. Recognizing the authority Jesus had, he assumed, *had faith,* that when Jesus issued an order it would be carried out even in the spiritual realm of healing. Once Jesus accepted the request as legitimate, he approved it and it happened.

One theology book used this story as the basis for prayer to Jesus but this is nothing more than a man needing help and asking someone for help. We can spiritualize it but *this is not an example of prayer, it is an example of worldview.* The universe has order. Recognizing this and following God's system, and assuming it works, is part of being in harmony with God so he can answer prayer.

Our Focus: The Father

When the disciples asked Jesus to teach them how to pray he began, "Our Father . . ." He did not say, "After I die, when you pray say, 'Lord Jesus.'" Often I hear people praying something to the effect, "Lord Jesus, I ask that you touch my son's life, in Jesus' name, amen."

This is both ungrammatical and wrong. When we use the formula "in Jesus' name" at the conclusion of our prayer, we are acknowledging the authority and right we have to come to the heavenly Father. Our position in Christ allows this. It is as if Jesus says, "Richard, when you talk to my Father, tell him I said to call." So I say, "Heavenly Father, Jesus said I could call you and that you wouldn't mind at all."

We have distortion any time we emphasize one person in the Godhead to the exclusion of the other two. God is three persons, but one. Not Jesus only, not the Holy Spirit only, nor God the Father only. We come to our heavenly Father in prayer through his son Jesus Christ (because of what he accomplished at the Cross and in his resurrection) and under the direction or guidance of the Holy Spirit.

Jesus said,

> *Which of you, if his son asks for bread, will give him a stone? Or if he asks for a fish, will give him a snake? If you, then, though you are evil, know how to give good gifts to your children, how much more will your Father in heaven give good gifts to those who ask him!* (Matthew 7:9-11)

God did not lightly choose the term Father to describe his relationship with us.

A Journey to Wholeness

When I accepted Christ's sacrifice as payment for my sins, I received forgiveness and a new position with a corresponding performance. God is now my heavenly Father and I am his child. I have a special claim on my father's attention. I am a joint heir with Jesus Christ. If I ask something good or needful from my father, he will give it to me.

Praying directly to Jesus is not wrong, or even to the Holy Spirit for that matter, but it should not be the norm. Often our prayers to Jesus are to him as Lord and Master. That perspective makes us obedient servants yet this is a small part of what we have through Christ.

Once I was driving alone late at night in Ethiopia. The road was rough and muddy. It was dark as only the Ethiopian countryside can be. I shifted into four-wheel drive and immediately started slipping off the road into the darkness. I felt rather than saw the chasm before me and, as I started over, I thought of the fifty-gallon drum of gasoline tied down directly behind my seat. I yelled, "Jesus, help me!" The Land cruiser stopped with the headlights pointed into nothingness. Beyond a doubt, Jesus heard my prayer.

I did not ask for forgiveness for calling on Jesus but our prayers should normally be to the Father, not to Jesus, nor to the Holy Spirit. In obedience to his Father, Jesus came to earth to die so we could live. He never intended to replace the Father but came so we could call God Father.

When people come to us for spiritual counseling through prayer, we require that they address their prayers to God as Father. Sometimes that is not possible until we deal with the betrayal of the parents (as in incest or molestation). Then the way is clear to accept God as Father in a right and wholesome way. Approaching God as our heavenly Father forces us to recognize our relation-ship to him as his children.

Our Relationship

Status and Role

Status refers to the *position* we have at any given time as we act and react to life around us. Status has labels: man, woman, policeman or policewoman, pastor, teacher, clerk, electrician. With each position or status comes a corresponding *role or performance*: a man dresses as a man (normally) and a woman dresses and behaves as a woman. A police officer may have a uniform and if not, still acts with authority.

A teacher behaves differently from her students. She has control of the class. The teacher may sit or stand while students sit unless asked to stand. She controls the black board, the assignments and the focus of the class that day. If she dresses seductively, chews gum with her mouth open and tells jokes just for the laughs then her behavior is not in keeping with her position as the teacher. We can honor her position as teacher (status) and, at the same time, evaluate and judge her performance (role) as wrong.

Status and role go together. I can have several status and roles; not all of them function simultaneously. For example, I am a man, a husband, a father, a grandfather, a reluctant or semi-Republican, a teacher, a former professor, a prayer and resolution counselor and even a handyman. Notice that a status and role can have a counterpart: with a husband comes a wife, father–children, grandfather–grandchildren, a teacher has students, a student has a teacher, a mentor has an apprentice or disciple. We do not function alone and neither do we function apart from the interaction of others. (Even a hermit interacts in the sense that he rejects the rest of us.)

Each *status and role set* has its own expectations: responsibilities, privileges and obligations. When I married, I became a husband and, with that came a change of status, I had new responsibilities to care for and provide for my wife. I needed to shape our life together so that she could grow and be more complete as a woman, as a wife and as a person with gifts, talents and education. As a husband, I had special privileges reserved just for me that I could now receive from my wife.

Between us, we had an intimacy that was for no other man or woman. I had a claim to her attention and she had a claim to mine that stood out from others. I had an obligation to provide for her needs. She also had an obligation to provide for my needs. Sex is not in focus here, I am talking about the special oneness that comes with marriage.

We complete each other; we give and take for the mutual benefit of each other. In marriage as "one" we are more than the two of us. We have certain expectations for each other. She will not flirt with other men or view them as fair game. Other women are not fair game for me. (If I respect women then I never consider them fair game.)

How we view our positions, and the performances associated with them, affect our relationships with others. After I married, I behaved in a different way when my role as husband was in focus. Once we are Christians, we have a special relationship with God as Father, with Jesus Christ as Lord and Savior, and with the Holy Spirit within us.

The Father/Child Connection

Sons and Daughters

If I see God as my heavenly Father then that makes me his son! The relationship I can now have with my heavenly Father is no less real than the one I should be having with my earthly father. I am his son because I was born into his family (that is what being 'born again' means). I cannot earn the right to be his son. I just am. No amount of work makes me more his son or less his son. I am one-hundred percent his son because I was born into his family through Christ.

If so, then I do what God wants because I want to please him. A son wants to be like his father and imitate his father's actions. We can carry the heavy burden of obeying God because he commands us or we can carry the light burden of being whom he made us and redeemed us to be. As a son, I should naturally act out of who I am.

Jesus did not come and die so I could be a servant. Nothing wrong with being a servant, in this we are imitating our Lord Jesus Christ but I want to be a son first. Part of being a son is service if God asks. As a son, I receive love; as a servant, I receive approval for a job well done. There is a world of difference. Why would I prefer being a servant instead of a son?

In the Gospel of Luke (15), the father in the parable had the right perspective. The prodigal son went off and sinned in terrible ways and, because of his behavior, he felt he could no longer be a son. Returning home, the son hoped that his father would accept him back even if father only let him live there as a servant. After all, this was all he deserved.

However, the father saw it differently. The prodigal left as his son and returned as his son. Our status as sons or daughters does not fall off like a coat. We are what we are. A son is always a son; a daughter is always a daughter. We might deny this but God will not.

The scriptures say,

For I am convinced that neither death nor life, neither angels nor demons, neither the present nor the future, nor any powers, neither height nor depth, nor anything else in all creation, will be able to separate us from the love of God that is in Christ Jesus our Lord (Romans 8:38-39).

However, is that completely true? Hebrews tells us,

It is impossible for those who have once been enlightened, who have tasted the heavenly gift, who have shared in the Holy Spirit, who have tasted the goodness of the word of God and the powers of the coming age, if they fall away, to be brought back to repentance, because to their loss they are crucifying the Son of God all over again and subjecting him to public disgrace (Hebrews 6: 4-6).

I spoke at a Haddiyya church in Hosanna, Ethiopia during the time the Communists were in control. Around that time, several Christians had renounced Christ to keep from imprisonment. I could not give comfort to them for doing so and used the example of Paul. He had been imprisoned, had not been afraid and had even led his jailer to Christ.

Jesus did say,

The Father/Child Connection

Whoever acknowledges me before men, I will also acknowledge him before my Father in heaven. But whoever disowns me before men, I will disown him before my Father in heaven (Matthew 10:32-33).

The point is that if people deliberately and with full awareness choose to reject their position in Christ, they do so at their own peril. God will not force us into the Kingdom. God does not violate our wills.

Until the day I die, God will continue to hold out his hands to me but I must reach back. I believe in eternal security. Nevertheless, I also believe that I could burn the bridge between God and me. However, nothing else and no one else can do that.

The prodigal had to reject his position before he could act in the terrible ways he did. A person truly accepting his position as a son acts like a son. Acting in ungodly ways without feeling contrite is not natural for a son of God. The prodigal son showed his true nature, he really was his father's son, when he could not continue in his wrong lifestyle and repented. As John in his epistle says, the children of God cannot consistently sin and be comfortable behaving that way. They are going against their natures.

We once prayed with Paul, a British man. He had a prior life of sexual promiscuity. After he had forgiven those involved and received forgiveness himself he sinned again.[54] Well, someone will say, "God certainly did not answer those prayers!" However, even as God's redeemed children we still sin.

---

[54] There is more to dealing with sexual sin than mentioned here, read the book *Cleansing: Resolving the Consequences of Sexual Sin* by the author.

A Journey to Wholeness

Paul did sin again sexually but he could not handle the conviction and load of guilt that came with his sin and he repented soon after. Paul's verification that he was a child of God did not come from being sinless but from his response to sin. He could no longer handle that which was now, to him, against his nature.

We can come boldly into God's presence because, as his children, we have a right to come,

> *because those who are led by the Spirit of God are sons of God. For you did not receive a spirit that makes you a slave again to fear, but you received the Spirit of sonship. And by him we cry, "Abba, Father." The Spirit himself testifies with our spirit that we are God's children. Now if we are children, then we are heirs–heirs of God and co-heirs with Christ, if indeed we share in his sufferings in order that we may also share in his glory* (Romans 8:14-17).

The name of Jesus has power. We can use his name for good but also, obviously, for evil. We want safety in numbers as we pray so that we do not abuse the power and authority given to us. Christ warns us,

> *A good tree cannot bear bad fruit, and a bad tree cannot bear good fruit. Every tree that does not bear good fruit is cut down and thrown into the fire. Thus, by their fruit you will recognize them.*
>
> *Not everyone who says to me 'Lord, Lord,' will enter the kingdom of heaven, but only he who does the will of my father who is in heaven. Many will say to me on that day, 'Lord, Lord, did we not prophesy in your name, and in your name drive out demons and perform many miracles?' Then I will tell them*

plainly, "I never knew you. Away from me, you evildoers!" (Matthew 7: 18-23)

The Servant Only Distortion

When we accept Christ as savior, we are the redeemed of the Lord. We are "sinners saved by grace" but it does not stop there. We quickly go from the label of sinners saved by grace to sons and daughters of the living God. Sinners saved by grace do one of three things: either they continue to sin because that is how they see themselves, they are preoccupied with not sinning, or they become servants as a way of somehow repaying God for what he did.

If God calls us into service, we want to hear and obey but let it be because he, our father, asks us to do a task for him. Service comes out of being sons and daughters. Otherwise, we do a task for God rather than letting God work through us. Sometimes we can do good works for God, without his direction, while God keeps trying to get our attention and says, "I would rather do it myself."

Let this mind be in us, who being the children of God, are willing temporarily to put aside some of our rights and privileges because God asks us to do a work for him.

> . . . *Do not merely look out for your own personal interests, but also for the interests of others. Have this attitude in yourselves which was also in Christ Jesus, who . . . emptied Himself, taking the form of a bond-servant and being made in the likeness of men . . .* (Philippians 2:4-7 NAS)

A Journey to Wholeness

We are a priesthood of believers but God did not save us primarily for service. He has thousands of angels to do his biding. He wants us for fellowship. We can still serve God but even our service comes out of our being sons and daughters. Jesus in the midst of his role as the obedient servant still viewed God as his Father.

We want to group everything around the core of the relationship of father/son and father/daughter. All our other relationships radiate out of this core of being: for examples, master/servant and teacher/pupil. Through Jesus Christ, God redeemed us from our sins to freedom and adoption as his children.

In Prayer and Resolution Counseling, when we keep our focus on God as our Father and ourselves as his children then getting his perspective on things gets easier. As his sons or daughters, we can stand beside him and look at an event, with all the actors, and see the rightness and wrongness of it all. From his perspective, we can see that *sin, in a point of time, is not near as important as sin as it grows, expands and continues to damage those involved, innocent or otherwise.* As his children, we want to be intolerant of sin because we see it through the eyes of eternity.

Jesus talked about our being in the world but not of the world. As God's children, we will be going against today's social norms that promote tolerance and freedom "as long as no one is hurt." We will begin to recognize the wrong messages that come through a comedy like *Fraser*.

I have been a missionary for many years and have lived outside the United States for more than twenty-five years. During those years, I have gained the ability to view culture with a certain amount of detachment. If I use my American background as the standard then another's cultural differences are bad if they make me uncomfortable. I am learning, to view my culture and other cultures as if I am looking through a window at them without emotional involvement. The differences between cultures are not necessarily bad, just different from mine.

My task now is to understand more clearly what my heavenly Father's standards are and recognize the universal principles that apply to all. I need to understand how much my own culture has affected my worldview and interpretation of what feels right, versus what is right. If I do not have an understanding of my culture and how it has shaped me then I am in danger of projecting a cultural (American) gospel instead of the pure gospel. I am in the world but not of it. As God's child, I want to live by his cultural standards.

10

Jesus and the Holy Spirit's Participation

Many Christians are afraid to assume the role of a prayer and resolution counselor because it is such a responsible position. They are right to hesitate if they are going to do a work for God but doing a work for God is not the same as being a channel for God to use. The first we do in our own strength, so we ought to be frightened of such a responsibility; the other we do out of obedience, as we see God's hand setting the stage for us.

When God controls and asks us on to the stage then he also gives us both the authority and the power to do the job.

In Christ

Our Authority

Christ's authority and his role as our Great High Priest and intercessor are in focus when he said,

> *And I will do whatever you ask in my name, so that the Son may bring glory to the Father. You*

Jesus and the Holy Spirit's Participation

may ask me for anything in my name, and I will do it (John 14:13-14).

Paul says that, "*In him and through faith in him we may approach God with freedom and confidence*" (Ephesians 3:12). He did not say that in Christ and through faith in Christ, we could approach Christ. Jesus constantly focused on the Father as the source of life and blessing.

If you, then, though you are evil, know how to give good gifts to your children, how much more will your Father in heaven give good gifts to those who ask him! (Matthew 7:11)

Many Christians focus on Jesus for everything. This is an error and against what Jesus himself taught:

Look at the birds of the air; they do not sow or reap or store away in barns, and yet your heavenly Father feeds them. Are you not much more valuable than they? Who of you by worrying can add a single hour to his life? (Matthew 6:26-27)

Our heavenly Father is the provider and normally answers our prayers. Christ, on the other hand, is the great High Priest interceding for us.

For this reason he had to be made like his brothers in every way, in order that he might become a merciful and faithful high priest in service to God, and that he might make atonement for the sins of the people.

A Journey to Wholeness

Because he himself suffered when he was tempted, he is able to help those who are being tempted (Hebrews 2:17-18).

As priest, Jesus intercedes for us and mediates between God and us. We do not pray to the priest though Christ did say, *And I will do whatever you ask in my name, so that the Son may bring glory to the Father. You may ask me for anything in my name, and I will do it* (John 14:13).

As we go further, we see that when we use Jesus' name we involve him,

You did not choose me, but I chose you and appointed you to go and bear fruit-fruit that will last. Then the Father will give you whatever you ask in my name (John 15:16).

We direct our prayer to the Father, who answers.

One theology book explained that when we pray in Jesus' name it means that we are coming to God with the same attitude that Christ did. This sounds good but the author is missing the point: "in Jesus' name" brings in Christ in his priestly role but also represents our authority and rights. It is like phoning God and saying, "Jesus said I could call." We are acknowledging that Jesus has already given us permission to go to the Father on our own because of our position in Christ, (God sees us as holy) and relationship with him, Jesus.

We do not come into the Father's presence with fear or apology but **BOLDLY** because, in Christ, we have a right to claim the Father's attention.

When Connie and I visited Washington, D.C., we went to the office of our state senator. He gave us passes to the Senate so we could attend a session. We did not apologize for entering and no one questioned us once we showed our passes, signed by the senator. Because of Christ, we have a pass that allows us free access to the Father.

Jesus gives us four distinct perspectives in Matthew 18 concerning him, God and us: (1) The two or three, (2) Binding and releasing, (3) The power of agreement and (4) Christ's presence. Recognizing these create a dynamic whole in prayer:

Our Community

All the authors of the scriptures have written from a relational point of view. American culture has an individualistic orientation that emphasizes the importance and priorities of the one as opposed to the many.

A constant theme in scripture, in both the Old and New Testaments, is that the group suffers when the individual sins. Therefore, it is the group's responsibility to hold its members accountable for their actions. This group responsibility carries over into prayer as well. "Bear one another's burdens" infers the community of believers in action rather than the member in isolation.

Paul cautioned that, "*Every matter must be established by the testimony of two or three witnesses*" (II Corinthians 13:1). Again, action or endorsement comes through several people, not one person. In the following verses, this theme of two or three is an unbroken thread that not only provides power in prayer but also safety in prayer. When three people (two safe others and the hurting one) are involved then there is more responsibility shared and more possibility for correctness of action.

Our Power to Bind or Release

To bind means to forbid; to release or loose means to permit or allow. These actions are especially important when Jesus says, *I tell you the truth, whatever you bind on earth will be bound in heaven, and whatever you loose on earth will be loosed in heaven* (Matthew 18:18).

This verse is widely used as the grounds for binding evil spirits so that they cannot manifest themselves or their power. As we will see later, breaking (to loose) the bonds of unholy marriage is an issue when, for example, a child becomes a bride to Satan in a Satanic ritual.

Paul talks about the union that comes through being with a prostitute. That union must be broken. Carmen mentioned earlier, lived in sin for many months with Pablo. One of the last things we did with Carmen was to have her forgive Pablo for his part in this sexual sin, confess her own sin and ask forgiveness. We asked for a special release for Carmen because of the sexual sin, and because of the commitment between her and Pablo. Because of her long-term sexual involvement with Pablo, we had her ask God to grant her a spiritual divorce, to break the bonds and to free her from any claims that Pablo might continue to have on her.

Knowing God's will in this matter, I also proclaimed that the bonds between Carmen and Pablo were broken in Jesus' name. We have the power to do these things but it is not enough to know we can break ties between people. We must know when doing so that it is appropriate. For this reason, we should use the power "in community," not alone.

Our Power of Agreement

A third perspective concerns the power of agreement. Jesus told us, *Again, I tell you that if two of you on earth agree about anything you ask for, it will be done for you by my Father in heaven* (Matthew 18:19).

In a sense, God has given us a blank check. We can fill it out but only if two or three agree on the amount and the purpose and are willing to sign the check.

His Presence

A last but important perspective concerns Christ's special presence, *"For where two or three come together in my name, there am I with them"* (Matthew 18:20). I do not understand all the implications in this promise. All I know is that Christ is with us in a different way when we are in community, so to speak, than when we are alone. Yet he is also with us individually. A major factor may be that with this special presence there comes added power and direction, covering (through his death) and protection (through his resurrection and defeat of Satan).

Any power we have *does not come from us* but from Christ in us. We cannot bring healing; we cannot recognize or extend forgiveness or have any authority apart from Christ. Any authority we have is there because he gives it to us and that authority is based on what he did at the cross.

Christ's presence is not an option; it is a necessity.

A Journey to Wholeness

The Jesus Only Distortion

When we are only Jesus focused, we have pushed aside God the Father. I heard a pastor tell of Jesus seeing the dilemma that God had with a sinful world and coming to earth to solve this problem. That is wrong.

The scriptures tell us, *For God so loved the world that he gave his one and only Son, that whoever believes in him shall not perish but have eternal life* (John 3:16). God was the initiator of our salvation. He sent his son Jesus. Jesus, obedient to the Father, came.

When a father and mother are irresponsible or betray a child, the child defines the father-mother position according to their behavior and response to the child. The father does not show love, only anger. The father is busy working or focusing on his own interests and he has no time for his son. Therefore, the child defines love as sterile. The parents only extend love when the son behaves as they want. The child must work to earn their love.

The child reasons that if he were worth anything or were precious then his father would pay attention to him. Thus the son views himself as worthless or lacking, neither precious nor special. The son lacks self-esteem, has no sense of belonging, and can even wonder if he has a right to live. Viewed in this light we can understand why the teenage population has such a high suicide rate.

In such circumstances, how might a son define God as father? He is busy doing other things. God is love but his love is sterile. He gives it only when the son performs. In addition, father can withdraw his love at any time. The son feels he has worth or preciousness, even in God's eyes, only as he is in Christ.

Thus, we look to God, or Jesus, for direction and orders, not for love. Obedience is the focus, not imitation, not pleasing the Father. The result is "Thank you Jesus.

I love you, Lord. I am your servant." Pious as such words sound, when we push away God as Father we also push away our position as his child. Instead of a relationship with acceptance and unconditional love, we take on the servant role with a task orientation that can give us approval, but never love. We must constantly prove ourselves worthy servants by producing good works.

Instead, we should be doing good works just because that is what a son does who is like his father.

Balance

Strange as it sounds, God did not send his son to replace him. God, through Christ, had to handle the sin question before he could get on with his real goal: making us his children. The focus I am suggesting is not new. Paul and other writers of the Epistles had the same emphasis. Jesus was there, but God the Father was too. Consider these examples:

May God our Father and the Lord Jesus Christ give you grace and peace (I Corinthians 1:3 GNB).

Let us give thanks to the God and Father of our Lord Jesus Christ, the merciful Father, the God from whom all help comes! (II Corinthians 1:3 GNB) (Also Galatians 1:3, Ephesians 1:2, Philippians 1:1)

Praise be to the God and Father of our Lord Jesus Christ, the Father of compassion and the God of all comfort, who comforts us in all our troubles, so that we can comfort those in any trouble with the comfort we ourselves have received from God (II Corinthians 1:3-4).

Praise be to the God and Father of our Lord Jesus Christ, who has blessed us in the heavenly realms with every spiritual blessing in Christ (Ephesians 1:3).

Paul, an apostle of Christ Jesus by the command of God our Savior and of Christ Jesus our hope (I Timothy 1:1).

Peter recognizes all three, Jesus, the Father and the Holy Spirit. Each has his place:

To God's elect, strangers in the world . . . who have been chosen according to the foreknowledge of God the Father, through the sanctifying work of the Spirit, for obedience to Jesus Christ and sprinkling by his blood: . . . (I Peter 1:2)

John was close to Jesus but he did not push God the Father aside:

We proclaim to you what we have seen and heard, so that you also may have fellowship with us. And our fellowship is with the Father and with his Son, Jesus Christ (I John 1:3).

Jude begins his epistle with,

Jude, a servant of Jesus Christ and a brother of James, to those who have been called, who are loved by God the Father and kept by Jesus Christ (Jude 1:1).

Notice that he calls God our Savior when he says,

> . . . to the only God our Savior be glory, majesty, power and authority, through Jesus Christ our Lord, before all ages, now and forevermore! Amen (Jude 1:25).

Through obedience, Christ did become our savior but God the Father set the salvation solution into motion.

John sums up God's place, the son's place and our place with when he introduces his epistle,

> *Grace and peace to you from him who is, and who was, and who is to come, and from the seven spirits before his throne, and from Jesus Christ, who is the faithful witness, the firstborn from the dead, and the ruler of the kings of the earth.*
> *To him who loves us and has freed us from our sins by his blood, and has made us to be a kingdom and priests to serve his God and Father . . .* (Revelation 1:4b-6a).

With the Holy Spirit

Real

We have power and authority in Christ, given to us by him, and approved by the Father. It is extremely important, however, that we use the resources that he has given us. The major resource is a person: the Holy Spirit. He must be guiding us when we bring our prayers to God. We do not have to listen to the Holy Spirit and we can deny him an active role but we do so at our peril.

The Holy Spirit is not an impersonal force. Paul blesses us with these words, "*May the grace of the Lord Jesus Christ, and the love of God, and the fellowship of the Holy Spirit be with you all*" (II Corinthians 13:14). "The fellowship of the Holy Spirit" tells us that this Spirit has personality so we have some personal and emotional benefits in relating to him.

In addition, the Holy Spirit is with us in an active way when we pray, according to Paul,

> *In the same way, the Spirit helps us in our weakness. We do not know what we ought to pray for, but the Spirit himself intercedes for us with groans that words cannot express. And he who searches our hearts knows the mind of the Spirit, because the Spirit intercedes for the saints in accordance with God's will* (Romans 8:26-27).

Partnership versus control

> *When the Counselor comes, whom I will send to you from the Father, the Spirit of truth who goes out from the Father, he will testify about me* (John 15:26).

The Holy Spirit's role is not to take over. We are not to surrender to the Holy Spirit. That implies we become captive to the Holy Spirit. This is not so. Rather, we have agreement and partnership.

Jesus called the Holy Spirit the comforter and the one called alongside us. Both words show a twosome, not a oneness. The one called alongside does not take over but is there to help. Therefore, a better word to use in our relationship with the Holy Spirit is *partnership*. That

Jesus and the Holy Spirit's Participation

means that I am responsible for my choices and actions but the Spirit is always there to guide me. He does not guide in everything but in important things. We do not need the Holy Spirit to help us decide on rye bread or whole wheat for a sandwich. After all, God did give us minds and the ability to use them.

The Holy Spirit is also there to poke us when we are on our way to a strip joint. As Christians, we have two safe guards within us while non-Christians have only one. We both have the prompting of our consciences but we Christians also have the prompting of the Holy Spirit. Both can be factors that slow us down and make us more responsible in our actions and decisions.

God is not interested in helping us decide whether we should have rice or potatoes. He is interested in whether we join the army, marry Jane, go to college and other life-changing decisions. We can take the wrong roads but the Holy Spirit is there to guide us toward the right ones, if we let him. However, God does not normally force us to do anything.

The Spirit and we should form a partnership in prayer. When we do not allow his participation out of fear or distrust, we shut ourselves off from his guidance and counsel.

I once read an editorial where the author said how much she had feared the Holy Spirit in the past but that now she felt free to surrender to him. If she meant surrender, according to what the word means semantically, then I disagree with her. God did not bring us into salvation so he could take away our lives or replace us and our abilities to live by letting the Holy Spirit "take over." Surrender implies that the person, the captive, is under the control and domination of the other. For the Holy Spirit, this is not true.

During World War II when the Japanese held Allied soldiers, the prisoners of war had no choices in their day-to-day activities or in what they could eat. The Japanese had total control of them even to the point of killing them at will. The soldiers could not voluntarily leave nor, except a few, could they escape. This was so because the soldiers had either surrendered or been captured by the Japanese forces.

The Holy Spirit does not act like a conqueror. The scriptures talk of our being able to grieve the Holy Spirit.

And do not grieve the Holy Spirit of God, with whom you were sealed for the day of redemption. Get rid of all bitterness, rage and anger, brawling and slander, along with every form of malice. Be kind and compassionate to one another, forgiving each other, just as in Christ God forgave you (Ephesians 4:30-32).

That we can go against the Spirit's wishes shows that we have a partnership with the Spirit in our Christian walk. He does not take over but we can let the Holy Spirit be our guide and control us to a certain extent.

Jude tells us. *"But you, dear friends, build yourselves up in your most holy faith and pray in the Holy Spirit"* (Jude 1:20) which means to let the Spirit guide our prayers. Jesus called the Holy Spirit the Counselor,

But the Counselor, the Holy Spirit, whom the Father will send in my name, will teach you all things and will remind you of everything I have said to you (John 14:26).

Later Jesus adds,

But I tell you the truth: It is for your good that I am going away. Unless I go away, the Counselor will not come to you; but if I go, I will send him to you.

Jesus and the Holy Spirit's Participation

When he comes, he will convict the world of guilt in regard to sin and righteousness and judgment: in regard to sin, because men do not believe in me; in regard to righteousness, because I am going to the Father, where you can see me no longer . . . (John 16:7-10)

In addition, Jesus told us,

When you are brought before synagogues, rulers and authorities, do not worry about how you will defend yourselves or what you will say, for the Holy Spirit will teach you at that time what you should say (Luke 12:11-12).

 He was referring to the times of persecution. However, the Holy Spirit can guide our words at any important time. This especially applies to Prayer and Resolution Counseling when we are seeking God's will and perfect resolution.
 I gave a talk once on the grieving process that takes place when missionaries lose a loved one, retire or have to leave people or tribe they have worked with for years. After the presentation, most of the people had left and I was walking down the aisle when a small cluster of women entered the aisle also. They shared that Betty had lost her husband and had left the people she had ministered to for many years. She had been crying and her friends were comforting her.
 I do not normally hug a woman other than my wife but I gave Betty a hug and said, "I just felt that you needed a hug."
 One woman said, "You know, we were just talking about how hard it is to lose a husband and Betty had said, 'I sure could use a man's hug.'"

That is how the Holy Spirit operates. He prompted me and I behaved in a way that brought blessing and comfort to this woman. This was not surrender; this was cooperation with the Spirit. These women saw it as from me but also recognized that God cared.

God honors the fact that we have minds, wills and the abilities to make right and wrong choices. Having the Holy Spirit in us does not take away from our freedom but does permit us to let the Spirit into our lives as a partner.

The Power Only Distortion

A distortion comes with a "Jesus only" approach. Christ came to reveal to us the Father, not to replace him. The same distortion occurs when we have a "Holy Spirit only" approach. The Spirit in us helps us to conform to Jesus Christ and to be in fellowship with the Father and the son. Seeking the Spirit merely for power or control is wrong. The Holy Spirit works with us as we minister to others. Still, both the hurting one and we are in control and using our faculties.

A friend we had counseled in prayer and resolution reported to us that a woman came to her mission center and spoke to the assembly. This woman put people to sleep and then had the Holy Spirit work in their lives to bring healing and forgiveness. Our friend stood up in the meeting and asked the question, "How can people receive healing and forgiveness without awareness and repentance, and without forgiving others who have wronged them?"

I question that this is God's way. Such a "sleep approach" appears to be an occult-like practice that emphasizes passivity. We must confess consciously and with awareness. God has not given us a painless way to

Jesus and the Holy Spirit's Participation

acknowledge what others or we have done. Extending forgiveness and seeking forgiveness is not easy. We cannot do it second-hand nor passively or asleep, supposedly as a work of the Holy Spirit.

We see God's greatest power today through the ministry of the Holy Spirit. The Spirit can reveal hidden things to us. He can bring back from beneath the surface issues and events that have life in the present unbeknownst to us. He exposes and this can hurt. Nevertheless, he also heals and separates us from the past and from its force in our lives. He does this in relationship with us. The knowledge he gives us permits us to do our part. His work in this area might be more important than his "power gifts." In this he covers a multitude of sins and brings the dead to life and sets the captives free.

The Holy Spirit wants to have a place in our lives but he is not a genie in a bottle, at our beckon and call; nor are we to use his gifts for private gain or power. In the book of Acts, Simon was a practicing sorcerer before he became a Christian. As Simon followed Philip around, the signs and miracles that Philip was doing astonished him (Acts 8:9-13).

Later Simon watched as Peter and John laid hands on people and these people received the Holy Spirit. Simons' response was to offer to buy the spiritual gift,

> *"Give me also this ability so that everyone on whom I lay my hands may receive the Holy Spirit"* (Acts 8:18). *Peter's response was, "May your money perish with you, because you thought you could buy the gift of God with money!"* (Acts 8:20)

Today there is a great deal of misuse and abuse of the power and gifts of the Holy Spirit. If we are going to involve the Spirit in our lives then we do so on his terms, not ours.

In Prayer and Resolution Counseling, we want to pray so that God can answer our prayers and bring resolution and healing. As important, is that we go away from Prayer and Resolution Counseling with a greater appreciation of ourselves as children of God and that God is our Father. Equally important is that we relate more fully to Jesus Christ our Savior and more fully appreciate what is available to us because of his suffering, death and resurrection: the power and authority that we have in Christ. Lastly, as God's children, we know that we are not alone. The Holy Spirit is always there as our partner and guide. Jesus said that we could have fellowship with him and the Father. Also we can have the fellowship of the Holy Spirit.

11

Satan's Opposition

We live in an age when people are becoming more "spiritual" but with a dangerous twist. Any time we seek to enhance our spiritual selves and yet do not recognize the different spirit forces around us, then we will be prey to the dark forcers of evil.

We have impersonalized evil and made it atmosphere. When people do evil things, we have redefined them as wounded, environmentally affected, unable to stop them-selves from doing hurtful acts. They really did not mean it. We increasingly talk about people being diseased. It is the disease that is at fault, not the person.

The more we explain away evil, the less room there is to consider evil forces such as demons and Satan. The more technologically advanced we are, the more spiritually removed we are from reality. Whenever we help another, using Prayer and Resolution Counseling, we will be threatening the Kingdom of Darkness and that kingdom will respond. Satan is the prince of this world and ruler over the forces of darkness. We must understand this special being who is the enemy of both God and humankind.

His Character

We must keep in mind that Satan or his forces are always in the background ready to interfere, disrupt or destroy the work of God. Satan is the *great accuser* of the saints before God and he is the *slanderer,* distorting the truth and confusing people with lies.

If we made a movie that accurately portrayed the fall of man and his subsequent history, we would give several actors important billing. The first couple, Adam and Eve, would be up there. We could not leave out Noah, Abraham, Samuel and David, just to name a few. However, top billing would only go to a few: God, the Holy Spirit, Jesus *and Satan.*

Satan is a key player, not because we want him to be, but because he is there. He would be among the major stars in this drama of man.

I taught a college class once on social structure and church growth. One assignment I gave my students was for them to go to their churches and get a copy of their church doctrinal statements, as summarized in their creeds. The church members often recite these creeds during a service.

When we looked at these various creeds as a whole, we came out with the following: they mentioned God, the Holy Spirit and Jesus. They mentioned the incarnation, sin, salvation, the church, heaven and hell. In all that we looked at, they either mentioned Satan at the end, as a one-liner, or ignored him. How unfortunate because Satan is a major player today. He is the Prince of this world and the enemy of all God's people.

I have heard people say that we should not mention the *Evil One* because, when we do, we give him honor through giving him attention. This is not true. We give him honor when we excessively fear him. Others think that the Evil One will just go away if they turn their backs on him. We give him power, however, when we ignore him and pretend he does not exist. The scriptures tell us to resist the Devil, not ignore him.

Satan is a *predator*. The scriptures characterize him as a lion, *Be of sober spirit, be on the alert. Your adversary, the devil, prowls about like a roaring lion, seeking someone to devour* (I Peter 5:8 NAS).

Common sense tells me that I want to be aware when he is around. In Kenya, the people build a thick hedge of thorn bushes around their camps to keep out lions. Ignoring a predator is both foolish and dangerous. We can try to ignore Satan but he does not ignore us.

His Activities

Over an eleven-year period, we lived with a group of Amazon Indians. Connie was the first foreign woman the Indians had seen. They spoke only their own or other, equally unknown languages. They knew nothing of Christianity or even that a supreme being like God existed. It took much hard work to analyze the language and culture and learn to speak their language.

A few years later, we brought in a slide projector that ran on batteries. One night we invited the Indians to a slide show in our house—make that a hut, all sixteen by twenty-five feet of it, made out of bark and tied with vines. That night I did not ask for God's protection. After all, it was just a slide show.

We were all sitting on the floor in the dark. I had turned off the gas lantern before the show. As we showed stories about Jesus, using filmstrips, we were explaining in their language, what they were seeing. After awhile, the Indians saw the scene showing Jesus on the cross.

A Journey to Wholeness

We began to explain why they were punishing him in that way and began to talk about salvation.

Connie and I could feel the atmosphere change in that hut as we began to talk. The Indians were quiet and listening intently. Suddenly the gas lantern flared up! It startled all of us and the spell was broken. The lantern was cool to the touch and had been off for close to an hour.

I try never to open a time of prayer without giving due to Satan. I say something like this:

> *"Heavenly Father, I know that Satan and his forces are ever ready to interfere and disrupt what you want to accomplish during this time. I ask that you build a hedge of protection around us, our families, and those people who are special to us and our properties so that no force of evil can operate or keep us from doing your will."*

Once we were visiting my sister. A neighbor dropped by while we were there and we found ourselves talking about the differences between Mormon and Christian beliefs. This woman was a new convert to Mormonism and knew little about it or Christianity. After a time we began specifically to explain why Christ came and had to die.

In the middle of this, the door suddenly burst open and four children rushed in. One had a scrape on the knee and it was bleeding. We were not able to pick up and continue the conversation.

We can say this was just a coincidence but the timing is too perfect. Satan and his forces are real and they are always alert to stop God's working when we leave the door open. Prayer can close the door.

Satan's Role

Satan is *our enemy*. He deceived Eve and eventually drove the wedge between God and humankind. I used to think that three groups of people make up the world. On one side were God's people. In the middle were a large group of uncommitted people and on the other side were Satan's people. That picture is false. Instead, the world consists of a dichotomy, only two groups of people. One group belongs to God and the other group is under "the prince of this world."

> *We know that anyone born of God does not continue to sin; the one who was born of God keeps him safe, and the evil one cannot harm him. We know that we are children of God, and that the whole world is under the control of the evil one* (John 5:18-19).

Jesus describes what the characteristics of each group are,

> *He who does what is sinful is of the devil, because the devil has been sinning from the beginning. The reason the son of God appeared was to destroy the devil's work. No one who is born of God will continue to sin, because God's seed remains in him; he cannot go on sinning, because he has been born of God. This is how we know who the children of God are and who the children of the devil are: Anyone who does not do what is right is not a child of God; nor is anyone who does not love his brother* (John 3:8-10).

The scriptures tell us that Satan *clouds the minds of people*. Even during a prayer time, the forces of evil can be active. Once we were working with John and he reported that he kept hearing a voice in his head saying, "Don't believe it. God isn't listening to you!" We told him to command the voice to stop and to command the spirit to leave. We joined him in prayer and added our authority.

Nothing much happened, except that John then went on with his prayer and finished. Shortly after that, he left. We had shopping to do so we immediately left also.

When we returned and entered the house where we were staying, the smell was awful! It was as if an animal had died and rotted. I moved some furniture to find the dead thing before I remembered what had happened before we left. The smell was the after-effect of a demonic presence.

We prayed and asked God to cleanse the room and the smell left.

Christine, while in the midst of prayer, suddenly could not concentrate. She said it was as if someone had turned on an eggbeater in her head. Connie told Christine to command the spirit to leave and to take the confusion with it. Christine did this and she was then free and lucid and continued her prayer.

Several have gotten the thought, "God isn't listening to you. You are talking to the air." Others, "This isn't working." Many times, we have worked with people afflicted to a degree by spirits. These spirits told them, "If you continue this, we will kill your child." (Often this last thought is confirmation that there is a degree of demonic affliction.)

We are in a spiritual battle and we must be alert to the forces of darkness. We must not fear because our position in Christ is what keeps us safe. However, we cannot be smug and think that the forces of darkness cannot trouble us or hinder us because we are God's children.

The World's Standard

Satan's work is not always apparent. More often, the interference is from what has come from the television or society. Both can be just as deadly as the straightforward demonic attack. On television, a man and a woman entered a house to stay for the weekend. The woman host knew they were not married but showed them to their room with its queen-sized bed. A lesson presented and learned.

In the movie, the hero finally corners an evil and cruel villain. Then there is the scene where the hero kicks, punches and brutalizes the villain. Only then does the hero kill him in some nasty way. The movie presented a lesson: we can torture and otherwise brutalize people if we feel they are evil enough.

If we define people as less-than-human then we can kill them without hesitation. The Turks applied this lesson to the Armenians. The Germans applied this lesson to Jews, Gypsies and other people during World War II. More recently, others have applied the lesson in former Yugoslavia and in several countries in Africa.

I saw an interview that concerned a priest whom they had accused of raping a woman. Part of his defense was that he had not been involved emotionally so the act was not sin! The world's standard cannot be our standard.

Do not love the world or anything in the world. If anyone loves the world, the love of the Father is not in him. For everything in the world—the cravings of sinful man, the lust of his eyes and the boasting of what he has and does—comes not from the Father but from the world (John 2:15-16).

This is not a popular view during these days when society is questioning almost every standard. The scriptures tell us, *"Do not be surprised, my brothers, if the world hates you"* (I John 3:13). Whether we need to accuse another or confess our own sin, we must do so using as our guide God's law and principles. He does not accept a man sleeping with his mother-in-law or two women and a man having sex together. He does not accept a man with plural wives, group sex or the men loving boys' movement.

God also opposes returning clothes after people have worn them once when they never intended to buy them in the first place. Through the media, all these sins are worth attention and money. We might consider such people cute, exciting or freeing but God says they are committing sin.

সে ৰ্ছ

We want to view the world and society with a certain amount of distrust and skepticism, always keeping in mind that the world is under the power of the Evil One. The world systems are not God's but Satan's systems. As God's children, we live in the world but we do not live under the domination of the Prince of this world. We must not give more due than necessary to Satan and his forces but we are foolish to ignore him and think that he will go away. We want to be aware and alert but not preoccupied with the forces of evil.

Satan's Role

In Prayer and Resolution Counseling, we do not hunt for Satan. Nevertheless, if his forces appear, we handle them in the authority we have in Christ. After all, Christ has already legally defeated Satan and his forces. God is just biding his time before he takes over what he has won.

If Satan's forces get a degree of control over people's lives, it is normally because they have chosen to sin with foreknowledge and deliberation. In other words, they have been rebellious and such a spirit of rebellion can give entrance to the forces of darkness. Another way they can gain entrance is through extreme trauma and fear. It is as if such strong responses create a briefly open door for the forces of evil.

This is not a detailed discussion of the Kingdom of Darkness but we must always consider the options. We should not fall back on human nature and a one-dimensional (earthly) approach to the issues of life.

Nor do we want to end up dwelling on sin and awaking each day to a task of searching out sin or spending our lives avoiding sin. The purpose of Prayer and Resolution Counseling is to get rid of *abiding sin*. These forces came because of power sins. Only God can free us from the power and forces that have been at work for years. Once freed, we can move on into life with a burden Jesus calls light and a yoke he calls easy. This happens when we fully accept and live who we are in Christ.

I am a child of God and as such, it is natural that I behave in righteous ways because otherwise is against my nature. As a son of God, although I may sometimes sin, I do not dwell on sin but am open to receiving blessing and being a blessing.

❧ 12 ❦

The Priestly Role

The Old Testament priestly order consisted of a High Priest and, under him, other priests. In the New Testament, we find another priestly order but the same hierarchy. This new priestly order consists of Christ, the Great High Priest, and, under him, other priests. John refers to this group when he says, *He loves us, and by his death he has freed us from our sins and made us a kingdom of priests to serve his God and Father* (Revelation 1:5b-6a GNB).

As priests, we have duties. We do not stand between God and man so people do not have to go through us to gain access to God. That changed. However, priests and sacrifices still go together. Our current task is to help people come to God in a way that satisfies his standards. We guide people in prayer, the only way Christ's sacrifice can be appropriated now, and make sure that the prayer is effective.

We use Christ's sacrifice in two different ways: First, we can help people accept the sacrifice for their sins and enter the new birth experience we call salvation. Second, we can guide people in prayer to receive daily forgiveness (I John 1:9). The priesthood exists and should function in today's world.

The Priestly Role

Priests as Facilitators

On television, I listened to an account of healing. A young woman had lived a wild life of sex and drugs and was dying from the physical effects of years on cocaine. In desperation, she and her parents went to Europe seeking someone to help her.

A simple country priest was receiving confessions and she went to him. Many people were waiting but the priest spent a long time listening to her confession. She did not ask for healing but for forgiveness and the priest gave her absolution. A few days later, she began to feel God healing her body and in a few months, God had completely healed her.

The moral of the story is that she approached a simple country priest who did not know enough to doubt his role as God's priest. God worked through him and his prayers, along with hers and freed him to bless her beyond anything she imagined.

When I first began to counsel using prayer, I considered this approach as nothing more than specific and focused prayer. In Turkey, after presenting a short seminar on our methods, a Christian worker came up and told me that what I was doing was functioning as a priest. Coming from a mainstream evangelical church background, this made me pause and think. I was uncomfortable with the idea of myself as a priest but he was right. This is what Peter said,

But you are a chosen people, a royal priesthood, a holy nation, a people belonging to God, that you

may declare the praises of him who called you out of darkness into his wonderful light (I Peter 2:9).

I had thought that I was praying in a different, legal way and that I was focusing on forgiveness in prayer more than Christians normally do. I was a priest, however, one of many operating out of the royal priesthood. In Turkey as I counseled Christian workers and coordinated their presentations to God as Father, I was helping them to apply the sacrifice of Christ to specific sins. Is not this the main role of the priest, to take charge of the sacrificial process?

I fully agree that Christ died once for all time at the cross, "*but he, having offered one sacrifice for sins for all time, sat down at the right hand of God*" (Hebrews 10:12). I am not talking about crucifying him daily but of appropriating this sacrifice whenever needed. The scriptures say, *Hence, also, he is able to save forever those who draw near to God through him, since he always lives to make intercession for them* (Hebrews 7:25).

So how can we best function as priests? We bear another's burden: "*Carry each other's burdens, and in this way you fulfill the law of Christ*" (Galatians 6:2). We affirm, clarify, and build up. We confess to one another; we are witnesses and we can intercede for another.

And so, as those who have been chosen of God, holy and beloved, put on a heart of compassion, kindness, humility, gentleness and patience; bearing with one another, and forgiving each other, whoever has a complaint against anyone;

The Priestly Role

just as the Lord forgave you, so also should you (Colossians 3:12-13).

As priests, we focus on our position in Christ:

Since, then, you have been raised with Christ, set your hearts on things above, where Christ is seated at the right hand of God. Set your minds on things above, not on earthly things. For you died, and your life is now hidden with Christ in God. When Christ, who is your life, appears, then you also will appear with him in glory. Put to death, therefore, whatever belongs to your earthly nature: sexual immorality, impurity, lust, evil desires and greed, which is idolatry (Colossians 3:1-5).

Notice, we are in Christ and he is our life but we still have our earthly bodies and sinning potential. This is why Paul exhorts us, *"But now you also, put then all aside: anger, wrath, malice, slander, and abusive speech from your mouth"* (Colossians 3:8 NAS). As priests, one of our tasks is to help our brother or sister do what Paul says.

We have considered it inappropriate in these days to confess our sins to another person. This is a carry-over from the Reformation's resistance to the excesses in the Roman Catholic Church at that time but confession is acceptable. James encouraged us,

Is any one of you sick? He should call the elders of the church to pray over him and anoint him

> with oil in the name of the Lord. And the prayer offered in faith will make the sick person well; the Lord will raise him up. If he has sinned, he will be forgiven. Therefore confess your sins to each other and pray for each other so that you may be healed. The prayer of a righteous man is powerful and effective (James 5:14-16).

As priests, when helping a sister, we must insure that forgiveness of others has truly happened. We cannot allow excuses such as, "He didn't know better." "That is what I learned from my parents." "I had no other way to go." The troubled sister must be completely honest if we are to help her fully appropriate the work of Christ.

> Do not lie to one another, since you laid aside the old self with its evil practices, and have put on the new self who is being renewed to a true knowledge according to the image of the one who created him (Colossians 3:9-10 NAS).

The principles of the Law are our guide since God provided these as guideposts for righteous living. We are not under the Law but accept the standards and principles behind the Law. Paul says, "*the law is holy, and the commandment is holy, righteous and good*" (Romans 7:12). The Law is God's standard whether or not we are in the Age of Grace. Paul says,

> Now we know that whatever the law says, it says to those who are under the law, so that every mouth may be silenced and the whole world held

accountable to God. Therefore no one will be declared righteous in his sight by observing the law; rather, through the law we become conscious of sin (Romans 3:19-20).

The Law condemns us when we violate godly standards. It also blesses us with a long life and health when we live by its standards. The Law condemns us and cannot save us. In the Law, however, we can see God's standard and an indication of his character.

This also means that the principles within the Law give us a standard that we all accept. The Law is a point of reference for recognizing sin, its consequences, and on-going force. Paul tells us that,

the sinful mind is hostile to God. It does not submit to God's law, nor can it do so. Those controlled by the sinful nature cannot please God. You, however, are controlled not by the sinful nature but by the Spirit, if the Spirit of God lives in you. And if anyone does not have the Spirit of Christ, he does not belong to Christ. But if Christ is in you, your body is dead because of sin, yet your spirit is alive because of righteousness (Romans 8:7-10*)*.

A sinful nature responds by not obeying the principles of the Law but, by implication, a nature controlled by the Holy Spirit, does obey the principles of the Law. The Law is a standard for us even now but it cannot condemn us if we are in Christ, nor can it save us. It does provide the grounds, however, for under-standing what sin is:

> *What shall we say, then? Is the law sin? Certainly not! Indeed I would not have known what sin was except through the law. For I would not have known what coveting really was if the law had not said, 'Do not covet'* (Romans 7:7).

In fact, when in Hebrews it says,

> *For the word of God is living and active. Sharper than any double-edged sword, it penetrates even to dividing soul and spirit, joints and marrow; it judges the thoughts and attitudes of the heart* (Hebrews 4:12).

This word of God includes the principles of the Law in the Old Testament.

Prayer and Resolution Counseling helps us understand the real issues and our parts in them. Real resolution only takes place when we truly understand what we are forgiving or confessing. We can hinder God's ability to act and answer our prayers when we forgive on false premises or confess without true awareness.

Priests for Resolution

It is important that we approach God as Father. We are sinners saved by grace, true, but not as a prominent

The Priestly Role

label we wear. Instead, we are adopted members of his family. As sons and daughters, we can come boldly into his presence because he has given us that right. As his children, we can anticipate that our behavior will be that which becomes a son or daughter of God. The scriptures talk about God giving us a new heart.

A sinner, even saved by grace, by definition commits sin. A son or daughter imitates and is like the father although he or she may sometimes sin. We come to God, in our position in Christ, as his children.

Through Christ, God has redeemed us and made us righteous, even holy. He has sanctified and justified us. He has forgiven and saved us. Just as importantly, he has made us joint heirs with Christ so we can come to God as father.

We need an understanding of the issues but we cannot deal with the issues involved unless God's helps us. To gain understanding we can use even secular counseling approaches unless they muddle rather than clarify the issues. For example, society, the psychoanalytical and behavioral approaches consider environment an excuse for behavior. Nevertheless, while environment is a factor and provides reasons, it does not lessen our responsibility for wrong acts.

Past grudges are present grudges until people acknowledge them and forgive the offenders or receive forgiveness. People need the past and the present and all the participants involved so that they can fully see and accept responsibility for their parts. There can be many players. Our role is often one part in the drama so we cannot take credit for the whole play. The script involves several parts with their players and, while our role is crucial, we cannot play ours without the others. Unless we recognize their parts and, if need be, forgive, we cannot confess with understanding our part in the drama of life.

Stacy was an older woman with a past. During her late teen years, she lived with a boy friend and became pregnant. He demanded an abortion and she gave in. Thirty-five years later, twenty years a Christian, she still felt the guilt of that act. She had prayed for forgiveness countless times. As Connie and I counseled her in prayer, we got her to share the whole story. Notice that, according to Glasser and Adams, this is the useless past.

We found that Stacy had been praying a prayer that God could not answer. God could forgive Stacy but not for all that happened.

Her boy friend warned her, "If you don't do this I'll leave you."

The girl friends she ran with told her, "Everybody is doing it."

The nurse at the clinic was self-assured and counseled her, "Having an abortion is not that big an issue. It is a minor operation."

For years, Stacy carried one-hundred percent of the burden of guilt when she needed to hand over some of this to the others—and forgive them for their parts. When she realized this, she accepted that others were involved as well. She suddenly felt anger and rage over what they had done to her. She faced the fact that they had encouraged her to do a deed that had haunted her for more than thirty years. After a struggle, she forgave each of them and then confessed her own part and asked forgiveness. God forgave Stacy and, for the first time in

The Priestly Role

her Christian walk, she felt fully forgiven and free of that terrible burden.

Bobgan would disagree with the way we handled Stacy when he says,

> *Psychological counseling attempts to deal with guilt through redefining standards of right and wrong [I agree] and by shifting responsibility from personal choice to such things as the 'unconscious,' the past, other people, circumstances, and so on, all of which encourage the victim role [I disagree] rather than reveal personal responsebility.*[55]

After Prayer and Resolution Counseling, one woman wrote, "It is amazing to me how much my past affected my NOW . . ." Stacy's past was her present burden. She was, to a certain degree, a victim—but still responsible for her actions. Her willingness to assume all the responsibility and guilt was wrong. Other people were involved. How could she possibly receive forgiveness for *everything* when she had but a part, significant as it was?

Forgiving or asking forgiveness outside the context of real life is shallow and meaningless—a rote that merely follows the rules instead of getting to the essence. God already knows what happened and its significance but how can we know the significance of what has happened unless we fill in the details?

---

[55] Martin & Deidre Bobgan, *Psychoheresy*, p. 218.

A Journey to Wholeness

Was this counseling or Christian theology? Could Stacy have received the help she needed from standard secular or Christian counseling, no matter how sincere the counselor? A change of mind was not enough. Feeling better about herself was not enough. Telling Stacy she did not do anything wrong, when she felt she had, was not enough. Stacy needed forgiveness but she also needed to forgive and she needed to see it from God's perspective and do it his way.

Stacy ended her time in Prayer and Resolution Counseling a whole person. When God intervenes, we do not come away as survivors, having learned to cope with life or anticipating a life burdened with the constant need to resist our wrong inward inclinations.

There must be resolution. It is only possible when we have handled all the details. Otherwise, the details will be a weight or a catalyst that continues to influence the present. *Resolution can only come when God acts for us to complete a heavenly transaction that touches our lives here on earth.* Only God can do this. We can appropriate Christ's sacrifice but only if we present the issues to God with a focus, presenting specifics so he can answer in specifics.

Prayer and resolution counseling does not focus on sins as much as on its consequences and power. The power is like a ball and chain hindering a person and dragging him down. Only God's power can break this chain. Prayer and Resolution Counseling accepts that we can do things on earth that God confirms in heaven.

For example, according to Jesus, marriage is a rite that God endorses in heaven. This means that a marriage creates spiritual ties between people that no earthly court can cut, only God can. If people divorce and marry again, the first marriage is still on the books in heaven. The spiritual union between the partners is still in effect. Unless God breaks those ties, the partners in the second marriage will bear the consequences. They will share the previous spouse and not be fully one with the present spouse. The tie can be broken, if directed by the Holy Spirit, through prayer by asking God to break the spiritual ties or bonds. Otherwise, the present marriage will not be on a solid foundation.

Normally, I do not consider divorce an alternative. Nevertheless, if a former spouse has already remarried and the bridges burned, then all we can do is make the best of the situation. We want to create the best possible foundation for the present marriage. The foundation is established through the closure of the first marriage. The former marriage bonds, spiritual ties, between the spouses must be broken so a true union can take place in the present marriage.

Too often the church has worshiped and made sacrifice to the idol of marriage. The sacrifices are the abused man, woman or children in a bad marriage. When there is emotional, physical or verbal (spiritual) abuse in a marriage and the offending member is unwilling to admit faults or seek help, then a divorce should take place for the sake of the health and safety of the spouse and the children. To suggest that the hurting members in a marriage should stay in harm's way is wrong. God is not nearly as interested in the institution of marriage as he is in the welfare of the individuals in that marriage.

We must also consider the spiritual bonds created through sexual sin. Paul is not asking a question when he says,

> *Do you not know that your bodies are members of Christ himself? Shall I then take the members of Christ and unite them with a prostitute? Never! Do you not know that he who unites himself with a prostitute is one with her in body? For it is said, "The two will become one flesh." But he who unites himself with the Lord is one with him in spirit* (I Corinthians 6:15-17).

One flesh emphasizes the sexual nature of the sin when the real issue is the spiritual union that takes place in both marriage and illicit sexual unions. Above, Paul equates sexual sin with marriage: "*For this reason a man will leave his father and mother and be united to his wife, and the two will become one flesh*"(Ephesians 5:31), but he also compares the sexual union (which seems temporal) with our spiritual union with Christ, which is eternal. The sin act can take only minutes *but the results are ongoing*. The people involved will not have release without the breaking of the union (and, of course, confession and forgiveness).

Through Christ's sacrifice, God has given us all we need to have life as a blessing, not a burden. Prayer and Resolution Counseling is not satisfied with helping people cope with life or survive. It should be solution oriented and provide a foundation for righteous, victorious living.

Priests for Completion

One counselor says that anger has no place in repentance. However, feeling hate, anger and even rage as part of the forgiveness and repentance process is not wrong. In fact, forgiveness given without feeling is suspect. Often others have encouraged us and "greased" the path we have taken to sin. When we truly understand what others have done with full clarity, as we stand beside God and look back, we realize the awfulness of what they did. We see not just the sin but also the ongoing consequences of their sins against us. Seeing it from God's perspective does not lessen the sin. Nevertheless, the scripture warns us, *"Everyone who hates his brother is a murderer; and you know that no murderer has eternal life abiding in him"* (I John 3:15 NAS). Recognizing and feeling again the sins others have done to us should make it harder for us to forgive. Still, we must forgive, and once we do, God can fully close the door.

The mind, heart, emotions and beliefs all work together. *Our behavior and expectations come out of our belief system and out of our feelings—not out of our mind and rational thought.* Pam was a missionary very focused on Jesus. A victim of her father's molestation, Pam could not easily relate to God as her heavenly Father. Yet Pam could give an excellent lesson on the fatherhood of God. She had information. She had learned the lessons and could teach them to others but could not accept them for herself.

A Journey to Wholeness

People often have a dual system at work within themselves. One system applies to other people, and one system applies to them.

"*I* know that God is a God of love as he relates to others but *I* can only relate to him through Jesus and as a servant. *I* know that God hears our prayers but, because my earthly father never listened to me, God does not hear *mine*. *I* am the exception."

People do not consciously say such things but they believe them and feel this is so. *We operate out of what we feel and believe, not out of what we rationally know.* If we think of ourselves as drunks then we will behave as ones. People will explain why we do not have to be or why we can change but we will feel within ourselves that we are what we are, drunks. *We are what we believe ourselves to be.* Knowledge does not bring release from the bondage of belief and feeling. Only God's intervention can change our innermost being and change our beliefs and feelings about ourselves, others and God.

Clearly understanding others and ourselves and the why behind our wrongdoing, is a step towards freedom: freedom from sin and freedom from wrong forces that control us. Confession consciously forces us to bring up what we believe and compare it with what God says. This is a useful exercise.

For example, John asked forgiveness for trying to take all the love that his wife had and not letting any of that love go toward their daughter. Of course, this is strange, but John had never verbalized what his belief system said: people give out love in only one direction at a time. That meant that when his mother loved him, she only did so until her boyfriend came into the room. Then

The Priestly Role

she withdrew her love from John and redirected it toward the other. John never taught this in class but, for himself, his system worked.

John got married and was never satisfied with his wife's love. In his perception, her love was never enough. She was constantly shutting off her love for him and giving it to their daughter. John was always the loser whenever his wife directed her love elsewhere.

The fact that John accepted Christ as his savior was only because, for a brief time, John felt God's love. Since then, he almost never experienced his love. To John, God was always busy elsewhere. John could only serve. Maybe in service, God would notice him. John was consistent in his reasoning at the belief level. He had operated this way for years and when he heard a different message, he created another system to handle that new information. This new system now existed beside his old one. John could even apply this new teaching to others but John's old system remained intact and continued to guide him.

It was not enough for John to confess his sin. He had to confront the error of his belief system. He had to recognize that it was controlling him, instead of him controlling it. He had to reject all the garbage in his system and accept the truths that God had all along for him in his Word.[56]

---

[56] This handling of foundational lies is a topic in my book *Freedom from Words of Power: Breaking the Chains of Harmful Declarations, Vows and Lies*. The complications in dealing with tearing down and rebuilding the foundation by which a person lives demands more detail than I can give here.

A Journey to Wholeness

Foundational issues can come to the surface during confession. We should be living by general principles. These are not "do this" and "don't do that" but "take this road" or "take that one." We need to understand the reason (principle) behind our choices, not just obey a rule. The Law said, do not kill. Jesus restated it as a principle and said do not even have hate toward another. It is the same as murder. The Law said, do not commit adultery and Jesus did not put it aside. He restated it in principle form and made it even harder to deal with,

> *You have heard that it was said, 'You shall not commit adultery,' but I say to you, that everyone who looks on a woman to lust for her has committed adultery with her already in his heart* (Matthew 5:27-28 NAS).

The scriptures say, "*Search me, O God, and know my heart; try me and know my anxious thoughts*" (Psalm 139:23 NAS) and implies that we have a choice in dealing with the sin. "*Come let us reason together*" (Isaiah 1:18) implies respect for us, his creation. This is a joining of minds. God is willing to come down to our level as a way of dialogue. He wants us to do it his way, not by force, but by choice.

The Priestly Role

As priests, we have an active role with hurting ones to see that they clearly understand the issues and accept their parts in them. This means that they need to confess sin or declare they are blameless. In our priestly roles, we level the ground and clear the brush away so nothing is standing between the hurting ones and God as their Father. This task means taking a certain amount of responsibility for what happens and requires a deep sensitivity to the Holy Spirit's guidance and prompting.

Theoretically, we are already qualified as priests in Christ. However, the only way we are going to be qualified in practical ways is to perform as priests when God puts hurting people into our paths. If he brings them, then he will also help us perform our roles as priests. This is a great responsibility but also a great privilege and honor. We should not be afraid to accept it.

13

Forgiveness a Key

The Necessity for Forgiveness

In Prayer and Resolution Counseling, we focus on God as the one who can help us. Only he can empower us for change, only he can forgive and break the chains of sin that dominate our lives. Sharing is not enough, nor is just talk. If God is not actively involved then we ignore the results of Christ's death and resurrection. We ignore the ministry of the Holy Spirit, not to mention our relationship to God as his children.

Often resolution of an issue involves sin, either our sin or the sins others committed against us. Jesus told us, *And when you stand praying, if you hold anything against anyone, forgive him, so that your Father in heaven may forgive you your sins* (Mark 11:25).

When sin shows its ugly head then the process of forgiveness must take place. Forgiveness does not come naturally but Jesus said we should go against our natural instincts to return like-kind (to get even, to get revenge) when he said, *But I say to you who hear, love your enemies, do good to those who hate you, bless those who curse you, pray for those who mistreat you* (Luke 6:27-28 NAS).

The scriptural focus is clear when it comes to forgiveness. If we realize that we have wronged someone then we go to that person and ask for forgiveness.

> *Therefore, if you are offering your gift at the altar and there remember that your brother has something against you, leave your gift there in front of the altar. First go and be reconciled to your brother; then come and offer your gift* (Matthew 5:23-24).

The focus is on us, as the wrongdoer, doing the right thing. If a person has wronged us and that person asks for forgiveness then we forgive him.

Forgiveness is the subject of an amazing body of literature. Much of it distorted. For example,

> *Forgiving others: specific prayer naming the person(s), naming the offense(s),* **releasing them from blame and responsibility***, accepting and thanking God for the situation as it now exists and for the good that He is bringing out of it, and blessing the offending individuals. (emphasis mine)*[57]

If we release someone *from blame and responsibility*, then we are saying either that a wrong did not occur or that the person was not able to behave differently. If real sin has occurred then it is wrong for us say the sinner is blameless. God does not and neither should we.

---

[57] Burden Bearers, Seattle, Washington, seminar notes (Seattle: n. p., n. d.).

Also, notice that this redefines sin as *good* and a blessing. Granted sometimes God can bring good out of evil but we cannot sanction sin because out of it comes good!

Here is a prayer Ruth Bennett suggests,

> *Dear Jesus, please tell [name the person] these words: 'I forgive you for [name injury]. I will no longer hold this against you.* **You did the best you could.** *Jesus is setting me free to forgive everyone. He has healed me.' (Emphasis mine)*[58]

This type of prayer excuses the wrongdoer. Holding people responsible is the first step in recognizing that a wrong has been committed and needs forgiveness. (This does not mean confronting a person.) More of a misconception is to redefine evil as good.

Sandi's mother bought her a piano. She told Sandi that it was hers and the daughter was overjoyed. A few weeks later, when Sandi came home from school, the piano was gone. Her mother had sold it without telling her or explaining to her why she did it. Many years later Sandi shared a poem with us that she had written. The theme? Everyone must have been laughing at me, talking about "my piano."

Should I guide Sandi in a prayer that says "My mother was not responsible for what she did. God, thank you for this blessing;" I do not think so. The mother sold her daughter's property without her permission and without any consideration of the hurt that action brought. (The mother is elderly now but plays a piano at socials. Until She forgives her mother, whenever her

---

[58] Bennett, Rita, *How to Pray for Inner Healing for Yourself and Others* (Old Tappan, NJ: Fleming H. Revell, 1984), p. 65.

mother plays the piano, Sandi remembers this wrong done many years ago.)

Kelsey, a noted author, writes of getting over feelings of unforgiveness toward others. He says that God can remove our unforgiving attitudes but that we must bear the feelings that come with unforgiveness until God gives us freedom.[59]

Nowhere in scripture does God take over our responsibility to forgive. Instead, the scriptures clearly state, *"And forgive us our sins, for we ourselves also forgive everyone who is indebted to us . . ."* (Luke 11:4 NAS) and *"If you forgive anyone his sins, they are forgiven; if you do not forgive them, they are not forgiven"* (John 20:23). In the Lord's Prayer, Jesus said, *"Forgive us our debts, as we also have forgiven our debtors"* (Matthew 6:12). The "as" here means "in the same way." God holds us accountable and says he will forgive us in the same manner we forgive others. When we withhold forgiveness we, to a certain degree, close the door of forgiveness to ourselves.

Sharon Wegscheider-Cruse says,

Forgiving is a gift we give ourselves. It implies that we admit that we do not know the complete circumstances of the people who have had an impact on our lives. . . . Forgiveness acknowledges that we do not have the knowledge or wisdom to sit in judgment and execution over people who may have hurt us in the past.[60]

---

[59] Morton T. Kelsey, "How to Forgive" (Glorieta, NM: Dove Leaflet # 75, 1995).
[60] Sharon Wegscheider-Cruse, *Learning to Love Yourself: Finding Your Self-Worth* (Pompano Beach, FL: Health Communications, 1987), p. 31.

A Journey to Wholeness

Nowhere do I see in scripture that we forgive out of ignorance or because we do not understand. Most of the time we need to forgive *despite the fact we know they have hurt us and planned it that way*—and we often know that God himself agrees with us.

Jesus said,

And whenever you stand praying, forgive, if you have anything against anyone; so that your Father also who is in heaven may forgive you your transgressions. But if you do not forgive, neither will your Father who is in heaven forgive you your transgressions (Mark 11:25-26 NAS).

We cannot claim to be Christians and yet continue to hold a grudge against another. When we do, the issue is not a loss of salvation but we will carry the unhealthy seeds within us that can only germinate into life-draining weeds.

Forgiving on God's terms means we do so as an act of will, if nothing else. Ideally, we do not forgive another because God is bigger than we are, demands it, and forces us to forgive. However, Jesus said,

For if you forgive men when they sin against you, your heavenly Father will also forgive you. But if you do not forgive men their sins, your Father will not forgive your sins (Matthew 6:14-15).

Nor do we forgive merely because God has forgiven us. As God's children, God expects us to behave as he does and that includes the ability to forgive on his terms. This means that we do judge despite the scriptures that say,

Do not judge, and you will not be judged. Do not condemn, and you will not be condemned. Forgive, and you will be forgiven (Luke 6:37).

We have emphasized not judging and forgotten that, in fact, we are *to evaluate* right from wrong! But, as we evaluate or judge the sins others have done against us, we want to use God's standard. Jesus said,

And why do you look at the speck that is in your brother's eye, but do not notice the log that is in your own eye? Or how can you say to your brother, 'Brother, let me take out the speck that is in your eye,' when you yourself do not see the log that is in your eye? You hypocrite, first take the log out of your eye, and then you will see clearly to take out the speck that is in your brother's eye (Luke 6:41-42 NAS).

If we hold ourselves as accountable to God's standards as we hold others, then we have the right perspective to judge, evaluate, the behavior of others.

Paul said,

*For through the grace given to me I say to every man among you not to think more highly of himself than he ought to think; but to think so as to have sound judgment, as God has allotted to each a measure of faith (*Romans 12:3 NAS).

Christians have taken this verse to mean that we have no worth and should not have any pride in self. Yet Paul is not saying we should think of ourselves as nothing. We should not exaggerate our position but better put, we should recognize who we are and not allow ourselves to be doormats.

When we have accepted our worth, we can then give worth to others as well. Giving worth to others includes holding them accountable for their actions. Jesus, the servant, criticized a host when he did not show Jesus the common courtesy of washing the feet of a guest.

Judging right from wrong creates the basis for exhorting and rebuking. This is a function that members in the body of Christ do for one another to maintain purity.

God created us in his image. One piece of that image includes our ability to determine right from wrong and the ability to make choices, even wrong ones. God holds us responsible, however, for our choices and actions. Normally, God will not violate our wills and stop us from sinning. He could intervene but usually he does not.

Also, we can evaluate the action when someone wrongs another or us and even react in anger—and yet not sin.

God created within us a built-in need for justice. When someone has violated our sense of justice, forgiveness allows God to see that justice is satisfied on our behalf. What we cannot do, without harm, is to hold judgment and demand payment when someone hurts us. Unforgiveness is our demand that the person pays our way. Only if the person pays our price—we get revenge—will our justice be satisfied.

But that is God's job, *"Do not take revenge, my friends, but leave room for God's wrath, for it is written: 'It is mine to avenge; I will repay,' says the Lord"* (Romans 12:19).

The approach in therapy that encourages a victim to confront and curse or vent their anger on the former perpetrator is neither godly nor useful. That is vengeance and it is God's job to exact vengeance, not ours. If anything, he is better at it.

When we judge another, we take God's place and stand between the wrongdoer and God. We get in the way of God's working when we withhold forgiveness. Yet to forgive, even for the right reasons, is not easy. Forgiving is a continuous process as others wrong us,

> *So watch yourselves. If your brother sins, rebuke him, and if he repents, forgive him. If he sins against you seven times in a day, and seven times comes back to you and says, 'I repent,' forgive him* (Luke 17:3-4).

Rebuking another is different from confronting for vengeance sake. When we rebuke another, we are emphasizing his wrong behavior so he can repent and ask for forgiveness. When we exhort another, we are emphasizing his correct behavior for encouragement. The emphasis in the verse above is on a wrong done against us: that is why we must forgive.

However, if a person is not acting correctly as a child of God, as opposed to wronging us personally, then we go to that one, with two or three witnesses and confront them. This is the Christian community in action.

We are wrong to think that since God is love everything will work out. This is not so. God's love for us does not eliminate his need to satisfy justice and maintain his holiness. Justice demands a payment for sin and this must be paid. How is it then that we deserve punishment or death and instead get release and blessing? It is because God is merciful and, out of his mercy, he forgives us. Mercy is receiving something we do not expect or deserve in the light of our deeds.

Mercy does not come free. Sin and its effects, like some evil energy, can only be displaced, not stopped. Christ's sacrifice provided both a substitute and a payment for sin that opened the door for God to show mercy to us. Without Christ's sacrifice, God could not, in justice, forgive us. God as a God of love *"is not willing that any should perish"* without knowing him and yet many people die in their sins because God also gave us the freedom of choice.

For our part, when we show mercy and forgive, we are not condoning sin in any way. We know the extent of the wrong and we extend mercy and forgive anyway. That is how God does it. He does not excuse sin. He has full knowledge of the deeds. He knows that the by-product of sin is death, legally and otherwise. Yet he does not demanding payment from the wrongdoer. When we forgive another, we give to God our judgments and our rights as witnesses and accusers and give him his proper place as the righteous judge.

Ron Price says,

> *Forgiveness is making a decision to tear up the emotional IOU we hold against that person, regardless of whether they desire our pardon or not.*[61]

He is both right and wrong. Tearing up implies throwing it away but we cannot take an IOU off the books that easily. The bookkeeping does not allow us to cross out the debt. *Someone has to take the loss.* That is where Christ comes in.

Tearing up the IOU means that we extend mercy. Mercy means that, although we may feel the wrongdoer deserves death, we are putting the matter into God's hands. Might the guilty one get away with it? No, because God will see that justice is done and he will exact a payment. We can depend upon him to do it in

---

[61] Ron Price, "Mental Health Attitude," in *The Healthy Cell Concept* (Nampa, Idaho: AIM International, 1989), pp. 68-69.

one of two ways: either he will make the guilty one pay *or* he will substitute Christ's payment on the cross. Notice that mercy and forgiveness are not free. In providing them, Jesus Christ paid a price. (He takes the loss, so to speak.) In providing mercy and forgiveness, God had to see his son suffer. When sin occurs, someone must always pay.

Forgiving someone in general terms is unrealistic. If we do so, we cannot expect a release from our unforgiving spirit or from our anger and resentment. This is especially true when we are the victims of molestation, rape, or incest. Extending forgiveness is hard but it is essential for our emotional, spiritual and physical health and well-being. Unless we forgive, we will remain tied to the perpetrator and the forces he or she created until the day we die.

Anger is not always sin. Sin comes when we hold on to anger or when we let it turn into hatred, or when the anger is not justified. God did not create us with the capacity to hold on to anger without paying a price in our own bodies, spirits and emotions. Holding a grudge forces us constantly to control our anger rather than resolve the issues that make us frequently angry.

I find it interesting, as a linguist, to see how many people try to get around using the phrase, "I forgive. . . ." They will say, "I give her over to you, God," or "I won't hold it against him any longer." "I want to let this go." The word forgive is a strong term semantically. It has a quality of finality to it. People like to use words that hedge or qualify: "I forgive Frank but give me a time when I can talk to him." Or, better still, "I forgive Frank, but I can still tell others about what he did, right?"

Extending forgiveness is often only possible if we forgive in small doses. Esther's elder brother molested her from her earliest memories and continued to do so through her early teen years. Esther could not possibly forgive her brother with a blanket prayer. Jesus said that we must forgive from the heart (Matthew 18:35) which means that for Esther she had to be fully engaged with her heart and mind.

Esther considered the first remembered time. She saw it as vile and her brother without excuse in any way, and, after a struggle, forgave him. She did not forgive him because he deserved it. He did not. Nor because God had forgiven Esther and she was a sinner also. She forgave to get this judgment off her back and on to God's, so to speak, so he could take his rightful place. Esther found it difficult to give up even this piece of wrong she held against her brother but, at last, she did.

The next incident was not any easier. Incident by incident she chipped away at her anger, resentment and urge to kill her brother. Esther understood what mercy meant: her brother deserved to die for what he did to her but she would not demand it any longer. She gave him over into God's hands even knowing that God might extend mercy and forgiveness by letting Christ pay.

Details are Important

If we look at the sacrifices apart from the Day of Atonement sacrifice, we can see a pattern. People came to the priest and had to acknowledge the type of sin committed (confession) so the priest could determine the appropriate sacrifice. The priest performed the sacrifice in a careful manner. The sinner participated through confessing his sin, placing his hand on the head of the animal, observing the sacrifice of the animal and, at times, eating a portion of it.

Every sin was considered. People either looked to the daily sacrifice to cover them or came personally to the altar. There was even a sacrifice for the sins people committed out of ignorance.

> *If a member of the community sins unintentionally and does what is forbidden in any of the LORD's commands, he is guilty. When he is made aware of the sin he committed, he must bring as his offering* . . . (Leviticus 4:27-28a).

Also,

> *Or if a person thoughtlessly takes an oath to do anything, whether good or evil—in any matter one might carelessly swear about—even though he is unaware of it, in any case when he learns of it he will be guilty (*Leviticus 5:4).

There was also provision for sins of omission (not doing something we should have):

> *If a person sins because he does not speak up when he hears a public charge to testify regarding something he has seen or learned about, he will be held responsible* (Leviticus 5:1).

In the New Testament, James takes this further and makes a general principle, "*Anyone, then, who knows the good he ought to do and doesn't do it, sins*" (James 4:17).

Sin was a serious matter and all were equal before God. Whether people were rich or poor, God made provision for them to come to him. The sacrifice could be for sin, for purification, for thanksgiving, for service. The sacrifice, once done, was absolute. For a particular offense, it did not have to be repeated. If a sinner came and fulfilled the regulations, the sacrifice was legal in that when the priest fulfilled his part, resolution came, regardless of feelings.

This careful approach that God demands we see also in his careful dealing with Israel to redeem the first born sons:

> *The LORD also said to Moses, "I have taken the Levites from among the Israelites in place of the first male offspring of every Israelite woman. The Levites are mine, for all the firstborn are mine. When I struck down all the firstborn in Egypt, I set apart for myself every firstborn in Israel, whether man or animal. They are to be mine. I am the LORD"* (Numbers 3:11-13).

> *"Count the Levites by their families and clans. Count every male a month old or more." So Moses counted them, as he was commanded by the word of the LORD* (Numbers 3:15-16).

> *The LORD also said to Moses, "Take the Levites in place of all the firstborn of Israel, and the livestock of the Levites in place of their livestock. The Levites are to be mine. I am the LORD. To redeem the 273 firstborn Israelites who exceed the number of the Levites, collect five shekels for each one, according to the sanctuary shekel, which weighs twenty gerahs. Give the money for the redemption of the additional Israelites to Aaron and his sons."* (Numbers 3: 44-48)

One Levi substituted for one first-born son. The life of one Levi, committed to God's service, redeemed the life of one first-born. When the Levi stock ran out, then a set amount of money redeemed every additional first-born.

To God, individual people are important and details are important.

Not all sin is the same. Just as in the sacrificial system, where different sins demanded different payments; different issues demand special transactions in prayer. We cannot pray effectively until we see sin for what it is, how it operates on both the earthly and heavenly levels and what is needed, besides forgiveness, to completely resolve the issue.

For examples, in sexual sin, besides forgiveness, people need cleansing. When people commit occult sins, they must renounce spiritual allegiances. In the sin of rebellion, people need to accept, before God, the place they or others have in the authority structure. If people sin in making unwise and wrong vows, they need forgiveness but, as important, God must release them from the obligation to fulfill those vows. This is not a game. We are dealing with spiritual forces at work.

The Lord rightfully criticized the Pharisees when he said,

> *But do not do what they do, for they do not practice what they preach. They tie up heavy loads and put them on men's shoulders, but they themselves are not willing to lift a finger to move them* (Matthew 23:3-4).

It is our task, as priests, to be burden bearers and burden lifters.

> *Brothers, if someone is caught in a sin, you who are spiritual should restore him gently. But watch yourself, or you also may be tempted. Carry each other's burdens, and in this way you will fulfill the law of Christ* (Galatians 6:1-2).

Above all, the priest's role is to see that the appropriation of Christ's sacrifice for the sinning brother or sister is done in a careful manner. If the Old Testament sacrificial system demanded anything, it was a specific, careful approach to the throne of God. It was not the haphazard, general and casual approach we often see today—as if sin's payment is a minor discomfort rather than the personal humiliation, suffering and death of Jesus Christ for us.

The Benefits of Forgiveness

The act of forgiveness creates a dynamic force that touches and heals us. Often forgiveness allows reconcileation. Also, when we forgive, we touch God and he touches others in a way we will not understand this side of heaven.

For Us

We benefit in forgiving. What was remarkable for Esther was that as she got near the end of the incidents, the rage and anger lessened and she began to feel compassion for her brother. That was God working within her. Even today, Esther does not trust him or excuse him for what he did. Neither will God, until her brother confesses his sin, but she is free from the burden of judgment and the anger and rage are gone.

God did not create us to hold in anger and hatred or to seek vengeance without damaging ourselves. We pay the consequences of not forgiving another in our own bodies, hearts, minds and spirits even when, as victims, we did nothing wrong.

Paul said,

Forgiveness a Key

Therefore, laying aside falsehood, speak truth, each one of you, with his neighbor, for we are members of one another. Be angry, and yet do not sin; do not let the sun go down on your anger, (Ephesians 4:25-26 NAS).

Tracy was an angry woman and, to a point, was justified. Her father abused her as a child. For years, Tracy held a grudge against him for his sins against her.

We forgive others within the context of the sin happening. The resulting feelings are a justified reaction to real sin. The issue is not to deny the feelings or reactions but, as victims, we want to get rid of the harmful effects of the sins. Often the harm is more in our reactions and feelings than the actual sin, horrible as it might be. Their sin cannot destroy us, but our own inner workings and responses can.

Tracy was obsessed with what her father did years ago and used most of her energy to feed the hate. When she brought to the surface the memories of what her father did, she would get nauseated. She felt intense pain in her joints and stomach to the point of wanting to die. Her father sinned against her but she was sinning against herself by giving up her life for her father. Her father was her reason for living. He dominated her life more than he ever did when she lived with him.

In forgiving, we are imitating our Father in heaven who wants to forgive all people coming to him on his terms. He is not willing that any should perish. When we continue to hold another accountable for their wrong against us, we stand between that person and God. To a degree, we limit God's working in their lives.

When we hold on to anger, when we remain as accusers, this will show through our feelings, speech and actions. In this state, we are imitating Satan, not God, for Satan is the great accuser and slanderer. Acting out this role for any length of time can only bring emotional and physical harm and possible early death.

God did give us the ability and right to judge another, to evaluate when things are right or wrong. Nevertheless, he never intended for us to take on the job of avenger. He can handle that role without harm but we cannot.

We benefit when we keep short accounts when others harm us. We do not want to make light of what others do to us; we want to hold them accountable for their actions just as God does. However, when we can forgive with awareness, we want to do so and give them over into God's hands to judge. *Do not take revenge, my friends, but leave room for God's wrath, for it is written: 'It is mine to avenge; I will repay,' says the Lord* (Romans 12:19).

God will see that justice is done in either exacting the cost of sin from that person or placing the cost on his son Jesus Christ. Either way, someone will pay for sin.

For the Wrongdoer

When Tracy finally forgave her father, she did not excuse his actions in any way. By placing him into God's hands to handle the wrongdoing, she took her hands off. She could now go into life without this burden and the darkness that it brought. Her father, on the other hand, was now fully in the hands of God (for these sins). This meant that Tracy was no longer in the middle, standing between God and her father as the accuser.

God now had a free field in working in her father's life. We increase God's power in another's life when we take our hands off.

Forgiveness a Key

Martha prayed for her husband Frank for years that God would save him. She mentioned his unsaved state whenever she was around other Christian friends. The time came when she spent several days with Connie and me dealing with her own issues in prayer. Martha was clearly a Christian but she had let her past sins and grudges create a huge burden that she carried day after day.

As we dealt with her past, we also dealt with her husband Frank and the wrongs she held against him. After she forgave him, we asked her to give Frank over into God's hands. If God choose to use her in bringing Frank to a saving knowledge of Christ, then fine. Otherwise, she was to give up the burden and stay out of the way.

Martha did pray and released Frank to God's care. He became a Christian soon after this, within a month, totally apart from her help. Away from her, in a motel room, he began to read the Bible and accepted Christ.

As Martha got herself right with her heavenly Father, including forgiving her husband, her heavenly Father began working in Frank's life. We do not understand the dynamic power released when we step aside, but we do recognize the cause and effect consequences of giving and receiving forgiveness.

Mike was angry with his father. His anger spilled over toward others as well. Because of his father's betrayal of trust, Mike did not trust anyone in authority. I directed a training program with Mike as a participant. When I asked the participants to fly into Malaga, Mike chose to fly into Madrid instead and take the train to Malaga. I asked everyone to stay in their hotel rooms the first night and rest. Instead, Mike went out and met a local fellow who cheated him out of some money. I would give an assignment and Mike would ask to do something else.

Once I recognized that this was a low-key pattern of rebellion with Mike, I confronted him. Mike was perfectly willing to discuss the issue. (By this time, he began to trust me, an "exception," to his rule of untrustworthy authorities.) We traced his unconscious pattern of rebellion back to his reactions toward his father. I guided Mike as he brought these issues to God in prayer and he forgave his father.

Prayer does release power for God to work. When Mike saw his father a few months later, his father had begun to change! Mike's prayer of forgiveness permitted God to work in his father's life with greater power and yet without Mike's presence. God is almighty yet our actions can hinder or release his working. I do not understand it, I just see the cause and effect in action.

We can restrict God in his actions. Jesus went back to his hometown Nazareth. This is what happened,

He was not able to perform any miracles there, except that he placed his hands on a few people and healed them. He was greatly surprised, because the people did not have faith (Mark 6:5-6 GNB).

For God

We can stand with God and accuse others based on his standards and declare the wrong as sin and even demand payment. God does all those things also. We want to "call a spade, a spade" if that is what God's standard dictates. Once we have done so, however, we need to hand the issue over to God whose job it is to satisfy justice. When we hold on to the role of accuser, judge, jury—and hangman—then we are taking God's place.

It is as if we go to a righteous lawyer (the Holy Spirit) who helps us understand the facts of the case. Together we gather all the evidence and arrange it in a logical order. We place all the evidence and supporting documents in a briefcase and take it to the courthouse. The court assigns a case number and we learn that the judge will view the evidence and render a verdict in a few days. The judge tells us that he will deal with this matter. We have his word. He has all he needs in the material we have given him and he has access to additional information. We can leave. It is no longer our concern.

As we leave the courthouse, the burden is off our shoulders. Justice will be done. Maybe not today; but soon. We do not need to check on the ruling later because, in God's perfect court, justice is always done. We do not have to hang around the courthouse. The court does not need us as witnesses. We have stated the crimes and we have nothing more to do with this case. We are free of this case, its burden and weight. We can concentrate instead on getting back to living.

When we forgive another, this does not mean that we have forgotten what has happened. History is history and we cannot erase it. Nevertheless, when we give it over to God, he creates the conditions so that our past history is exactly that, past. It no longer has the power to create the same harmful emotions and responses. It is not forgotten, but it no longer has power, nor is it any longer a present reality.

Sounds Pollyanna? Greta's father raped her for years before she fled her home. Years later, she was physically and emotionally unable to do anything except stay in her room day after day. She wanted to commit suicide. When the Christian ministry center allowed her to walk in the garden, she would stomp out the life and beauty of any flowers she saw.

A Journey to Wholeness

Forgiving her father was hard but she did. Hour after hour, she accused and forgave him until we had covered every remembered instance. Today she knows that she is a victim of incest but it is knowledge without emotional reaction. It does not hurt anymore. It is as if it happened to an actor in an unpleasant movie and she saw the movie. She does not think of the movie unless she is counseling other victims of incest. Her history is a background for insight but not for pain. Greta has not learned to cope with life and survive. God has healed her.

Only God can do such healing. (Greta is now a licensed counselor working with abused children.)

Several things happen when we forgive another with clarity and understanding. First, we put down a load. We expend a great deal of emotional energy holding on to grudges, however right they seem. When we give over these feelings to God and forgive another, we have more energy for living in the present instead of using that energy to maintain the past.

Also, we label the sin for what it really is. We verify that the sin is or is not a violation of God's standard. We want to see things as God sees them. We want his standard and we want to imitate our Father in heaven in his actions and attitudes. The start of doing so comes from focused thinking and evaluating the real issues.

When we forgive, often we are able to see past the sin and begin to see the person behind the sin. We begin to understand how God can hate sin and yet love the sinner and want to bring that person to himself. After we forgive and after we receive forgiveness, we can see the possible good, without the bad distorting the image. We can have compassion. We consciously can accept the good and we can consciously accept the bad. We can be better partners with the Holy Spirit to allow changes in ourselves. We can see things the way God sees them, as if through his eyes.

When we hesitate to forgive, we are condoning and endorsing wrong behavior. Not forgiving means we accept their wrong behavior as okay, even for us. So we continue to empower that force in our lives and in the lives of others as well. Allowing wrong behavior to go without judging it will not free us but may create the force within us to repeat it ourselves.

This is especially true when it comes to wrong parental models. I have met many fathers who hated what their fathers did to them as children and yet they are now doing the same things to their children. The only way to kill the force, power, pattern of past and present behavior is to confront it. We recognize the people involved (including ourselves), judge them, reject the pattern and ask God to step in and kill it.

Kay's mother was always afraid of what Kay might do. She always suspected that Kay would do wrong whenever Kay was out of her sight. Her mother would phone to check on her daughter. Her mother did not prepare Kay to step into life except as she lived it her mother's way.

Since Kay refused to forgive her mother, she endorsed that her mother's behavior was okay. This was a form of love and concern, according to Kay, when actually it was distrust and a kind of curse that her mother had placed on her: Kay was no good and could not be trusted. She could not live life without her mother's help. Kay forgave her mother and no longer excused her—just as God did not excuse her. Now she was able to reject her mother's model of mothering as her future model. If Kay had not done so, then likely she would have a daughter and continue the same pattern. Is this a conscious choice? No, it is an unconscious acceptance of a wrong model and the regeneration of a sin from one generation to another. The harm will continue unless we allow God to intervene through our prayers.

When we rightfully hold another responsible for their actions then we also create greater responsibility on our part to do right. We are more consciously aware of the right standard and more aware of the consequences of doing it the wrong way. When we realize that putting our finger in the fire burns then we are more hesitant to do it again! It can seem that sinning is fun on the surface but there is always a hidden cost involved. Just good sense tells us to go the right way and avoid the consequences of doing otherwise.

We want to forgive out of who we are, the children of God. As his son, I want to have his attitudes, his perspective, and his emotional responses regarding the things of the world. As his son, I want to imitate my Father in heaven. When Jesus said his words were not his own but his father's in heaven, he did not mean that he was parroting God. He and God were in harmony with one another so that their thoughts were the same. Jesus spoke and they were his own words but agreed with what God himself would have said.

When we worked among a primitive tribe in South America, the Indians had a phrase *baba citigi*. A *baba citigi* was a close friend, a buddy. To their way of thinking, when you had such a friend and you said, "Let's go fishing," your friend would respond, "You know, that is a great idea. I was thinking the same thing."

Sin is usually a social and relational activity. There is a circle of responsible people, a circle of effected people and partners, models and encouragers. Sin seldom occurs in a vacuum. It happens in the context of other people. When we sin, those around us either encourage or discourage us in what we plan to do or what another will do to us.

We did Prayer and Resolution Counseling with a Swedish young woman. The issues were the sexual sins that she had participated in when younger. Because of the cultural climate of Sweden that encourages sexual experimentation at an early age, Oona had to recognize and fault her father for encouraging her to sin. Her mother was a poor example and encouraged her. She was responsible for her wrong deeds but she had to take into account the part that her parents played. They modeled, encouraged and endorsed her actions at that time.

Oona's parents violated her trust and God will hold them responsible for what they did. In accusing and forgiving them, Oona rejected their actions and attitudes for herself. She will not duplicate their lives in herself when she becomes a parent.

If we are going to be useful and a blessing, we need to recognize the part we play in lessening or increasing the forces of righteousness at work around us. We want to encourage others toward righteousness. We can under-stand this when we also recognize and acknowledge those in our lives who have encouraged us to do wrong through word, deed, or example. We want to act in righteous ways because it is a natural part of our behavior as sons or daughters of God. This is what John meant when he said,

> *Whoever is a child of God does not continue to sin, for God's very nature is in him; and because God is his father, he cannot continue to sin"* (I John 3:9 GNB).

The children of the Evil One sin and it doesn't matter or bother them but sin should bother the children of God because it is against their natures.

Part Four

The Hindrances to Resolution and Healing

For I can testify about them that they are zealous for God, but their zeal is not based on knowledge. Since they did not know the righteousness that comes from God and sought to establish their own, they did not submit to God's righteousness (Romans 10:2-3).

Our view of the world and of God affects the way we pray and, in turn can affect the rightness of our prayers. God will not answer our prayers if, in doing so, he is endorsing our distorted thinking.

One hindrance to answered prayer is to think we can by-pass Christ's sacrifice and still have our prayers consistently answered. Our prayers are hindered if we have a distorted view of God's part in lives because this affects our perception of reality and, in turn, affect the correctness of our prayers.

A Journey to Wholeness

Others factors that can hinder our prayers are such things as giving false forgiveness, not fully understanding the details of a situation, not covering all the effects that come out of wrongdoing and so on.

14

Misconceptions about the Way

I was staying with a Christian worker in Egypt when he shared his doubts. He had met a Muslim man whom he felt was about as righteous in his life style as one could be. Would God save that Muslim if he died without accepting Christ?

There is much talk about respecting people of other religions and not trying to convert them to Christianity. After all, the reasons go, "Aren't there many ways to God?" That is a good question. The answer effects how we view the need to tell others about Christ. Should we support missions that have the goal of converting people of other religions? Is it possible that there is more than one way to God?

A pastor wondered why a couple was going to Russia to proselyte Jews: if they are God's special people then possibly God has a special salvation plan for them.

This ignores the facts. Jesus was a Jew. The first Christians were Jews. Christianity began as a Jewish movement and involved many Jewish religious scholars (the Pharisees). The Gentiles did not dominate the movement until after the fall of Jerusalem and the general rejection of Jesus by the religious and governmental leaders of that time. Is the *Jews for Jesus* movement valid? Of course it is. It is bringing Jews back to their roots.

Many Christians, even in places of leadership, ask the same question in various ways, "Isn't Christianity the way for the western world but perhaps there are other ways for other peoples?"

This lack of certainty concerning the way to God is certainly a hindrance to receiving resolution for the issues of life troubling us.

The Way

Instead of starting with the question, "Does humankind think that there are many options in seeking God?" we should ask the question from God's point of view: "Why would a loving God demand only one way to approach him?"

In order to answer this question we have to accept three basic premises: (1) God exists, (2) God is holy and (3) God is just. If he is holy, then that is his primary attribute. Everything else must yield to it. For example, he cannot permit injustice to go unpunished. To do so would jeopardize or undermine his holiness. He is a God of love. Yet while he can display his love in acts of goodness, he cannot bypass his holiness or his sense of justice in order to satisfy his desire to show love.

The scriptures tell us that God is not willing that any should perish. Because he loved the world (the people in it) he sent his son Jesus, not to condemn but to save. It also says that he does not find any pleasure in the death of the wicked.

Just

If there is a standard, there is also the possibility of violating that standard. That is where sin comes in. Sin happens when we do wrong; when we violate the standard. Wrong can be an action or attitude. It can occur in ignorance or through omission: not doing a right action when necessary can be sin. For example, a man knows his friend is raping and murdering a girl and does nothing because he does not want to be involved. That man is guilty according to the scriptures. Standing by and doing nothing when evil occurs is the same as helping the offender, although an American court may say otherwise.

When wrong occurs, justice must be satisfied. Payment must be made or God's holiness is compromised. God cannot just let it go. Created in his image, we also have within us the desire to see justice satisfied when another wrongs us. In a sense, when sin occurs the universe gets out of balance, in that a debt is incurred. The only way to bring it back into balance is to "pay the piper."

One Muslim man said, "God is so great that he can overlook sin." No, that is not possible. If justice is not served then God's holiness is affected and that cannot happen because the central core of his essence is holiness. Everything gives way to his holiness.

So God has a problem. He loves us and wants to bring us into fellowship with him but sin stands in the way. Sin must be paid for and justice must be served. So how can God satisfy justice and, at the same time, allow us into his presence and fellowship? How can he allow us to come to him as our heavenly Father?

Since the beginning of time, humankind has felt a need to satisfy God through a sacrifice when they have sinned. Most often, the sacrifice involved blood—the killing of an animal or a person. People recognized that they needed to make a payment to offset the sin that occurred. People have beat themselves, starved themselves or otherwise tried to atone for the sins they have committed. We recognize God's need for satisfying justice even when we may know little about God.

Logical

God is a unique being, one of a kind. We are like him but he is not like us. He is God. We must come to him on his terms, not ours. God sets the standard for right and wrong, not humankind. Society may think that sleeping around is okay if no one is hurt but God says it is sin. God's standard goes across cultures and applies to all people—both those claiming to be Christians or his followers and those who do not.

Those who worship God, those who say there is no God, those who do not know if there is a God, and yes, even those who have never heard of God, all are still accountable to live by the same standard: God's standard and his definition of right and wrong.

The scriptures tell us that our righteousness is as filthy rags. This does not mean our righteousness is not worth something; just that in comparison to God's standard it does not count for much. It is not enough to cancel out the debt owed. When compared with God's holiness, our righteousness seems dirty instead of clean, dark instead of light.

So, any sacrifice or payment for sin that would allow us access to him (with justice satisfied) cannot come from our level. Even the best that we can do or pay is not

Misconceptions about the Way

enough by his standard of holiness and justice. Any sacrifice we make must be on God's terms. We can only approach God his way.

The dilemma is that nothing we can do will ever satisfy God and pay off the debt we incur because of sin. Humankind cannot render justice. If there were going to be provision made for humankind to come to God without sin or with the sin payment satisfied, it was going to have to start with God, at his level. A human-level payment would never be enough. There is only one way justice could be satisfied: the sin payment must *be a God-level payment.*

This is where Jesus Christ comes in. It is as if God says, "I will send a part of myself. He will be both God and man. He will live as a man but without sin. When the time comes, he will die on a cross and that will be the payment needed for sin."

In this way, both God's holiness and justice are satisfied and he is freed to express his love fully. Now he can see us in or through Christ as righteous because he allows Christ to pay for our sin. *"For our sake he made him [Jesus] to be sin who knew no sin, so that in him we might become the righteousness of God"* (II Corinthians 5:21 RSV). In this way God's justice is satisfied without violating his holiness.

Nothing we can do can compare with or satisfy what God's standard demands. Even the best of another way would fall short by comparison. We fall short by comparison (our goodness versus God's) and we fall short due to inherited sin (members of the human family).

Any sacrifice we humans could give would lack completeness: it would not fully satisfy the need. It would also lack durability: it would not last forever.

Only God himself—deity—could be the perfect sacrifice. Because the sacrifice needed must be inclusive—total and complete, covering everything, it could only come from God himself. Because the sacrifice needed must be for all time, only an eternal being—God—could be that sacrifice. Because the sacrifice had to pay for all ungodliness, only a sinless being could be that sacrifice. Only deity, a complete, eternal and holy God could provide such a perfect sacrifice.

Peter, speaking before the Council, tells us that there is only "one way": *"Salvation is to be found through him [Jesus] alone; in all the world there is no one else whom God has given who can save us."* (Acts 4:12 GNB)." He lived and walked with Jesus over a three-year period. He knew what he was talking about when he made such an absolute statement. For some reason, modern scholars seem to think they know more than Peter did and can reinterpret what he said. Peter only said what Jesus himself said, *"I am the way and the truth and the life. No one comes to the Father except through me"* (John 14: 6).

Are there many ways to God? If there were other ways for us to go, would God have picked the one way of the many that was the hardest—the cross and the pain and humiliation that it involved? Certainly not. The only way to God is the way provided by him through Jesus Christ.

15

Misconceptions about God

A major hindrance to resolution is the misconceptions we may have about God. If we see God as harsh and unforgiving, it is very difficult to ask for forgiveness and to feel forgiven. Believing that God is the author of evil—that he causes bad things to happen for some ulterior motive—will make us hesitate to approach him. The less we understand about God and his character, the more likely we will pray in a faulty way that does not permit God to answer.

Misunderstanding God's Role

The sovereignty of God is a mystery. He is all-powerful and, for that matter, can be all-controlling, but he has chosen to limit his control for a time. It is difficult to understand how God can be all-powerful and all-knowing and not use his power but he has chosen to let us make our own choices. He controls the general picture, so that the end does not come sooner than his schedule, but within the general picture, man has charge.

A Journey to Wholeness

The world is like an arena with games going on. Overall, Satan and humankind are running the games. God controls the lighting and air conditioning but normally does not interfere. Not because God does not want to, but because we told him long ago that we wanted control.

Sometimes a player or team wins even though he would have preferred they did not win. The only time he steps in is when the game gets out of control, or they so totally violate the rules, that bedlam will happen. Then he intervenes so things get back into reasonable boundaries. Still, not his boundaries, but his intervention puts off total disaster for a little longer.

The day will come when he takes back total control of everything—air, lights and the game itself. If a player goes over the line, even a little, God will immediately deal with him. People will play the game God's way. For now, however, until Christ comes again, people play the game, for the most part, their way.

For now, God permits this. Pecks says it best,

Having forsaken force, God is impotent to prevent the atrocities that we commit upon one another. He can only continue to grieve with us. He will offer us Himself in all His wisdom, but He cannot make us choose to abide with Him.[62]

This means that good people die for no apparent reason. Their death is not God's will, but they die anyway. Does this mean that God does not care? The scriptures give us two verses that give insight into God's character and feelings about all this. One concerns the righteous and is in Psalms where it says, *"Precious in the sight of the Lord is the death of his godly ones"* (116:15

---

[62] M. Scott Peck, *People of the Lie*, p. 205.

NAS). The other concerns the wicked. In the book of Ezekiel, God says, *"Do I have any pleasure in the death of the wicked,"* declares the Lord God, *"rather than that he should turn from his ways and live?"* (18:23 NAS).

In the New Testament Peter tells us that,

The Lord is not slow in keeping his promise, as some understand slowness [regarding his judgment]. He is patient with you, not wanting anyone to perish, but everyone to come to repentance (II Peter 3:9).

I read an unpublished manuscript that explained why there are many famines in the world in these days. According to the author, God has created famines as his way of saving children. When the thousands of children die before the age of accountability, they go to heaven.

I disagree with his conclusion. Often famine has come as a form of judgment but never, some bizarre way, has it come as some form of blessing. Nevertheless, I can see the author's reasoning: if God is sovereign then how can we explain the terrible things that are happening? Evil comes that good will prevail. If God is controlling the world, as the author believes, then his paper answers the dilemma, but it also takes away the responsibility from humankind.

God's Limitations

Misunderstanding the nature and character of God can create the grounds for inappropriate prayers that hinder God from answering. God does have restrictions. He cannot operate contrary to who or what he is. God has three major attributes of character that work in balance and harmony: his holiness, his justice and his love. One attribute cannot be in conflict with the other two. Here is an example of such a conflict: many Christians and non-Christian feel that God's love is an all-covering attribute that is going to overrule everything else. God loves every-one; therefore, he will save everyone. It does not work that way. God cannot let his love rule if it jeopardizes his holiness and sense of justice.

God is Holy

Because God is a God of love, we do not want to believe that any of us will go to hell. Somehow, God's love will permit him to forgive us no matter what, even without Christ's sacrifice. This is not true.

His desire to love cannot distort who he is. He has two other attributes that must be satisfied before God can fully express his love. Above all, God is holy. He cannot tolerate anything or anyone that is less. This also means that God cannot tolerate sin in any form or to any degree. God is not the author of evil.

God is Just

A hindrance to answered prayer happens when we fail to recognize that God's system of justice needs to be satisfied as part of his answering our prayers. Resolution includes forgiving others and asking forgiveness. When sin occurs, it creates an imbalance in the universe. Giving forgiveness and asking forgiveness opens the door for satisfying justice through Christ's sacrifice and bringing balance back.

Misconceptions about God

God is a just God. That means that God's standard of right and wrong exists in the universe, not just the world, and that standard continues right into eternity. When sin occurs, justice must be satisfied. This is where payment for sin comes in. The guilty one must pay a price for justice to be satisfied or payment must come from another source. Either way, justice must be served.

God, the holy one, wants to bring us to himself because he loves us. Jesus said, *"For God so loved the world that he gave his one and only son, that whoever believes in him shall not perish but have eternal life"* (John 3:16).

His love is not like our love because,

> *Very rarely will anyone die for a righteous man, though for a good man someone might possible dare to die. But God demonstrated his own love for us in this: While we were still sinners, Christ died for us* (Romans 5:7-8).

God is an amazing being but he cannot jump in and solve the problem of bringing us into his realm just because he wants to, or because he loves us. *His holiness and justice take precedent over his love.* God cannot violate his nature. He cannot violate his own standard and make an exception for us.

The problem is that we, on the human level, can do nothing to satisfy the demands of God's justice system. In a sense, nothing at the earth level is big enough, good enough or worthy enough to cover the demands at the heavenly level.

God's way of fulfilling his justice was to provide a satisfaction for justice at his level. We need a God answer for a God need. Therefore, he sent a part of himself, his son Jesus Christ. His son's mission was to become a man, walk blamelessly throughout his life and, in the end, fulfill his purpose. He was to die and through his death provide payment for our sins. Instead of our paying with our lives to satisfy justice, Christ paid that price with his life.

His payment is powerful enough for God to see us through Christ as if we had never sinned. In Christ, we are no longer sinners but the redeemed and righteous. Now God can make us holy. Being holy, we can have a relationship with God as his children.

We must start with God as holy and out of his holiness he is also just. Only when these two attributes are satisfied can he also fully operate out of his love. The first step in resolving the harmful events of life is to satisfy his justice by appropriating what is available through Chris's sacrifice.

Our Limitations on God

There is a difference between a lack of faith, or not enough faith, and disbelief. Disbelief can hinder God from answering our prayers while it takes very little faith on our part for God's system to work.

For several weeks, Connie and I worked in Prayer and Resolution Counseling with a young woman, we will call Janice. We tended to work for four days, mornings and afternoons and then take three days off to do personal and ministry business. We accomplished a lot during our days of prayer and she and we experienced God's working in her. The problem came when we stopped for a few days. During our off-days, Janice would ponder what God was doing and begin to reason why he could not be healing her.

Invariably, when we started a new cycle of Prayer and Resolution Counseling, we would have to re-

Misconceptions about God

process—repeat some of what we had handled before—or spend time explaining why God's system works regardless of her feelings.

A little faith or a lack of faith does not seem to hinder God's working. What does hinder his working is when we do not believe that he can work. The people of Nazareth had such a debilitating attitude and lack of expectation that this actually hindered Jesus from working.

> *And when He had come to His own country, He taught them in their synagogue, so that they were astonished and said, "Where did this Man get this wisdom and these mighty works? "Is this not the carpenter's son? Is not His mother called Mary? And His brothers James, Joses, Simon, and Judas? And His sisters, are they not all with us? Where then did this Man get all these things?" So they were offended at Him. But Jesus said to them, "A prophet is not without honor except in his own country and in his own house." Now He did not do many mighty works there because of their unbelief* (Matt 13: 54-58 NKJV).

ೞ ೲ

Holding a wrong view of God's role in the world can blur our reason for forgiving another. A young woman, a victim of incest, can find it hard to hold her father accountable for his horrible actions if she feels that God was in control. Such distorted thinking goes on to conclude that God had this happen so good could come or she could learn a lesson.

When the van carrying a pastor and his family crashed and burned, people wondered why God did not stop it from happening. People question how a loving

A Journey to Wholeness

God can permit children to die in famines. Why doesn't God do something?

Well, it depends on your view of God and his sovereignty. Is God in control of the world? If he is, then we have a right to question his performance and competence. We should question whether he is doing a good job of running the world. On the other hand, what does scripture say about God's control? John says, "*We know that we belong to God **even though the whole world is under the control of the Evil One***" (I John 5:19, emphasis mine).

When Adam sinned, he took our destiny in his own hands and went into the world to live and mold it his way. He did so without the fellowship and guidance of God as he had it in the Garden. Man wants to do it his way. Man, aided and abetted by the Prince of this world, Satan, have made the world what it is today.

When Israel decided they wanted a king like the other nations around them, God told the prophet that they, in wanting a king, were rejecting him. The people of Israel wanted to put themselves under the rule of a king rather than under the rule of God.

Is God in control? God would like to be. He has the power to take over any time he decides but he has chosen to let us do it our way. He has shown us the right way and now holds us accountable for the choices that we make.

Unfortunately, we have usually made poor choices since all this began. Our world is increasingly an unpleasant place to live. We have disease, terrible injustice, horrible crimes, cancers and mental disorders.

Our earth is a dying planet, with fewer species of animals, birds, flowers and trees than before. The earth is a polluted planet that began as paradise. Blame it on humankind and blame it on the Prince of this world but do not blame it on God.

16

Misconceptions about Forgiveness

To feel forgiven is the greatest need Christians and the non-Christians have today. We hear much about forgive-ness as a concept but often we do not understand the dynamics of what it means. Yet our prayers of confession that bring us forgiveness hinge on our correctly forgiving others and in our understanding what it means when God forgives us.

One way to get healing, according to some, is to confront the wrongdoer and vent our rage. Others tell us just to let it go. Still others urge us just to forgive and forget. Christ, however, teaches that we must address offences and resolve them. He said that when we recognize that someone thinks we have wronged her, or if we know that we have done something wrong, we are to go, confess, and ask forgiveness. Notice that the wrongdoer begins the healing process by confessing and asking forgiveness. On the other hand, Christ also tells us that we must address the issues that we have against someone else and resolve these through forgiving. In Chapter 13, I discussed the topic of forgiveness at length. Here I am discussing some of the misunderstandings concerning forgiveness that hinder resolution.

A Journey to Wholeness

The first misconception has to do with God. What do we do when we are angry with God?

Being upfront with God

During my growing up years in Redondo Beach, I had a neighbor, a lovely elderly woman who never went to church. One day she told me the reason: God had taken her baby and she was angry with him for this.

Can we be angry with God? Does God need forgiveness? Can we forgive God? Won't God be angry if we accuse him? The scriptures show us at least two examples where people felt God had let them down. The prophet Jonah trusted God to destroy Nineveh and he did not, leaving Jonah feeling betrayed and angry. The prophet Elijah had given his all in the service of God but he had to flee from Jezebel who was trying to kill him. He was angry with God for not protecting the other prophets from death and for not protecting him from Jezebel. "After all," he complained, "I have always served you." God's response to both of these men was not anger or rebuke but gentleness and a quiet voice.

"Why didn't God intervene and divert the plane that crashed into my son's plane?" Why didn't God delay the van so that the brick missed the windshield? Instead, the resulting crash killed the pastor and his entire family. God does intervene at times but, overall, we humans have created the kind of world in which we live. God did not leave, we threw him out and we are paying the consequences. People die young. Evil people seem to get richer and righteous people poorer. Cancer robs a child of life.

Sometimes people blame God for getting them into tough situations. During Prayer and Resolution Coun-

Misconceptions about Forgiveness

seling with me, Jamie was angry with God for not stopping him from marrying Mandy. This despite the fact he had seduced Mandy as the first step in marriage. He misunderstood God's role. God wants us to decide to follow him because we choose to, not because he forces us to do so. The time will come when God truly controls the world through Jesus Christ. When that time comes, he will rule with an iron hand.

Jane's stepfather touched her the first time when she was seven and continued to do so until she left home for college at eighteen. Technically, he never committed the full act of incest but he claimed her body and soul until he died.

Later Jane married and, after years of trying, was elated to find she was pregnant. It devastated her when she later lost the baby. She was angry with God.

What do we do when we are angry with God? Why didn't God stop her stepfather from molesting her? What had she done to deserve such treatment? When the baby was stillborn, where was God? Jane was a Christian, in Christian work, yet God did not stop these tragedies from happening to her.

For a long time Jane did not admit her anger towards God. She stopped reading her Bible, however, and stopped praying. When her friends had their babies, it only renewed her angry with God. He had taken her baby from her and she could no longer have children.

If we are angry at what God has done then we need to forgive him. We need to forgive so we can reestablish trust in him. Our forgiveness is on different terms, however, than with humans. We do not base our forgiveness of God on the blood of Christ, but on trusting his character and love. Because we have a relationship with God, we can tell him anything we want. A misunderstanding of God's character and role causes much of our anger. We need to express that anger to God

A Journey to Wholeness

aloud. Because we want to be reconciled to him, we want to take care of this situation. When we forgive God, we "give up" our judgment against him because we choose to believe that he really does know best. We may still disagree with him and what he did, or did not do, when he did not intervene, but we choose to trust him and his decision. In the eternity, when we fully know the circumstances, we will agree with his actions. We choose to trust God to work within his holiness, justice and love.

No Excuses

Repeatedly I have had to stop a person from praying, "Father, I forgive them. They didn't know what they were doing." Ignorance is never an excuse for sin; nor is it ever the grounds for forgiveness.

While overseas, I met Jane, a Christian and a trained counselor. She asked for help. She had been gang raped as a teen and the memory of it continued to haunt her. Both Christian and secular counselors had counseled her as part of her training. She had experienced being the client, on the other side of the desk, and had shared her rape experience. Yet years later, this past trauma continued to be a present part of her life.

I did not have much time so I asked the most important question: "On what grounds did you forgive the men who raped you?"

"On the same grounds," Jane replied, "that Christ did. 'Father, forgive them, for they know not what they do.'"

In the context of Christ's suffering, where he uttered those words, he was clearly referring to the soldiers. They were nailing the Son of God on a cross. We cannot imagine what his Father was feeling at that time. In this

Misconceptions about Forgiveness

context, Jesus asked God to pardon them. Was Jesus saying that they did not know how to crucify someone or that they did not know that nailing him to the cross would kill him? No, of course not. They knew their jobs well; they were professional crucifiers! But, they did not know to whom they were doing it—the Son of God.

What Jane did sounds spiritual, even pious, but it is not forgiveness by God's standard. As God's children, we want to operate as our Father does. This means that we hold people accountable for their deeds, without excuse. We fully understand the awfulness of what they have done but we extend mercy and forgive. This may be easy to do with minor offenses; doing so with major ones—molestation, rape, incest, humiliation, cruelty or betrayal, to name a few—is difficult.

Even when we fully understand what they have done, God would have us forgive—not excuse. When we excuse someone's evil then we eliminate the need to forgive. Is that what we want to do? Here are some excuses:

- They are just human.
- They did the best they could.
- They did not know what they were doing.
- They lost control.
- They grew up in a terrible home.

While these are possibly reasons to help explain their behavior, *there can be no excuse for sin,* not from God's point of view, and therefore, neither from his children's point of view. There is no reason good enough to make wrongdoing acceptable.

A Journey to Wholeness

I explained to Jane that she had been excusing these men. I helped her see their sin through God's eyes in stark reality and without excuse. I then asked her to forgive them.

Suddenly forgiving them was hard. She felt anger and rage. She wanted to hurt them back for what they had done to her.

I am always leery when forgiveness comes easy. True forgiveness comes hard. The sinners deserve to pay for what they did. God commands us to forgive, not because they are blameless, but because God will see that justice is done for us.

As priests, we must help people understand the issues so they can clearly present these to the Father. We are priests, burden bears and we expose, as scripture says, "*Have nothing to do with the fruitless deeds of darkness, but rather expose them*" (Ephesians 5:11).

Exposing is different from excusing. I attended a weekend Christian counseling seminar a few years ago that defined forgiveness as "releasing them (those who harmed you) from all responsibility and blame." Recently I read another counseling help that said we forgive others because "they are victims too." A pastor forgave his father because "He had done the best he could." If, in any way, we say people cannot help themselves then we are saying that they are guiltless. That is not the basis for forgiveness.

Sinning in ignorance is still sin and we need to deal with it before God. For example, Carmen told us about a time when she went into a temple. She said it was a beautiful experience and smiled as she remembered it. She could see no reason why the Holy Spirit brought it to her memory. As we questioned her, she added that she had placed flowers at the foot of the Buddha. We explained to her that her sin was in doing an act of homage to the Buddha, an idol. Once she understood, she confessed this and asked forgiveness.

The Blood Plus

We can forgive another and then feel that God has not answered our prayer. This happens when we go through the motions of forgiving and hold back. Jill forgave her former boyfriend for sins committed against her. Nevertheless, she felt that he had portrayed her as an evil woman to the community. He had given *his version* of their break up to many of their mutual friends.

The next day Jill did not have peace or release. We went back over her prayer and found that she had forgiven with reservations. She had forgiven him, sure, but she still wanted the freedom to give *her side of the story*. If people asked, or did not ask, Jill wanted to tell all the gory details of what *he* had done. Since she hung onto the desire to tell others, she wanted to get even. She still had not forgiven him. Jill wanted revenge. That is not forgiveness.

Shirley was angry when she finally forgave her father but had no release at all. As she later realized, she had forgiven him conditionally. She would not fully forgive him until he came, admitted what he had done and asked forgiveness. That is forgiveness with strings attached.

The blood of Christ is enough to pay for any offence. It is enough to satisfy justice. It is enough to satisfy God and enough to satisfy us. However, there are times when our thinking is faulty and we believe, most often subconsciously, that full payment takes the blood of Christ *plus* something else. Until that "something else" is paid, justice is not satisfied. For example, if we ask for God's forgiveness, it takes the blood of Christ *plus* us beating ourselves up or we serving God to help pay for our wrongdoings. Penance, as a way of earning forgiveness, falls into this category.

If I am trying to forgive someone else and it takes the blood of Christ *plus* making sure everyone else knows just how bad the offender is, or obtaining the offenders apology, then this is not forgiveness. This is retribution, not forgiveness. Such faulty reasoning will most certainly hinder resolution.

Limiting Mercy

After a Prayer and Resolution Counseling session, Tom came back and said that he had nightmares that night about the sexual partner he had forgiven. The next day we searched for the reason closure had not happened. I did not try to persuade him that the dreams meant nothing. Instead, we went to prayer and asked God to reveal *what part of the prayer* Tom had made was faulty. (Normally, when prayers are thorough, there are no such after-effects)

When we pray and know God's will, then we expect him to answer. If he does not answer, then it is our problem, not his. Something in Tom's prayer violated God's character, standard, or other principles found in scripture and thus hindered God from answering. Remember, much as he is a God of love, he cannot violate his holiness or his justice system.

The Holy Spirit led us to consider the forgiveness part of the prayer. The issue had been sexual sin of a particularly awful kind. When Tom talked about perpetrators like this fellow, he was extremely emotional.

I asked him, "How do you think God views such people?"

Misconceptions about Forgiveness

Tom replied, "He hates them."

"Do you think that God can save such people?"

"No," Tom said.

"Tom, if you believe what you just said, then this *class of people* is beyond God's redemption. Right?"

When Tom had forgiven his sexual perpetrator, his unspoken opinion was that all such people were damned. So had he really forgiven? No. Tom admitted that he felt this class of people was beyond redemption.

We went back into prayer and dealt again with just that part of the prayer. Tom confessed his sin of judging and condemning this class of people to hell and limiting God's mercy and he asked forgiveness. Then he forgave this person again—permitting God to show mercy, if God decided to, to whomever he wanted. Tom no longer stood in the way. The issue was resolved.

We know missionaries who left Ethiopia when it went communist because "Communists don't deserve the Gospel." We can substitute transvestites, molesters, rapists, serial killers and so on, but when we place such people beyond redemption then our words of forgiveness are empty words.

Hard Forgiveness

God never said forgiveness was easy. God created the grounds for his extending forgiveness only at a great cost to himself and his son Jesus Christ. For us, forgiving becomes especially difficult when the other people are not willing to acknowledge their wrongs. More so, when they say they are sorry and ask for forgiveness but we do not believe they mean it. Sometimes, the offense is so horrendous it seems unforgivable. Yes, forgiveness is hard to give at such times.

A Journey to Wholeness

Neither "Forgive me" nor "I forgive you" should ever become trite statements. I personally feel that we should not make children constantly ask forgiveness for every little thing they do wrong. They will soon hate the word. Asking forgiveness becomes a form of punishment instead of a way for release from the burden of sin, condemnation and guilt.

Forgiveness comes with a built-in need for an object: we forgive *for* something. Whenever people are constantly misusing the formula "Forgive me" or "I am sorry," we need to confront them. The formula approach is not the wrong being done but the defense mechanism being used to avoid taking responsibility for their wrong actions. "I did this or that, and I am very *sorry for* what I did, please *forgive me for* doing that." This is true repentance. True confession involves recognizing the wrong, remorse and repentance.

Remarks such as, "If there is anything I did wrong, forgive me," "If you think I need to say I'm sorry, I will," "If I sinned, God, please forgive me," are remarks not about remorse and repentance but simply trying to clear the air without any real admission of wrongdoing.

When we feel that someone is faking it or is not facing up to the wrongdoing, we then have opportunity to say, "Yes, I forgive you for (name the offense)" but we want to make it clear to them that we have put them into God's hands in this matter. Unless they are repentant, he will hold them accountable. Repentance means that they determine not to repeat the offense. We take our hands off and, once we do, *we can no longer hold their sin against them.* (Nevertheless, if they have robbed us and we have forgiven them, we will still lock our doors.)

There are two sides to giving forgiveness. One is for our own good, to get rid of the burden of judgment we have toward another. This means forgiveness shuts the door for us to the wrong. The other is to release another from our judgment, but we do not want to give false comfort.

Is there a sin that is unforgivable? In this century, several criminals have done terrible crimes, including sexual perversion, torture and cannibalism. I have heard people say they could never forgive such people. This is especially true of the families of the victims. Nevertheless, sin of every kind was placed at the cross when Christ died. There are no exceptions. Christ is willing to take on himself whatever man has done, no matter how horrible, if that person comes to God and asks forgiveness.

Whatever the perpetrator has done, not matter how badly we were hurt, we do not want to stand in that judgment role. God did not create us to carry that burden and it will only bring us harm if we do so for any length of time. It keeps us in the middle between God and the wrongdoer. We want to move out of that place by offering forgiveness so that God has a direct line to the person.

When we choose to offer forgiveness and allow God to see that justice is done on our behalf, we can then offer up to God all of the anger and pain connected to the offense. Since God will see that justice is done, our healing can now take place.

Holding on to a Grudge

We do not want to be a hindrance to another receiving forgiveness. If someone asks us for forgiveness, we want to forgive but on the right basis and for the right reasons. Forgiving only because God commanded us to do so is a poor reason. We do not want to forgive because we are forced to do so. Such forgiveness will not bring healing to the heart. To forgive, because we want to be free of the burden of holding on to the judgment we have placed on the offender, may be perceived as a selfish reason, but it will certainly bring healing.

When a person feels he or she has committed sin against us and needs our forgiveness, we cannot give peace or release if we deny that anything happened. We avoid the issue when we say, "It's okay." "There is nothing to forgive." Or, "Don't worry about it." We need to say, *"I forgive you."* It is amazing how hard it is to say those words.

Sometimes we do something that unintentionally offends the person. We may not have to repent of what we did because it was not wrong, but we may want to apologize or ask forgiveness for having done anything (from their perspective) that brought hurt or offense.

I once spoke at a meeting and afterwards was intently focused on a conversation with a man. The mission pastor came up and then went away. Later I learned that he felt I had slighted him and he "blackballed" me with the regional representative. I wrote to him and explained the situation and asked forgiveness. His response was, "Don't worry about it." He did nothing to reinstate me. Neither of us had release—he from feeling slighted or me from feeling condemned. And, I was still 'blackballed."

If we feel someone has sinned against us and we withhold forgiveness then we are seeking vengeance! Forgiveness means releasing the other person from our demand that he pay the price and allowing God to see that justice is done on our behalf, even to the point of extending mercy to the offender and allowing Christ to pay for it.

This sounds good but can be very difficult when a terrible sin has been committed. Extending forgiveness

Misconceptions about Forgiveness

on God's terms can be hard. It should be. Forgiveness by God comes with a price tag: Christ bore the penalty for sin in his own body on the cross.

When we truly forgive with full awareness and understanding, we reap benefits ourselves.

- Forgiving another free us to get on with life.

- The memories and emotions are no longer lying just under the surface.

- In many situations, we restore the relationship between the wrongdoer and us.

- We see more clearly the awfulness of sin and its results.

- We begin to operate more naturally as children of God.

- We become more aware of the role of the Holy Spirit.

- We more fully appreciate the cost that Christ paid on the cross for our sin.

- In forgiving, we close a door for Satan to tempt, accuse and attack.

- In forgiving, we cease to imitate Satan, the accuser.

Ultimately, when we forgive another, no matter how much they have hurt us, we benefit the most. We forgive to protect ourselves from the spiritual, physical and emotional ravages brought on by long-term judgment, hatred, bitterness, pain and sorrow. If we deliberately withhold forgiveness then we put a cork in the bottle of forgiveness God has for us.

The concept of forgiveness is the most important item in Prayer and Resolution Counseling because everything else hangs from this issue. However, the concept of forgiveness continues to be misunderstood, glossed over or forgotten as we strive toward our goals and desires.

God knows everything others or we have done in every situation we bring before him. He does not need the information we bring but we need to bring all the garbage out into the open to see it for what it really is. Then we must forgive or ask forgiveness out of the reality of the truth—no more distortions or half-truths.

Forgiveness is the area that we spend the most time on in Prayer and Resolution Counseling, not because we like dwelling on sin but because so many other issues in life build on those sins. We want to forgive out of knowledge, not obedience. We want to forgive because we are children of God and see life as he sees it. We want to be merciless toward sin and, on God's terms, merciful toward people who sin.

Part Five

The Procedure for Resolution

Thank you so much for being His channels from which we've gained perspective and wisdom. Through you God has exposed lies and broken their power, revealed unforgiveness, and then replaced them with truth and forgiveness.

K & M

This section focuses on the setting for Prayer and Resolution Counseling. In Chapter 17, there are various approaches to consider depending on the personality of the hurting one.

I have found the general checklist in Chapter 18 helpful and in chapter 19, there is a brief example of what a Prayer and Resolution Counseling session looks like in working with someone.

A Journey to Wholeness

This section concludes with Chapter 20: how people have gone on in life after Prayer and Resolution Counseling and Chapter 21: suggestions for people after they have received resolution.

🙣 17 🙢

Counseling Considerations

Commitment

Prayer and Resolution Counseling is time consuming. Many pastors and Christian workers have set routines and schedules, which makes Prayer and Resolution Counseling inconvenient because the prayer team must adjust the sessions to the people and their circumstances, rather than to artificial schedules.

We associated with the spiritual counseling staff of one agency where a staff member normally worked one hour a day, one or two days a week with a person. The hurting one would share; the counselor would bring out some scripture verses and send the person away to act on these truths. The staff tried for five years to help one young woman, Gay Lyn, and failed. We spent a total of twenty-four hours in Prayer and Resolution Counseling with Gay Lyn over a ten-day period. Because we were teaching a cross-cultural communication course, our sessions with Gay Lyn were in our off-hours in the evenings and over a weekend. Each session was at least two to three hours long.

God fully healed and restored Gay Lyn. She is now a licensed family counselor. Her agency counselors acknowledge that what God did for Gay Lyn in Prayer and Resolution Counseling was a miracle (their words). What God had done amazed them—but not enough to change their methods or schedules or to ask how we did it.

Jim, a pastor, can focus on a topic for about ten minutes before he loses concentration. This means that unless the hurting one is able to lay out the problem to Jim clearly and quickly, he becomes impatient, offers advice, which may or may not be to the point, and often the hurting one goes away frustrated.

When Tracy started having flashbacks about molestation, she went to counseling. In fact, her Bible School ordered her to do so. However, when Tracy ran out of money, her Christian counselor ran out of time.

Jane needed at least an hour just to get her thoughts in order. It was no wonder that her professional counselor could not help her in a fifty-minute session.

Another counselor, who was also a medical doctor, would listen for a short time to people and then hand them a verse or a passage of scripture written out like some prescription.

If we are going to take people's needs seriously then we must be willing to adjust our approach to fit their needs, give them sufficient time and be committed to them. Fast answers, pat memorized verses and shallow analysis are not acceptable.

Different Approaches

There are several approaches that we, as counselors, priests, burden bearers or safe others, can use. Which approach or approaches we utilize depends on the issues, circumstances and the personality of the hurting one. *Prayer and Resolution Counseling is a supplement to, not a replacement for, many other approaches.* We owe a debt to secular counseling and their findings. Not recognizing God can distort findings, but we have gained many insights into humans because of the work of these people. An example of this is the book, *Reality Therapy,* by Glasser, whose premise is that, before resolution can take place, we must take personal responsibility for our behavior. This spawned a Christian book that used and adapted his approach. We want to use whatever works, if it does not violate a scriptural norm.

The Analytical Approach

In Prayer and Resolution Counseling, we use the analytical approach to clarify and verify the issues. We must help the believer understand the background and dynamics of the problem but if we stop here, we have intellectual knowledge without resolution. Background is essential because it forces the believer to accept responsibility for actions or gives responsibility over to others, in part or completely (if a victim).

It is the Holy Spirit's task to convict of sin, but in Prayer and Resolution Counseling, we do confront if necessary. We need to expose irresponsible, hurtful, sinful behavior. However, if we confront the person too soon, we will destroy any atmosphere of trust. As Prayer and Resolution Counselors, we do not view the believer as a sinner but as a brother or sister in the Lord who has sinned. We accept the depravity of man, but we also accept that God created us in his image. Even more so, after we are born again, we are redeemed children of God.

A Journey to Wholeness

Connie and I prayed with one young woman guilty of sexual sin. An abusive, alcoholic father had raised her. During a session, she shared that she had had an abortion. Every time abortion has come up in the past, the people have brought it up out of guilt and shame. This woman mentioned it as an aside. When we began to ask questions, she clearly did not feel any need to deal with this episode so we did not. We are not the Holy Spirit; it is his job to convict people. Later, after we have built more trust, she may want to bring this up again. On the other hand, it may never come up.

Confronting others who have wronged us before we have forgiven them is an act of revenge. We are attempting to get them to see how bad they are and how much they have hurt us so they will beg for forgiveness.

The Holy Spirit reveals sin and convicts people of sin. Until he does, going through the motions of prayer is pointless. Waiting for the right time, we confront people but do not condemn them. We may not lord it over them nor force our views on them, no matter how right we may be. The others are ultimately responsible before God to account for themselves.

Just the listening, sharing the burden, empathizing or validating the hurting one will bring that person relief. One of the greatest things we can do in Prayer and Resolution Counseling is to empathize with the hurting one. Often we have been the first to share another's hurts and validate that she has the right to be hurt or angry. Yes, anger is acceptable. God himself can be angry. His children can also be angry, if they do not do so unjustly or carry the anger for too long a time. We must keep in mind, however, that just validation will not bring resolution.

People, victimized as a lifestyle, they may feel that what happened was their fault. It was something that they deserved. It takes safe others to validate the awfulness of what happened and to place the rightful blame where it belongs. What happened was not their fault. This will help them to bring their prayers to God with greater assurance that the issues are real. If they see it from God's perspective then they can have confidence that God can and will answer.

Listening carefully, asking questions for detail and clarification, and discussion are all part of the analytical process to arrive at the truth of a matter. It is a necessary tool to knowing what needs to be resolved and what steps are necessary to arrive at resolution.

The Directive Approach

The safe others of the Prayer and Resolution Counseling team help define the issues and guide toward resolution and solution. Being directive is the most efficient way to deal with a fellow believer's problem but we can appear judgmental and to have not really listened if we let time pressure us.

Prayer and Resolution Counseling cannot be aimless. We must be *directive* to ensure focus and clarity. Otherwise, we will have too many issues or side-issues up front, exposed, and without the means to handle them in the time we have. We must guide them to pray as specifically as possible and with full awareness of the people involved and what happened.

As far as I have seen, *God does not answer general prayers*. My rule is to talk only in detail about episodes or issues that we can handle in prayer during the session. Ideally, there should be no carry-overs, though that does not always happen. Nevertheless, ideally, what

A Journey to Wholeness

is "put on the table," so to speak, must be cleared before the session is over.

We are also directive in setting a pattern for prayer. There are principles that must be included. While the order of some steps may not be important, there are other steps where the order is crucial.

Praying aloud – We, the safe others, must hear the words, monitor what the hurting one is saying and, eventually endorse, come alongside, be in agreement with his prayers as our own. We have the responsibility to keep this person from making foolish promises, unclear or faulty confessions, or in some other ways voice something that is a distortion of the truth.

To the heavenly Father – Our view and understanding of issues will come out of our relationship with God as Father. Jesus clearly taught that we should address our prayers to the Father; he is the one who provides for our needs.

Through the Son – Jesus is our Great High Priest and intercessor. We also have his authority to come to the Father in his name. He also gave us the power and authority of his name.

Under the Holy Spirit's direction – We have authority through Jesus in bringing our prayers to the Father but we want to be careful in using this authority. We want to be in partnership with the Holy Spirit so, under his direction, we use this great power and authority wisely.

Accusing & Forgiving – We have a believer declare to his heavenly Father what another has done to harm him. Until he is clear about the parts others have played, he cannot clearly see his own involvement in perspective. (Notice that forgiveness comes after accusing: "Father, I accuse ___ . . . I forgive ___.")

Confessing & asking forgiveness – Only after extending forgiveness, can a person confess his own sins and ask forgiveness. Unwillingness to forgive another will hinder his forgiveness. (Notice that confession comes before asking forgiveness: "Father, I confess that I . . . Forgive me.")

Full closure – People involved in sexual sin need spiritual cleansing. People involved in occult activities need a different kind of cleansing due to contact with the profane. Praying believers will only receive what they ask for. People involved in sexual sin need God to break bonds since in sexual sin people's spirits are united (as in the oneness of marriage). This oneness also occurs during rape and molestation. People can have created allegiances and obligations due to occult involvement. They need to renounce and reject these ties to the Kingdom of Dark-ness. To have full closure to any one issue or instance, all of the pieces must be resolved.

Shared responsibility – As Prayer and Resolution Counselors, we are responsible to see that people pray according to God's will, in keeping with his standard and permitted by the scriptures. Every word said in prayer can be important so we must concentrate. We are coordinators and facilitators and, simultaneously, stand with people as priests before God witnessing and endorsing their prayers with our prayers.

Shared burdens – As a community of believers, the scriptures say that we should *"Bear one another's* *burdens, and thus fulfill the law of Christ"* (Galatians 6:2 NAS). We need to validate or invalidate what people share with us. We want to exhort, encourage and admonish when necessary in gentleness and love. Many, in both secular and Christian counseling, discourage our getting involved emotionally with people and their issues. I do not see how we can honestly share another's burden without feeling something. The hurting ones need to see that we care.

Prayer, a group activity – Technically speaking, we pray in the midst of a crowd. Even when we are alone, we are with the Father, Son and Holy Spirit. Some Christians say that prayer is a private matter, done alone. Prayer and Resolution Counseling says that only the simplest issues should be handled alone. It is crucial that others share this time and burden if the issues involve a degree of trauma. If the people do not clearly understand the issues, or if the issues are sexual or occult, they will need help.

People should not share deeply personal issues in an assembly. They should not accept a leader's encouragement in a meeting "to give their burdens to the Lord," unless there is very clear instruction as to how' to do this. Prayer and Resolution Counseling provides the SOP—Standard Operating Procedures—for how to give it to God.

Each issue and person is unique and we should handle them as such. *Working with several hurting people at one time may seem more efficient but it is not more effective.*

God with skin on – We may know that God forgives us when we ask. Nevertheless, it often helps to hear a brother or sister confirm this. "According to God's word,

'When we confess our sins he is faithful and just. . . .'" The rape victim needs to hear us say, "You are cleansed in Jesus' name." We can also say, "I declare before God our Father that you are blameless in this rape."

Safe others – We best achieve balance with a Prayer and Resolution Counseling team of two, ideally consisting of a man and woman. The two provide a whole that cannot occur otherwise. Men and women approach a problem differently and they process from different perspectives. Both perspectives are needed.

In the case of a female rape victim, this is very evident. While it may be true that a rape victim will find it easier to share her story with a woman, it is not true that she does not need a man around when working through the issues. The woman needs to set apart the rapist from other men or she will consider all men potential threats. As part of the grounds for healing, she needs to establish a trust bond with a safe man. Most of all, she needs to see a man angry on her behalf for what another man did.

The woman on the team can say, truthfully, "You are without blame" but a man saying this carries more weight because he is judging his own kind. The woman can say, "You are cleansed in Jesus' name" but a man saying this represents all men.

We did Prayer and Resolution Counseling with a man, a former convict. When he was five years old, his mother was very ill. The family took her away to the hospital one day without explaining anything to him. He never saw his mother again. His family also kept him at home during the funeral. Thirty years later, Connie held this man and comforted him as he wept and finally said good-bye to his mother. It would not have been the same

A Journey to Wholeness

if I, as a man, had done that; he needed a mother's touch.[63]

I relate to certain people better than Connie. It depends on the particular man or woman we are helping. On the other hand, she relates to certain others better. Cathy, a young woman we trained, related best to me. Kate, another young woman, related best to Connie. When that happens then the team member who relates best takes the forefront in leading the Prayer and Resolution Counseling times until greater trust is established.

As a substitute – There are times when people in the life of the hurting one has failed to do their job. For instance, a father or mother has not released the child to full adulthood. A person in authority has failed to recognize a job well done. There are any number of times when what is needed to put the final touches to full resolution is for the appropriate safe other to stand as substitute and do what is necessary. Of course, we do not do this until all of the other steps in resolution have been taken.

Sharon had spent several years establishing an orphanage in Central America. During that time, her field director raped her several times. When it was time for her to return home, he did not allow her to say her goodbye to her friends and to the children. Nor did he permit them to express their love and appreciation. He also forbad her from speaking to her supporting churches when she returned home.

---

[63] Normally, neither Connie nor I have physical contact with people we are praying with but there can be exceptions.

After guiding Sharon in accusing and forgiving this terrible man—and giving him over to God to see justice done, I placed my hands on her head. Before God, I blessed her for her service as a missionary. Then Connie knelt before her and thanked her in the name of the children she had provided for. To finish off this period of her life, I then prayed a prayer of blessing on her as she went on to new things.

Recognizing Satan's interest – We must keep in mind that the act of Prayer and Resolution Counseling automatically creates the grounds for spiritual battle between the Kingdom of God and the Kingdom of Darkness. Satan's forces will try to interfere unless we ask God to build a hedge of protection around our session and us.

The Non-Directive Approach

The non-directive approach can be useful if the Prayer and Resolution Counselors are sensitive to the leading of the Holy Spirit as believers reflect on their feelings and thoughts. The session can end up, however, as a time of aimless wanderings without some control and direction.

This approach should not dominate the session. Nevertheless, sometimes people need to reflect and internalize the truths before they can pray. *The fallacy is that truth and right perspective come out of mid air or from within ourselves. Damaged people may not have a reservoir of truth within themselves on which they can draw.*

People may not realize their gap in knowledge or recognize another alternative until they can formulate a question. When people have a question, they acknowledge a need for information or clarification.

Sometimes, when people cannot get past the big picture and begin to wander, I have them ask God, through the ministry of the Holy Spirit, to bring to their memory what is an important piece to consider for full resolution. The Holy Spirit can do this and most often does so directly to the people in need rather than to us as safe others.

Confrontational Approach

In Prayer and Resolution Counseling, I have been confrontational at times. I have done this to expose irresponsible behavior. For example, a pastor molested a woman at a seminar. When he was with us, he thought it was a minor thing, "All I did was try to kiss her." I made him realize what God had to say about people in authority abusing their positions. It was not a small kiss but molestation and a violation of trust.

Confrontation can destroy an atmosphere of trust and hinder the Holy Spirit from working. I did not confront this pastor until *later in our time together*, after trust had been built and love shown.

Empathetic Approach

In the empathic approach, we affirm what the hurting one is feeling or thinking. This gives hope to the hurting believer but just burden bearing does not bring resolution.

Counseling Considerations

The emphatic approach can be misused. For example, one Christian counselor says that as we step into the shoes of the offender we can begin to see his or her side and out of this can come understanding and forgiveness.[64]

He talks about appreciating the pressures the wrongdoer was under at the time of the offence. We should learn to see what happened from the wrongdoer's point of view.

This result of being empathetic is unacceptable and excuses, rather than condemns, the action. We cannot excuse wrong behavior even though we may appreciate the emotions and the circumstances around that behavior.

In Prayer and Resolution Counseling, the best approach is to use any method, or combination of methods, that considers the unique personalities of the people and is timely and useful. *Whatever approach we use, information alone, without resolution, accomplishes little.* We must use whatever is necessary to clarify and to get at the truth. Only then can prayer be specific, focused, and validated by the Prayer and Resolution Counselors and the people.

Other Considerations

There are other issues to consider in the process of prayer and resolution. This is not an exhaustive list but these things do influence the whole process.

---

[64] Everett Worthington, *Forgiving and Reconciling: Bridges to Wholeness and Hope,* InterVarsity Press, 2003.

Concerning Safe Others

People must trust us – By definition, safe others are ones people trust. It is not safe to put oneself into the hands of someone who is perceived as unsafe. We can build trust in different ways: Sometimes trust comes because of an existing friendship or when friends introduce us and, in that way, endorse us. People can begin to trust by listening to us teach. Trust can come after a relaxed time of sharing and coffee. We often have people meet us, or at least have a good chat on the phone, before they decide on whether or not they want us to work with them.

We are not judges – We must be careful not to show facial or oral indications that we disapprove of people when they share. The point is to have unrestricted flow of information from the beginning. Later, when the people trust us more fully, we can help them evaluate actions and face the reality of their parts in a situation.

Rebuking and exhorting both involve value judgments where we strongly attempt to change a path or encourage people to keep in it. The only reason we may be forceful in evaluation of right and wrong is to help them come to the Father in a prayer that he can answer. As we often tell people before they pray, "God already knows all this. The question is, do you know and accept it?"

Counseling Considerations

Concerning the Hurting One

Theology and worldview – There will be times when people's religious backgrounds or theological training get in the way. Normally, people are resistant to our focus on God as Father. Often people have prayed only to Jesus, Lord, or God. This may be habit or training, but more often it is a rejection of an earthly parent and they have projected this on God as Father as well. God is the ultimate victim when parental betrayal takes place.

People from Charismatic or Pentecostal backgrounds may want to pray in tongues. It does not matter whether we are for or against the use of tongues, they are not appropriate in Prayer and Resolution Counseling. We, the Prayer and Resolution Counseling team and the hurting one, need to know what is being said. We cannot endorse a prayer we do not understand, nor can the hurting one. Nor should a hurting one permit someone to pray over them in a prayer that she does not understand. (Despite what I have said, if tongues *are used*, then there must be an interpretation by a third party.)

Some people pray in a legal and formal way. Others are emotional, others relate to God almost as if they are watching a movie with him—with them and others starring in it. While we must always consider run-away imagination and even occult interference, methods can vary if the basic elements are there.

God does relate to people in different ways. For example, Americans consider dreams suspect but, in truth, our culture has programmed us to operate at a lower spiritual level than other people, even pagan ones. I know of people in Ethiopia, Mexico, Morocco and Sudan whose first encounters with God were through dreams.

A Journey to Wholeness

We have worked with Anglicans, Assemblies of God, various Baptists, Roman Catholic, Church of God, Dutch Reform, Evangelical Free Church, Fundamentalist, Independent, Lutheran, Nazarene and Presbyterian, to name a few. These included Calvinists and Armenians, Charismatic, non-Charismatic, and Pentecostal. We have worked with Americans, Brazilians, Canadians, a Chadian, Cubans, Dutch, English, Filipinos, Finnish, French, Germans, Irish, a Kenyan, Malaysian, Mexicans, Native Americans, a Nigerian, a Puerto Rican, several Senegalese, Swedish, Swiss and Vietnamese, to name a few.

In some areas, God is more broad-minded than we are. We work in different ways with different people and cultures. As Prayer and Resolution Counselors, we must maintain an absolute standard where righteousness, right principles and procedures are concerned but we must be flexible when God has not set clear guidelines.

The personal history – It is important that we know more than the (apparent) immediate problem. We *do not have people write a personal history.* We take down a chronological history of the people as we talk together. This may take a few minutes or several hours, depending on the people and the issues. We can best understand issues in the context of all of life. People's lives will naturally group into distinct stages because of age, grade in school, moves, marriages, divorces, traumas, jobs or other changes.

We need to be sensitive to the Holy Spirit during this time. We take notes and ask questions to clarify. *However, we do not bring up details nor stop to handle anything.* The team needs to have firm control so people do not expose the details until the right time. When the team can handle the issue is the time to share in detail and guide people in prayer. Before that time, exposure only creates an added burden and possible attack from Satan. Above all, this history gathering time is to give us a general picture of people's lives.

During this overview, we want to get an idea of their attitudes about life and expectations for themselves and for others. The hurting one needs to be a Christian to make effective use of these tools of Prayer and Resolution Counseling. How grounded are they in the scriptures? Are they growing, dead in the water, ignorant or educated about the Christian life? Did they go to college? Where and why? What were their life styles at different times in their lives?

What type of relationships do they have with others on the emotional level, involving sexual activities (as perpetrators or victims) and occult activities (passive or active participation)? How do the people relate to parents and other members of the family? Are there other significant people in their lives?

What about recurring habits, good or bad? Nightmares? Headaches? One woman was committed to working hard–on the surface it looked good–but turned out to be an indication of bondage/addiction. Another woman vowed to read three chapters of the Bible right after she got up each morning. This promise became a curse when she could not skip her routine even when she was sick or traveling.

Often out of this initial time, we see patterns revealed that, although not central, are significant and need to be dealt with. Notice that simply solving an immediate problem is not the issue—unless time is limited. We want to help people put their lives into their proper perspective and be released from all of the chains of the past and the forces of sin.

A Journey to Wholeness

In this way, we begin to pinpoint the main issues. The concerns that people bring may suddenly be less important than other concerns. Ideally, we want to deal with everything. The order of presentation to God the Father needs thought, insight, wisdom and guidance from the Holy Spirit.

We usually go back through the chronological timeline period by period. A period might be birth to preschool or the college years, it might be the married years or the period lived in a foster home. The Holy Spirit guides us as we seek to maintain control and create boundaries. Without manageable pieces, we have a huge unmanageable heap of data, some significant, some not, none of which we can handle effectively for resolution.

In the field of logic, *induction* reasoning goes from the specific to the general. In Prayer and Resolution Counseling, using the chronological map as our guide, we use the *deduction* method that goes from the general to the specific. In other words, we go by general time periods, and by themes, and within those we begin to create focus and direction. Well meaning people use the *abduction* method where they talk at random in the hope of inspiration that either does not come or does come but is unmanageable when it does.

We go from the general to the specific, by period and by theme. If people have been heavily into sexual activities, we normally handle this first. We start in the preschool years to see if there was been molestation. We do not consider anything as insignificant if the Holy Spirit brings it to mind. (Remember, we asked the Holy Spirit to bring to mind those things we needed to resolve.)

Then we look at the early school years. If no issues appear then we move on eventually to the present. We start at the earliest times because it is there that people have formed patterns that have been reinforced as time has gone on. Notice that this can take time, however, we are not talking about months or years but merely hours.

Personal Learning Style – It is important for the Prayer and Resolution Counseling team to begin to understand how people think, process information and make decisions. It is helpful to know whether people need to see the whole picture first (the holist) or if they are more comfortable dealing with the parts (the dichotomist). Do they need help in seeing how the details fit into the big picture or help in picking the details out of the big picture?

Do people need time to express themselves fully or are they focused on the mere facts without going into all the background? How about the amount of time they need to think through or process in order to make a decision? If we end up pushing too hard for an immediate decision, concerning whatever, the answer will most likely be an emphatic, "No!" or at least a digging in of the heels.

We need to know enough about people to make the process go smoothly and effectively. There are enough issues to get through without adding problems or obstacles due to our unawareness or insensitivity.

Concerning Process

Opening the box – Ideally, we do not want people opening up and sharing unless they feel the issues are important. Until we have the time to bring resolution, we never bring things into the open if they can cause pain, anger, suffering or anguish.

A Journey to Wholeness

Scheduling – We do not rigidly schedule our sessions. They should be long enough to bring resolution for an issue or episode but not so long as to be exhausting. Different issues are more demanding and draining than others are. One man was exhausted after twenty minutes; another person could go for an hour; while yet another was still going strong after four hours.

People may need to rest a bit before going on. We need to take a break at a good stopping point. We cannot rigidly schedule this. We do not want to break for lunch or the day unless we are at a good stopping point. We continue praying over a specific issue until we have at least some resolution.

Quality, not quantity – Focus and quality of time are more important than quantity. We are dealing with serious issues, standing before the heavenly Father in prayer and appropriating the results of Christ's death and resurrection.

Over all, we must always keep in mind that the Father is the focus but Jesus is our avenue to the Father. We must have the Holy Spirit as our guide so we rightfully use the authority and power we have in Christ. As Prayer and Resolution Counselors, we are only channels that God can use.

Role of the Spouse – Usually, the spouse *should not* act as the prayer witness for the other spouse. The spouse is too involved in the issues to have detachment. Also, the people in focus often have a relationship with both spouses. For example, if George has something against his brother, Pete, he should not use his wife as his prayer witness as this could easily affect the relationship between his wife and Pete. Or, if Margery has a problem with her mother-in-law, she should not ask her husband to be her prayer witness to deal with this.

If sex sin is involved, the spouse should not be hearing the details of the other's sexual exploits. Even in the priestly role, the witnessing spouse cannot "let it go" in the same way as when praying with a friend or stranger.

The openness in marriage: where we are encouraged to share *everything* with our spouse and hold nothing back is not the best advice. While we do not advocate lying or the keeping of secrets, we simply do not need to know all the gory details of our spouse's past life. We may need to talk about some issues. For instance, we may need to tell that we have a sexual history or that we have had an abortion—but not details.

Once these things have been resolved by the heavenly Father, however, there is no need or value in sharing any of the details. If he considers it finished and remembers it no more, neither should we. Present sins should be resolved before God first and then ask the spouse for forgiveness for the transgression without any of the messy details. The sin against the spouse was not in the details but in the mental act. As to present temptations, we must be selective in what and how we share with our spouse. For example, what can a wife do with her husband's confession that he has a problem of lusting after tall blue-eyed blonde-haired women?

After hearing this, every time they go out and come across a blue-eyed blond-haired woman, the wife will feel threatened or uneasy. It becomes a burden for her to carry and she cannot lift the burden from him. Worse yet, she may be given or take on the role of policing her husband.

A better way of handling this would be for the husband to go to another man for help in whatever way necessary. If the wife needs to know then she can be assured that her only role is to continue to love him and to pray for him, because he is getting the help and support he needs from another man.

The principle then is this:

If knowing the information is only going to add a burden to our spouse–because there is nothing he or she can do with the knowledge but store it away–then we should not share. We should share instead with a trusted friend.

The Prayer and Resolution Counseling team must be "outward focused" in that they adapt their approach to best fit the personalities and needs of the people they are helping. If the team is "inward focused," then there will be rigidity and insensitivity to the needs of people.

That said, the Prayer and Resolution Counselling team should be in charge! They do know more about achieving resolution than the hurting people and they need to show confidence when guiding people, even when they don't feel it in the early days of ministry.

There are many approaches available and the team needs to be comfortable in using a variety of approaches but, within the approaches, the principles underlying resolution cannot be put aside.

18

General Checklist

God Sets the Stage

Anyone can help another in Prayer and Resolution Counseling if they understand the basic principles. If you generate trust then people will come and ask for help.

We helped Cathy in prayer and resolution to deal with incest and sexual sin. Later, she found herself with a friend who shared her deep hurts about a rape. Confronted with her friend's need, Cathy thought of us but we were not there. She was and that was the time to help. She did the best she could, following our prayer and resolution procedures with her friend. God answered and gave cleansing, release and healing. Richard and Connie do not bring resolution, but God does.

Normally, people ask for help from us or share a burden with us. Anyone who has the trust of others can help them but we cannot help resistant or untruthful people. None of us can tackle the world but we can help those people we meet who really want help.

On the other hand, no one can do Prayer and Resolution Counseling unless God sets the stage. The Holy Spirit must prepare the heart and provide the time. Doing anything in prayer on our own has its problems because we can use and abuse the authority we have in Christ. We can do things for God he did not want done or were not in his timing. Prayer and Resolution Counseling is a source of power. Doing Prayer and Resolution Counseling with the wrong attitude or seeking to control through religious actions can be destructive to us and to others.

Who is Involved

We need to consider all the possible participants; what I call the "greater circle." We cannot assume that people understand the parts that others have played. Ingrid's first sexual sin happened with her high school teacher. We must consider the relationship of teacher–student. Others are involved as well. Both her parents encouraged Ingrid to experiment before marriage so their relationship to her is that of parent–child. A girl friend egged Ingrid on so we also have a friend–friend relationship to consider.

Each one of these relationships has its own privileges, responsibilities and obligations. Parents should protect their children. Friends should consider the other's welfare and encourage their friend toward the good. A teacher is in a position of trust and should stay within the guidelines of teaching and ought to be a model for good behavior.

Ingrid should have been able to trust her parents, friend and teacher but instead all of them violated her trust. In a sense, it took more than two to commit fornication.

Point of View

One purpose of Prayer and Resolution Counseling is to bring people into the center of reality. Then they understand what life is all about and can have a full and satisfying walk with God. We know God does not want us to have a fuzzy or blurred view of life. Prayer and Resolution Counseling should lessen the distortion.

We need to focus on Ingrid first and see how others have related to her as wrongdoers. Then we help Ingrid see herself as the wrongdoer. Her right perspective for her part in this sin is dependent on appreciating the parts others have played. This knowledge may lessen or increase her own accountability for her actions and it will increase her responsibility for right living in the future.

The Deed

People often talk in generalities that lessen or disguise the fact of real sin:

"I hurt my husband when I went with Bobby" really means, "I lied to my husband and did not consider my marriage vows when I slept with Bobby." (This means, "I committed adultery with Bobby.")

"We sinned together" can mean, "We stole the car," or "we committed adultery," or a thousand other acts.

"I fooled around" is not the equivalent of "I molested the little girl."

It sounds better to say, "We made love," than to say, "We committed fornication."

When Helen says, "I told my mother off," it can mean, "Leave me alone, I'm not a child!" Not serious, or more so when she really said, "I hate you, you bitch! F___ off! I'm not a child!"

Gene "borrowed it" instead of "stole it."

Tom "knocked her around a little," but more specifically means, "I blacked her eyes, punched her into a wall and when she fell I kicked her unconscious."

What were the actual wrongs committed? The truth is not always pretty. God already knows but does Ingrid understand and accept what her sin was? Sleeping together can mean anything; fornication means just that and is sin. Perversion is perversion. Are there additional sins to consider that grew out of the first? Is there an attitude or judgment involved that pushed Ingrid or the teacher toward this sin? For example, did the teacher consider all young women fair game? That makes him a predator. Does Ingrid consider herself a worthless person that neither she nor God could love? Did Ingrid seduce the teacher? After committing fornication, the teacher dumped her. Did Ingrid try to get revenge (return evil for evil)?

What Emotions are Involved

What emotions or attitudes came out of this situation? People can feel hatred, disgust, a sense of betrayal, a feeling of worthlessness or shame, a craving for more. Molestation and rape victims may be blameless but often feel guilt. Moreover, they always feel shame.

Resolution

Ingrid first forgave the teacher, her friend and her parents for their parts in this. She did it for each, praying a separate prayer for each person involved—including her mother and father individually. She then confessed her own sins with clarity and understanding and asked for forgiveness.

She needed to consider additional issues, but not until she had forgiven her parents and others and confessed her own sins and received forgiveness.

For example:

Cleansing: because of the special defilement of the spirit that fornication brings, she needed to ask for spiritual cleansing.

Bonds/ties: sexual sin creates a union of the spirit, a oneness, with another. Even if Ingrid had been a victim of rape, that act would have created a union. She needed to ask God to break that bond.

Bonds: The behavior of the parents created a lessening of the bonds between Ingrid, the daughter, and her parents. She needed to ask God to restore these bonds. (In incest, for example, sometimes the bonds need to be more fully broken between an unsafe father and a child.)

Release: If Ingrid had made a vow to never again permit a man to arouse her, for example, her vow would extend into marriage and Ingrid's relationship with her husband. Such a vow would be unwise and she would need to confess her sin and ask God to release her from the power of that vow.

Renouncement: If Ingrid pledged herself to the teacher then she would need to ask God to release her from that pledge.

Perspectives

Uniqueness

Every person is different. Every situation develops differently. The core sin might be the same but the situation changes as the participants change.

For example, Helen has had three abortions and feels guilt. Each time an abortion happened, there were different people involved. She had the first abortion without seriously thinking of the consequences. A friend encouraged it and Helen was only sixteen. She had the second abortion to keep from losing her boyfriend. She had the third because her husband did not want a baby. Each one is not a carbon copy of the other so we need to handle each one separately.

Different issues demand different considerations in our prayers. We must think through the issues and see what is happening from God's perspective or we will not receive the resolution needed. For example, when we deal with a believer having an occult background, we must see heaven and the earth from God's perspective. Did a dedication, fear or sin create a link to the Kingdom of Darkness? Is the person displaying a gift, such as prophesying or tongues that could be from either God or Satan? Was the person baptized during a satanic ritual?

Reality

The world is under the control of the Evil One, according to I John. Jesus said that we are either under

God's rule or under Satan's rule. Therefore, we are concerned with control and influence in a person's life.

Her mother and friends dedicated Helen to Satan as his bride. We have a satanic marriage here. What does that mean in affecting the form and specifics in our prayer? In Christ, we can handle all this in victory but we must do our part as well as ask God to do his part. Just saying, "I have a problem, God" is useless.

Often God's children, because of sin, are under Satan's control or have given to him a certain license to work in their lives. Or, like Helen, she was given to Satan by her mother. The believer must consider ownership by Satan and citizenship in his kingdom, allegiance to him or obligation because of relationships accepted or favors received.

If a believer has received a spiritual gift inherited or otherwise, we must validate it as from God, from Satan or of a natural origin. We have encountered two cases where tongues were of demonic origin but other cases where we validated the prayer language as from God.

Neither Connie nor I speak in tongues or have a prayer language but we know Christians who do. Our task is not to defend our church doctrine. As Bible Translators we learned to translate God's word for what it said, not what we wanted it to say. For example, Baptists should not translate in keeping with Baptist doctrine but in keeping with what the passage says.

We should test everything but not automatically reject what we do not understand or what we find uncomfortable. Whatever the issues, we must deal with them carefully, specifically and prayerfully.

Prayer and Resolution Counseling has long-term consequences but the quality of the prayers determines the quality of the results attained. We must use the authority and power we have in Christ with thoughtfulness and always under the guidance of the Holy Spirit.

Opportunity

I directed a five-month study abroad program for Christian workers in a non-Christian and non-Western society. I told the participants that *they could not witness to non-Christians* they met until the non-Christian opened the door by asking a question about the participant's faith or behavior (in contrast to other westerners' behavior).

These were my reasons: (1) It was illegal to proselyte in this particular country and (2) They should let God through the Holy Spirit set the stage and create the opening. Their job was to recognize when the Holy Spirit did so.

The scriptures tell us *to be ready always to give an answer:* that means someone asks a question. Zeal without the Holy Spirit is both dangerous and harmful. It is a great responsibility and privilege to help another in prayer but we should not go hunting for people to minister to as Prayer and Resolution Counselors. Let God bring people to us.

On the other hand, we can be timid and afraid to do our part even though God leads. Nevertheless, if not us, whom they trust, then to whom do they go for help? If not when friends come needing our help, then when? If the power of the Gospel is only good enough to get us to heaven then of what use is it to us now?

If God brings someone into our lives and prompts us to help them then he will guide us. If he has chosen us to help only one person in our lives, then for that one person we will have all we need in gifting, discernment and guidance from the Holy Spirit.

General Checklist

In Prayer and Resolution Counselling, it is important that we strive for *quality* of time with people, not *quantity*. Quality of time comes through preparation. The team needs to hear what people say are their issues and, by asking questions, understand what the real issues are. They are not always the same.

In many cases, people have not considered all the factors nor had a balance perspective about an issue. For example, often people's focus is on their forgiveness without considering the other participants who hindered or helped.

If people are unwilling to take the time for preparation, to give the team a chance to understand fully the issues—then we do not even start the prayer and resolution time. The team, not the hurting people, must control the quality of the time.

Normally it takes hours and weeks, not months and years for God to bring healing in a person's life. We want to go slow and be thorough so there is nothing left out. When Prayer and Resolution Counseling is done carefully and to a finish then the door to the past, as far as harmful effects is concerned, is closed.

19

Putting it All Together

This chapter is abbreviated compilation of several case studies in order to present an example of how Prayer and Resolution Counseling progresses from start to finish. Sometimes we cannot deal with all of a person's life and must handle just one important issue. Prayer and Resolution Counseling works either way but, ideally we should work with a person several hours at a time at least once a week. Better yet, work several hours morning and afternoon every day for three or four days and then take two or three days off. On average, people we have worked with have needed some twenty to thirty hours of Prayer and Resolution Counseling to handle all the significant issues. There is, of course, greater resolution and freedom if all of the issues are dealt with since all of one's life is intertwined.

Ideally, a man and a woman team help the hurting one. That is not always possible, so one person can help another. There is a loss, however, because the load is on only one set of shoulders and only one detached perspective is available. Also Prayer and Resolution Counseling is tiring and there is not the possibility of the other partner taking over while the other is less engaged.

Here we will cover only one situation where normally we deal with several issues during a session. Included will be the major aspects that need to occur in any Prayer and Resolution Counseling session, once discussion has taken place. These are:

Chronological History
    General
    Specific

The Circumstances
    The sin
    The participants

Discussion
    The issues
    The direction

Prayer
    The opening prayer
    The prayer for resolution
    The witnessing prayer
    The covering prayer

Chronological History

We take down the chronological history as we ask questions starting with where the person was born, the parents' names, their work, brothers and sisters, and so on. We must maintain strong control during this time. The person may want to gush out all the gory details. We cannot let that happen until we are ready to take these things to God in prayer.

A Journey to Wholeness

The chronological history gives us a time line and a point of reference and control. Without such we can aimlessly wander around and be overwhelmed with the complexity of a person's life.

GENERAL

John Doe - born April 1970, Dallas TX
Parents - Henry Doe, office manager; Mary Doe, housewife
Older brother - Harry (four years older)
Younger sister - Martha (six years younger)

Lived in Duncanville K thru 4th grade
Lived in Fort Worth 5th grade thru high school
1989-93 - Attended UT Arlington , B.A. History
1995 - Married Betty, two children: Mark and Sharon
Job - a computer hardware technician
And so on . . .

SPECIFIC

Now we go back and fill in the general with specifics but not in great detail. We do not want to "open the box" until we are ready to handle an item in prayer. So, specifics here mean looking into possible issues: sexual, the occult, rebellion, abuse, vows, lies and so on.

Putting it all Together

The father was physically abusive; the mother was passive.

Mr. Taylor, a neighbor, molested John when he was eight.

John molested his sister Martha when she was four, on and off until she was ten.

Preschool - Did anything happen that you know or others told you that was traumatic or of significant, and so on?

Grades 1 thru 6 – (Going grade by grade) Did anything happen during 4th grade? Good or bad grades? Why? Were there special teachers? What about fellow students? What did you really enjoy? Really hate? Any molestation or sexual messing around?

How was your home life? What was the atmosphere of the home? Did you feel loved, protected, cared for? Any negative words of power or judgments?

We keep the information less detailed, just enough to know or think there might be issues to bring up later.

College years: Did you live in the dorm? Party? Did you date? Did you have girl friends, sleep around? Were you engaged?

John first began a relationship with Betty - Did you respect one another? Did you violate each other's boundaries? Did you engage in sexual activities? (We will probably need to help them understand or define *when* sexual activities become sin.)

Again, we would be looking at the four major areas of sin by or against John: (1) *sexual,* (2) *rebellion or betrayal,* (3) *words of power* and *(4). the occult.* Words of power are vows, judgments or strong statements about John's character made to himself or by significant people: "You will never amount to anything;" "I'll never do anything right!" "You are a real slob!" are just a sampling.

THE CIRCUMSTANCES

We start with one topic and follow it through to the present. The best place to start is with sexual sins. This is for several reasons:

- These are usually on the person's mind and are garbage that needs to get out no matter what else.

- The person feels a release and cleansing that is initially experienced more deeply than other prayer answers.

- Often the person can see with greater clarity other issues and destructive patterns once he or she has handled sexual sins.

Therefore, we start at the beginning with a prayer of accusation: against Mr. Taylor, the neighbour, who molested John.

THE SIN

We all understand that the sin is molestation but we need to ask questions and get more details before we can help John take this issue to God in prayer. It is important to understand just what it was that Mr. Taylor did that was sin against John. What was John's reaction? Did this happen more than once? Did Mr. Taylor know that what he was doing was wrong? How do we know? We ask whatever builds enough of a picture so the accusation(s) is clear enough and specific enough to cover the reality of the issue.

THE PARTICIPANTS

As we ask questions, we find that Mary, John's mother, had Mr. Taylor baby-sit him often. One day John said to his mother, "I don't like Mr. Taylor; he isn't a nice man." She answered him with, "Don't *bother* me. You know I have a thousand things to do." So he thought she did not care.

THE DISCUSSION

Just sharing with someone does not bring resolution. Discussion and sharing are for validating or invalidating what the person is reporting. Maybe Mr. Taylor was just rubbing John's head and John did not like that. On the other hand, maybe Mr. Taylor was taking John's pants off and fondling him. There is a difference. Also "bad touch" and "good touch" come in here. John's perception of what happened needs to be carefully considered.

THE ISSUES

After John shares more, in specific details when possible, then we validate that what happened to him was really molestation. We point out that this action, in a point of time, is affecting his life even now. Mr. Taylor's actions likely played a part in that. John became more aware of sexual things at an early age and, in this case, perversion. John molested his sister. He does not trust Mark, his son, around their daughter Sharon although Mark has done nothing.

John and we agree that his mother is partly to blame. She was too busy to pay attention to him and gave him a wrong message. Whether she intended to or not, is not the issue, John feels that she did not care. Since he has held this grudge for years, he must handle it.

We go into as much detail as necessary to get all the facts. We want to make sure that John fully realizes all that happened, especially as sin carried over into other times and areas of his life.

As John sees the greater picture, he begins to appreciate God's perspective on sin and its effects and why God is so down on sin. We want to get John to stand beside God, so to speak, and look back and see the reality of what happened to him.

THE DIRECTION

Once we have the facts we now map out a plan of action to take this situation to prayer. Praying without understanding or awareness creates empty words that God cannot answer. The issue is molestation; the people involved are Mr. Taylor, John and his mother. John will need spiritual cleansing (from the effects of Mr. Taylor's sexual sin) and a breaking of the spiritual ties that came although John was a victim.

THE PRAYERS

During prayer, we need to keep in mind that we are dealing with God's system. That means that we do it his way. Often people feel such guilt that they only do *prayers of confession* when there is also a need for *prayers of accusation*. Grudges do not just go away. We can misinterpret what has happened unless we have Safe Others to help us gain perspective.

Resolution has no short cuts. If confession is needed then he needs a full and clear confession without hedging. Not "I fooled around" but "I tried to rape her." Confession is not for God's benefit, as if he did not know what we did, it is for our benefit.

One by-product of true confession is a greater awareness of the awfulness of sin and its consequences. If we did it, we do not want to do it again because we now understand the impact it had on the one we wounded. If someone did it to us, then we will not do it to another because we more clearly understand the impact it had on us.

There are four aspects of prayer presented here:

1. The Opening Prayer
2. The Prayer of Resolution
3. The Witnessing Prayer
4. The Covering Prayer

As part of the introduction or overview of the prayer process, it is important to emphasize the act of accusation. We tend to emphasize receiving forgiveness and slight the act of accusing and forgiving others. *First, we accuse* and forgive, *then we confess* our own sins and ask forgiveness.

This is important. As we accuse the others in our situation, we more fully realize and accept their parts. Sometimes this makes it harder to forgive. In turn, when we now confess our own sins, we are more fully conscious of our lesser or greater part.

Words are important. We do not let people start with, "I forgive John for . . ." but rather, "I accuse John for . . . I forgive him." In the same way, our prayer of confession should not start with, "Forgive me for . . ." but rather, "I confess . . . Forgive me."

In both the accusing and our asking forgiveness, God already knows all there is to know about the situation but do we? Accusing with knowledge makes us aware of mercy: forgiving others who have harmed us and do not deserve forgiveness. Confessing with knowledge make us aware of the cost of our forgiveness: the fact we do not deserve forgiveness or mercy but that God does forgive us.

The Opening Prayer

Normally the team leader gives the opening prayer. This sets the stage and tone of the session. It should not be rote and it should include all the Godhead, our relationship and even Satan! There are certain elements, which I always include in this particular prayer:

The Opening Prayer sets the stage for us, as his children, to come before the throne and to ask our Father for his help. Everything we say in prayer is significant. Therefore, we want to be careful in what we say and how we say it. Nevertheless, we do not want to pray rote prayers.

A proper relationship with the Father, Son and Holy Spirit should be acknowledged and maintained. In our prayer, we might recognize what the Heavenly Father has done in the past, praise, even worship him but we do not

A Journey to Wholeness

want to turn the session into a time of praise or worship. We must maintain focus. The point of the Opening Prayer is to open a session, not a church service!

Excluding the heavenly Father is often the result of wounding such as, when our parents have betrayed us in some way and we reject them. We then carry over that mistrust and rejection to God the Father. We must be careful in the use of the term *Lord* by any of the team. *The majority of people we have counseled started by approaching Jesus as Lord rather that God as Father.* Jesus clearly taught us to pray to the Father. The term Lord, although it is appropriate for both Jesus and God, often shifts our focus to Jesus and away from the Father, to servant and away from our being his children.

Without the work of Christ, none of this would be possible. Therefore, we will want to thank him for what he has done, and acknowledge his presence with us.

We always ask the Holy Spirit to guide and direct so we rightfully use the authority we have in Christ, never assuming that he automatically takes control. Actually, control is not the issue; we want to be in partnership and harmony with the Holy Spirit.

Our prayers should always contain the basic elements but no prayer should be a carbon copy of another.

Putting it all Together

The Opening Prayer

1. Praying to the heavenly Father
   a.) As his children
   b.) Adopted as part of redemption
   c.) Through Jesus Christ

2. Accepting the promise of Christ's presence

3. Taking authority in Christ's name
   a.) When two or three
   b.) When in agreement
      — To bind or loose
      — To forgive or withhold forgiveness
      — To agree on anything

4. Recognizing our power and authority in Christ

5. Putting the power under the Holy Spirit

6. Giving permission to the Holy Spirit
   a.) To lead, guide and direct
   b.) To reveal and convict

7. Stating the purpose and result
   a.) Pleasing to the Father
   b.) According to his will
   c.) For his glory and honor

8. Asking for protection against Satan during prayers: For ourselves, for our families, for other special people and for our properties

A Journey to Wholeness

Here is an example:

Father, we come to you in the name of Jesus Christ. We recognize that through his death and resurrection we have been saved and adopted into your family. As your children, we can come into your presence with confidence.

We accept Jesus' presence in the special way he promised when he said that where two or three of us are gathered together in his name he would be here in our midst. We also accept the power and authority of the name of Jesus for he said that when two or three of us here on earth agree on a matter in his name that you would do it in heaven.

We recognize that this authority can be misused so we ask the Holy Spirit to lead, guide and direct us so that all that we do is in keeping with your will, is pleasing to you and you receive the glory and honor.

We know that Satan and his forces would like to interfere with what you want accomplished today. We ask that you build a hedge of protection around us, our loved ones and our properties so that the forces of evil cannot attack in any way.

We also ask that you govern natural interruptions so that these things do not interfere with our concentration and focus. We ask this in Jesus' name, amen.

Putting it all Together

The Prayer for Resolution

Resolution involves a number of elements. To have full resolution, all of the essential elements need to be included in our prayers. If we focus simply on our need for forgiveness and leave out the other elements, only partial resolution takes place. There is a natural progression: First we accuse others and forgive them and then we confess our own sin and ask for forgiveness.

The Prayer of Resolution

1. Accuse the person before the heavenly Father

2. Forgive

3. Confess

4. Ask for forgiveness

5. Ask that bonds be broken
   a.) physical
   b.) emotional
   c.) spiritual

6. Ask for cleansing from sexual defilement

7. Other issues related to the situation
   a.) judgments
   b.) memories
   c.) emotions, etc.

A Journey to Wholeness

As we deal with each layer, once we have dealt with the elements of accusing and forgiving, we need to decide if we have anything to confess concerning that person. If not, we move on down to the next element.

Sexual activity creates bonds at the physical, emotional and spiritual level. In order to rid ourselves of unholy and illegitimate bonds, we have to ask God to break them since he is the only one who has the power to do so.

Sexual sins are of a defiling nature. Therefore, the next logical step is to ask for spiritual cleansing. With forgiveness of sin comes a cleansing from sin and unrighteousness. This differs from spiritual defilement, which is a stain put on us when sexual sin is performed by us or against us, from which we need purification. It is a cleansing of the spirit.

In determining what the layers are, the Safe Others and the wounded one often need to discuss the whole situation, sometimes at great length. This is one time when the perspective of Safe Others is most often needed.

John does this prayer. He may try to pray to Jesus but we do not let him. *John needs to stand in his position as a son of God who is addressing his heavenly Father.* Since John's father has been abusive, he probably will have a hard time at first talking to God as Father. If he shifts to "Lord" we remind him to whom he is talking to since Lord usually refers to Jesus and is not a term we would use with a father anyway.

During John's prayer, the team may interrupt him for clarification or to correct a misconception. *Notice the order of accusing first then forgiving, confessing first then*

Putting it all Together

asking forgiveness. Here is an abbreviated example of his prayer:

> *Heavenly Father, I accuse my mother of not caring enough of me to listen and for placing me in danger . . . There is no excuse for what she did but I forgive her.*
>
> *I accuse Mr. Taylor of molesting me. He tricked me by telling me it would be fun and using candy as a bribe. He made me promise not to tell . . .* **He couldn't help himself. ...**

(We break in - If he could not help himself, then it was not his fault. That is wrong. Mr. Taylor made a choice. He could help himself. He knew what he was doing was wrong and he did it anyway and with premeditation.) I agree. He knew exactly what he was doing . . . (We prompt John at times so nothing is left out.) . . .

> *I forgive Mr. Taylor.*
>
> *I confess that I was wrong when I promised to keep quiet. Forgive me, Father and release me from this promise. But I also acknowledge that I was a victim in this and Mr. Taylor carries the full weight of this sin of molestation.*
>
> **(We prompt John to ask for the following:)** *When Mr. Taylor molested me he defiled me, I felt dirty. Nothing I could do with soap and water would take that away. Cleanse me through the blood of Jesus.*

> *When Mr. Taylor molested me, I recognize now that there was a special tie created between us. I ask that you break those ties, on the physical, emotional and spiritual levels.*
>
> *I ask that you take away from me the shame and sense of helplessness I felt then. Take the memory of that time under the control of the Holy Spirit so it can no longer trouble me. I ask all these things in Jesus' name, amen.*

The Witnessing Prayer

A member of the Prayer and Resolution Counseling team makes the witnessing prayer. The point of the Witnessing Prayer is to add legality. According to Jesus, where two or three of us agree on a matter in his name, he said God his Father would do it. That means that we have the responsibility to rightfully use the authority we have in Christ.

God gives us what we ask for. When we do not ask, we cannot assume that he will fill in the blanks and answer. The hurting one has done his or her part in presenting this incident to the heavenly Father for resolution. Now, it is the Safe Other's turn to add their agreement and authority in witnessing that person's prayer.

As Safe Others, we witness John's process of working through the issues he faces and acknowledges that all was done on God's terms. We bring an additional authority and strength to the prayer as we pray in agreement. This in turn releases John from the burden

Putting it all Together

he has been under. As well, we rely on Jesus' authority to bind or loose whatever is needed given the situation and witness together that the process of healing, forgiveness, and resolution has been done according to the pattern of Scripture.

Another aspect of what the Witnessing Prayer does is to declare or speak out the completion of the different transactions, i.e. that forgiveness has been granted, cleansing has taken place. We speak out that which God has done.

Our prayers as Safe Others should not replace the hurting one's prayers. We helped guide John as he prayed to his heavenly Father. He answered his prayers. Safe Others only join in when needed and by adding their agreement, endorse the validity of the prayers. After John prayed an issue through to completeness, I prayed a prayer of agreement, witness and declaration.

Witnessing John's prayer means that we are endorsing that his prayer is in keeping with God's will, character and the Word of God. This is why we sometimes have to interrupt John's prayer to clarify and correct. We do not want to endorse what he said unless we fully agree with it.

The Witnessing Prayer repeats, to a certain extent, what John has said but we may also add a blessing and so on. This is where the Holy Spirit sometimes leads us to pray an intercessory type prayer or blessing.

A Journey to Wholeness

The Witnessing Prayer

1. Acknowledgement, agreement and declaration concerning accusing and forgiving, based on
   a.) Accusation of wrongs done
   b.) Offering up forgiveness
   c.) Giving up rights
      — As an accuser
      — As a continuing witness

2. Acknowledgement, agreement and declaration concerning confession and forgiveness, based on
   a.) Forgiving of others
   b.) Confession
   c.) God's faithfulness, trustworthiness

3. Acknowledgement, agreement and declaration concerning bond-breaking on the physical, emotional and spiritual levels

4. Acknowledgement, agreement and declaration for cleansing from sexual defilement

5. Acknowledgement, agreement and declaration concerning memories, emotions, etc.

Heavenly Father, Connie and I acknowledge that we have heard and participated with John in his prayers. We have witnessed that he has accused and forgiven his mother and Mr. Taylor without excusing them in any way. ...

John, since you have confessed your sin and you have forgiven those who wronged you, we can say that you are forgiven in Jesus' name (because of I John 1:9).

Because of the nature of these sins, a special bonding was created. Based on John's prayer and the work of your son Jesus Christ, we can declare that the physical, emotional and spiritual bonds are hereby broken between him and Mr. Taylor. They are on longer one in spirit.

We also recognize that through molestation, spiritual defilement took place. We can say with absolute assurance that John is cleansed through the blood of Jesus Christ and is pure.

John, you are cleansed. The unholy bonds that were created through this man's sin are hereby broken.

The hurtful emotions of those times have continued to be in force. We join with John in his request that you would take the harmful emotions related to this event. They are no longer needed or wanted. In addition, the memories have been a source of discomfort and an avenue for Satan to attack John. We ask you to put these memories under the control of the Holy Spirit so they can no longer bring harm or hurtful reactions and to close this door to Satan.

The Covering Prayer

Once we have brought the past to light and the wounds uncovered, but not yet resolved, it is extremely important that we protect people from themselves and from the forces of Satan. We must not leave them vulnerable or liable to greater damage because of a lack of care or protection.

If we are in the middle of an issue or finishing for the day, and there are still issues to deal with, then it is important that we end the time with a covering prayer. God will then keep the lid on the box, so to speak, until we come together again. If we neglect to pray then the issues continue to be on the surface and can be a tremendous weight on the hurting believer. The person cannot get the rest he needs and Satan's forces can attack him. This is especially true when dealing with occult issues but applies anytime.

When it comes to keeping the lid on occult issues, I have found that a covering prayer usually lasts about a week and then I need to "renew" it.

The Covering Prayer

1. We ask the Father to build a hedge around the believer so Satan cannot have entrance.

2. We give permission to the Holy Spirit to continue his ministry through the Word, contact with others and while the believer is sleeping, etc.

Also, the Covering Prayer is for the time that we are not in session together. For example, in our first meeting with John, we got as far as taking his life history, when it was time to close the session. During our discussion over

Putting it all Together

what we were going to deal with the next day, John told us that the previous couple of nights he had had difficulty sleeping. His dreams were about Mr. Taylor in which he felt that Mr. Taylor had some kind of power over him.

Also, John kept hearing a voice inside his head, saying that his prayers would be useless. Therefore, we prayed this Covering Prayer over him.

> *Heavenly Father, thank you for what has been accomplished today. We know that there are other issues to deal with and that these can be a weight or burden on us until you bring resolution. We ask that you take these under the control of the Holy Spirit until we meet again so they do not trouble us nor permit Satan to trouble us.*
>
> *We reject any messages that are coming from the Kingdom of Darkness to trouble John. We ask that you build a wall of protection around John so these thoughts and messages cannot get through.*
>
> *We ask this in Jesus' name, amen.*

The Prayer of Release

People have spent many hours sharing with us the intimate details of their lives because they trust us. They have put themselves in our hands. We are an authority and a guide. These are not positions to take lightly and such a relationship should not continue after the last Prayer and Resolution Counseling time is over.

A Journey to Wholeness

If our position of dominance continues it becomes a detriment to these people: it will be a hindrance to them ever standing on their own two feet; they may never learn to live their Christian lives trusting their heavenly Father; nor can they learn to appreciate and appropriate for themselves what Christ has done; reliance on the Holy Spirit within themselves as they live as true children of God could be delayed.

Therefore, I close the final session with a Prayer of Release:

Heavenly Father, Connie and I acknowledge that John has put his trust in us and put himself under our authority. It was right that he did so for a time but that time has now ended. We release him from our authority and ask that you restore us to our positions as brothers and sisters in Christ so we can be free to give and receive advice, counsel, exhortation and admonition one to another.

John, you are hereby released.

Putting it all Together

Here are the elements of the prayer of release:

> **The Prayer of Release**
>
> 1. Acknowledge to the heavenly Father that he has put himself under our authority.
>   - a.) It was right to do so for this time
>   - b.) We commend him for his willing to submit
>
> 2. Ask God to restore us
>   - a.) As brothers and sister in Christ
>   - b.) With the freedom to exhort, rebuke and give counsel as equals
>
> 3. We release him from under our authority.

In counselling, prayer is more than a formality or "bookends" marking the beginning and end of a session, as if to sanctify what comes between. Rather, prayer, under the guidance of the Spirit, the authority of the Lord Jesus, and the healing touch of the Father, is the avenue through which resolution takes place.

There is a logical, natural flow to the ordered progression of these prayers, which keeps us focused, on track and with proper attention to details. Even then, we cannot pull out a printed form for this sin or that sin. Each person is unique; even similar problems take different shapes, can come from different sources and can be quite complex.

I do not, even yet, completely understand the importance of the ordered progression of these prayers or the *why* behind its emphasis. Because the *why* is not always obvious, there is a tendency to downplay the significance of these specific procedures. I used to think that God was an understanding God and would overlook the lapse in proper *protocol* if our hearts were in the right place and we just prayed in some general or haphazard way. However, I have simply not seen this to be true. On the other hand, I have seen God consistently answer our prayers as we have approached him on his terms, with the proper *protocol*.

20

Some Emotional Responses

After Prayer and Resolution Counseling, people do not normally leave full of energy! Their responses are often like those who have gone through major surgery. Instead of a high, sometimes there is a low. God is working within them and this process saps their energy and emotions. Here is what some have reported:

Extreme Fatigue

Prayer and Resolution Counseling is a physically and emotionally draining time; we feel very fatigued. It is best if we can have a break or down time, away from people we know, before we enter back into the full pressures of life with its demands in our jobs and families.

One man, after a two and half hour session, had to take a nap. Another was exhausted after less than an hour because of his emotional reaction to confronting the reality of what he had done to a young woman.

One man went back to work immediately and felt that his struggles were greater than they needed to be because he had not taken the time to process what had happened.

I remember you telling me it would be better if I stayed away from work for a few days but I felt so good after what God had done that I went to work the day after I got home. Boy, was that a mistake! I had no energy and no reserves to fall back on when I was faced with relating people, even my friends! – FS

Emotional Numbness

Often the emotions are so raw and so draining that we shut down for a time of recuperation.

All I have doing this past week is to work in the garden and stay away from everyone! I don't feel bad; I just need time alone. – AC

Need for Quiet and Reflection

One woman spent several weeks working in her garden, processing all that had happened.

All I wanted to do was to isolate myself from family and friends so I went to a ____ tournament where I did not have to interact with others except at a very superficial level. – AG

Some Emotional Responses

Delayed Emotional Response

We prayed about some deep issues of abandonment, neglect, etc. but I felt nothing during the [Prayer and Resolution Counseling] sessions. Months later, I visited my father. Suddenly I was overwhelmed with anger at him. After experiencing this for a few minutes I declared that it was OK to feel the anger but now that I had dealt with these issues the anger no longer served me and I was ready to give it up. – CA

Several weeks after dealing with very strong words of power against me, I confronted another person using nega-tive words of power on a third party, a child. In doing so, I began to cry. I sobbed uncontrollably for a time before gaining control and was able to explain I was weeping over the wretchedness I had felt in living out those words of power spoken against me. – SS

Almost a year after dealing with my parents and my growing up years I began to feel deep grief and loss and anger concerning my lost childhood. This grief and sense of loss lasted for several weeks. – RD

When watching a video about the abandonment of some children by the parents, I again felt the awful emptiness, anger, and sorrow of abandonment. In talking it out, it seems that this was a delayed reaction and one in empathy with those children and not another issue that needed to be dealt with or the redoing of something already finished. – TP

No Dramatic Change

Many have reported seeing no big or dramatic inward change but finding they are unconsciously behaving and responding differently.

Another way I say it is that you restored my self-confidence in a way like never before. Gone is that feeling of insufficiency, as well as the feeling of being dependent on E__ and her approval. I just do things now, also practical things. On the surface, it may look like nothing big, but for me it's an enormous difference. And it's not that I have to do this, but it comes from the inside. Like I said: I just do things. And only now I realize how destructive E__'s judgment has been in my life. The song, 'I am a new creation, no more in condemnation, here in the grace of God I stand' has been one of my favorites since long, but now it got even more meaning to me. In one word: I celebrate my independence and feel free now to listen to E__ without losing myself. – BD

More Energy

When M__ was about 5 years old, her father had an accident at work. He was taken to the hospital where he died. Not allowed to go to the hospital or to the funeral there had never been any closure. M__ had "searched" for her father for 40 years. Her heavenly Father allowed her to "find" him and to tell him good-by:

Once I don't need to spend a lot of time and energy searching for my Daddy anymore, I have found I am not so tired. I can do just fine on about six hours sleep.

I have much more time to think about others—to do other things. – MC

Desire to Embrace Life

Several people have mentioned that their thoughts of suicide ceased and that life was now extra special. They looked forward to getting up in the morning.

I woke this morning no longer filled with pain. . . . I realized that God was not a majesty of authority sitting on a throne waiting for me to do what is right so I can be in his presence, but that he is a spirit that dwells inside of me with as much power and strength as I will allow him to be. I saw his spirit blanket everything I saw from my window and KNEW for the first time, from deep inside my being that GOD IS ALIVE. We need only to awaken that spirit to live ourselves. I knew I AM ALIVE and I WANT TO LIVE! – DL

More Confident to Handle Life

Many have reported a new confidence in their ability to deal with life and that living was no longer a burden.

I have come to realize just how far I have come. Granted, I still have problems I need to cope with which is indicative of being human. However, the past just does not have the pull or force like it once had. In fact, I almost forget how I felt. I apply how I feel now and interpret my past with it, as if I never had a problem. It's sort of funny. I always thought I'd be forever trapped in my self-made prison of low esteem, etc. . . . But I don't want to forget how I felt. Not that I want to relive it. But that enables me to understand others who have this problem. I guess, in the nutshell, I feel free. Free to be who J___ is, whatever that is. . . . Sometimes I'm still battered with fleeting paranoid thought but it just doesn't have the hold. It goes away. – JS

Thank you for the wisdom and tools which you and the Lord imparted to (my sister). She was able to spend 2-3 days with me and the Lord broke many of the chains which I also carried. O Lord, how GREAT THOU ART! Just even in my relationship with others, I can sense more of God's freedom and ability to move through me. We really had some powerful times of breakthrough and victory, I believe. Of course, there are still struggles and battles in life, but I guess I feel better equipped. – JK

Even though I have new problems in my life, I have the tools you gave me to deal with them. What a gift! – SF

I feel so blessed to have learned the way to talk to God, receive His healing powers, and grow in Him. You taught me a most valuable tool. – GR

Struggles

After Prayer and Resolution Counseling, life may not get better. Several have reported that the next year was rough but that, after that, life was a special blessing and adventure.

Occasionally, now that the problems have been resolved, there is the struggle to make some necessary life changes. Some have broken engagements because they now realized that they got engaged for the wrong reasons or that the other party is not at the same place in their walk with God and are not willing to change.

Some Emotional Responses

Pam's fiancé was not willing to accept her healing and demanded that she renounce it. She was not willing to do this and so he broke the engagement.

One couple having both gone through the entire process decided to break off their engagement because they saw they were not compatible after all.

Fay told her beau that she would not get engaged until he had gone through the process of Prayer and Resolution Counseling so that he would know what she had gone through and also that he, too, would be whole. He did and they had a beautiful wedding and marriage to match.

There are more and more difficulties with my marriage the closer I get to God. The closer my walk, the more distance is put between me and my husband. I am learning to serve God through my marriage. I serve as I provide for my husband and fulfill my biblical obligations. It is difficult to be intimate when there is so much distance and such different views. [God, of course, will work this out]. – RG

Sometimes what we expect from life after resolution does not happen. Mick thought that now that he had dealt with all of the sexual sin in his life that this would restore his marriage. However, his wife did not want him back even though she had forgiven him. She felt that he had not accepted the fact that he was a poor husband and father in the first place. And he was unwilling to deal with those issues.

Several missionaries have left their missions after resolution of their issues. They found that the mission was an obstacle to what God was asking of them.

Others working for Christian organizations have left for many of the same reasons. A whole healthy person will no longer be satisfied working in an unhealthy environment and organization.

CONFIRMATIONS

We encourage people not to talk about their receiving healing and about their being changed people. Instead, let people come up and tell the healed ones that they are different.

When I got home, neither my sister nor her hubby knew who I was when I left a voice mail message. She said it did not sound at all like me because I was so happy. My eldest daughter said that I didn't sound like myself on the phone either because I was so happy. My best friend said I sounded so "soft" and she was amazed by my trans-formation. My youngest daughter said that I looked different; I looked so happy and pretty. People at work have been responding very positively to my face and body language. They stop and talk to me way more than they used to. One of my co-workers who has not been particularly interested in my life in the past, stopped me today and said that she really wanted to sit down and talk with me about my experience in Virginia. One of my bosses, the one that I have some difficulty with, has been so smiley and receptive to me since I got back. We have had some genuinely nice chats. – NO

Gay Lyn spent her vacation each year with a friend. She normally stood in the background while her friend arranged their travel plans at the agency. God healed Gay Lyn of some terrible issues through prayer. A few weeks after this happened, when her vacation came around, Gay Lyn again went to the travel agent with her friend. Without realizing she was behaving differently, Gay Lyn joined in the discussion with the agent. Her friend turned to her and said, *"What has happened to you, Gay Lyn? You are so different this year! It is as if I am vacationing with a different person!"*

Prayer and Resolution Counseling can drain the team if the issues are deep ones. This is especially true for people receiving the help and guidance. It is not easy to take the cover off the past and face the reality of what they or others did.

To have emotional and physical responses is to be human and in many cases is a healthy part of the grieving process over what happened or what might have been. Prayer and Resolution counselling may actually start the grieving process but it also begins the process of closure so necessary in the grieving process so that life can go on.

21

After Resolution

Prayer and Resolution Counseling is not the end-product but rather it is the means for removing the obstacles to being transformed into the image of Christ and to being all that God created us to be. When Prayer and Resolution Counseling ends, we are now *free* to make choices instead of being bound to negative patterns. Freedom implies free to make good or bad choices.

Thank you over and over again for your willingness to love me and to teach me what I have longed all my life to know, how to experientially live a life with the Father's hand in mine. I will love you both until the day I die for that wonderful gift. – ON

A new set of considerations come into play after the Prayer and Resolution Counseling process has been completed. Among these are: post emotional responses; how do we move on with our lives and what do we do when new issues do come up? How do we build new and healthy patterns for living?

Sometimes we experience dramatic resolution of issues in our lives but go on to make bad choices that lead us further astray until we find ourselves back in a quagmire. The issues that have been resolved stay resolved. Nevertheless, we can build new harmful patterns and resurrect old issues by new bad choices.

How do we go on from here and walk in the new found freedom, to live out whom God created us and then redeemed us to be. The first step is actively to walk with God.

PARTNERING WITH GOD

The most important principle to remember is that this has been, is, and will be, a work by God. The new life, freedom and more healthy patterns in confronting life will come out of what he, the heavenly Father, the Almighty God, has done and is continuing to do in the inner person. Behavior, feelings, actions and reactions will all flow out of the inward changes.

It is not up to us to make these changes happen. It is up to us to work in partnership with the Holy Spirit so that we do not get in the way or hinder his work in our lives.

I feel like God is teaching me things and speaking to me directly again and I'm not being controlled by every wave of adversity and temptation. The challenges are still there but I'm learning to meet them in partnership with God instead of in my dysfunctions. All this has been . . . to let you know God used you to reveal Himself and bring healing that may not have been possible any other way . . .. You opened doors of consideration that left me in awe after our sessions. – JB

A Journey to Wholeness

I now realize that God loves me just the way I am, and I can come to Him at any time and ask Him for anything I need. I feel so liberated and free and am no longer carrying around the many events that I wanted to hide. Stuffing can be a very destructive thing and I do it no more. You have given me the tools to breathe free and deal with feelings and events in a more productive way. I no longer have that overwhelming feeling of insurmountable sadness, guilt and yearning for love. – GF

I already used the words 'free' and 'judgment'. That's again another way to say it: I experience a totally new freedom; freedom from bondages, from guilt, and from lies and misconceptions and—very strongly—from the judgment of people. It's not that the old patterns are gone completely, but I'm learning very fast to live out my newly found freedom. And a nice thing is that someone said, "You are even more free than before you went to the States." I can see that. – DB

The work that started during my stay with you is going on. One of the last, but not least developments: some weeks ago I suddenly realized for that for many years I did not really see my wife as a person I had to take care of. In the beginning of our marriage I cam home from work, thinking: Now I'm going to be taken care of, going to be served. That was my conviction, deep down, and when I gave her time and attention, it was out of a sense of duty. About twenty hears ago I found out how selfish my attitude was and I wanted to change it. I was not very successful. Ten years ago I saw that one of the roots was that I was spoiled as a boy (no excuse!). But I still acted out of that sense of duty. This was my new discovery a few weeks ago: I lived out the model my parents had shown me!! That was the model of a wife as a person who takes care of her husband and of a husband as a person to be taken care of, and that's it. The duty of a man lay in his work. When I was with you, I rejected that model and you broke its impact on my life. And only now I feel that I really want to take care of her, from within. Isn't it amazing? And awesome! – BD

Satan has come at me from all directions to steal what has been done and I almost gave in to it as Suicide thoughts began to assault my mind along with thoughts to doubt God's love and care of me. BUT I believe due to the counseling something new was working in me—I could go to <u>MY FATHER*!!*</u> – SG

Here are a few suggestions of what *partnering with God* looks like:

Giving God Time

God made us with the ability to create habits. Habits are useful in that we can live and behave without conscious thought about many things. We automatically turn the key a certain way when we unlock the car door. We tie our shoes without thinking of the procedure.

It normally takes *twenty-one days* to create or break a habit.[65] God has made us this way. Habits are useful in that we can live and behave without conscious thought about many things. We can breathe without thinking about it.

We need to reject bad habits and have God destroy the force and power of these in our lives. Even after God has answered our prayers, however, the habits do not just go away and die. God can have answered our prayers but we can continue to have recurring habit patterns surfacing for a week or more. Nurture the good

---

[65] Maxwell Maltz, M.D., *Psycho-Cybernetics* (New York: Pocket Books, 1969), pp. xiii-xvi.

ones and starve the bad ones. We can continue automatically to look at women with lust. Nevertheless, God is working and we must work in partnership with the Holy Spirit. It takes some twenty-one days for a habit to die completely.

God has cut the root and broken its force. Nevertheless, like a chicken with its head cut off, it continues to run around. It still looks and acts alive for a time. Either we can nurture it by using it or we can starve it by not feeding it. We can bring it back to life or help put it fully to death. We want to cooperate and partner with the Holy Spirit during these important three weeks to permit him to complete the job.

We are not talking about taking on the task of breaking the habit. We are talking about recognizing the work God is doing within us and helping it along by not feeding the wrong. During this period, our job is to partner with the Holy Spirit as he brings about these changes.

The same applies to good habits. They take time to establish. At first, we may need to consciously practice and act out the new pattern. As time goes on, again the twenty-one days, the new wholesome pattern will take root and become a natural part of us. Our task is to feed the good and starve the bad but it is not our job to do God's work for him.

Giving Myself Time

It is good to remember that, while the specific intervention by God was at a point in time, the outworking of that resolution is a process. We must love and respect ourselves enough to give ourselves time for this on-going process. When we get impatient and want it *all* right now, then we disrespect ourselves and begin to distrust our heavenly Father. Partnering means that we do all that we can do, ask God for help in all that we cannot do, and ask for him to do his part, leaving to him all those things that are not ours to do.

"I do believe [my part]; help me overcome my unbelief [God's part]!" (Mark 9: 24 NIV)

. . . I sense a greater ability to rest and an ability to be confident in God and his work in my life. – GS

Rejecting the Lie

Normally, with sexual and occult related sins, the results are complete at the end of the prayer time but we often have to face down for a time the lies, labels, and harmful emotions attached to bad memories. This does not mean God has not answered, it means that the roots are dying but are not dead yet. We should not feed them or they will come back to life!

When a lie or a past/poor response to a situation resurfaces then we must:

- ✓ Recognize it
- ✓ Reject it
- ✓ Declare the truth

This evening Satan was trying to use an old memory to accuse me . . . make me feel guilty . . . But I reminded him I had dealt with that and he could no longer use it against me. What a good feeling that was. – MC

I've had the opportunity to experience a situation here . . . that I felt shame and fear, but as I began to feel grieved—I did not allow myself to continue, I spoke truth to myself that there was no reason for shame or fear. I had not dishonored God, my heart and motive were pure

and that I was a good, respectable lady here... Now, that's significant! – GS

Focusing on Truth and Righteousness

We must consciously focus on truth and uprightness throughout the day until it becomes an unconscious habit.

When we set our sights on the light of righteousness and truth there is no place for darkness—darkness is behind us. However, if we turn and begin to focus on the darkness of unrighteousness we will quickly lose sight of the light.

There must be a conscious focus on and looking for input from those things that are:

- ✓ Righteous
- ✓ Lovely
- ✓ Pure
- ✓ Of a good report
- ✓ Uplifting and encouraging
- ✓ True
- ✓ Good and right

We must make a conscious effort to recognize and ignore or put aside those things which are lies, negatives or ungodly. These things do not draw us closer to the Kingdom of Light.

Satan has not let me alone since I left Virginia, but I am practicing what I learned and I realize now that he cannot defeat me when I am partnered with my Heavenly Father, Jesus Christ and the Holy Spirit. He can growl really loud but he has no power in the face of God. What a force there is along side me and what a wonder that I am privileged enough to be the Child of the Heavenly Father! – ON

So I'm living my 'old life', but I feel quite different! When I try to explain and describe to people what the difference is like, I'm looking for words. Till now I think the best way to describe it is to say 'I feel straightened out'. Through the lies and misconceptions I had about myself and the things I was guilty of (better: the measure in which I was guilty) I grew crooked (like the tower of Pisa). God through you corrected that and now I feel like I'm standing straight on my feet. – BD

Making Decisions

When we have decisions to make, part of the input is:

- ✓ What would be consistent with who we are as created beings and who we are as redeemed children of God?

- ✓ Does this lead us towards our goals or away from our goals?

One thing I have especially begun to like is being able to make a decision and feel confident in what I have decided . . . being ready to accept responsibility for my decisions . . . no matter if others don't agree with me. People keep telling me what a difference there is in me. – SJ

Be Wise

It is not a sin to be tempted, even Christ was tempted. It is, however, a sin to yield to or give too much credence to that temptation.

We should not put ourselves in harm's way. We should avoid unhealthy places and people. If we know we have certain areas of temptation then we should stay away from them and focus on something else.

When we stop looking for those areas and focus our time and attention on something righteous then when we inadvertently come upon those old areas of temptation, we will find them powerless.

With resolution comes a change in the way we view life. For example, instead of lusting after every woman with pretty legs, NG found he was now seeing these women as precious creations of God and lust was no longer there.

When I was at the mall recently, I came across the porno magazine _____. Talk about God's healing! Instead of being tempted, I only felt repulsed by such material! – SP

I now realize that God loves me just the way I am, and I can come to Him at any time and ask Him for anything I need. I feel so liberated and free and am no longer carrying around the many events that I wanted to hide. Stuffing can be a very destructive thing and I do it no more. You have given me the tools to breathe free and deal with feelings and events in a more productive way. I no longer have that overwhelming feeling of insurmountable sadness, guilt and yearning for love. – GF

Regular Time with God and the Word

If we are to have a relationship with God, we need to have a regular time with him just as we would with any other. We encourage people to get another version of the Bible to read, one they are not familiar with and have not marked up. We want them to read the Scriptures from their new perspective. As one man put it, "*It is as if I have never read it before and it is written just to me!*"

I have begun to read in the Old Testament as you suggested. It amazes me how different it seems now. My feelings are so changed [since resolution]. It's almost like someone rewrote the Bible! – MC

- ✓ For feeding: Reading the Word and listening to him
- ✓ For meditating
- ✓ For prayer
- ✓ For worship
- ✓ For praise
- ✓ For confession
- ✓ For supplication
- ✓ For intercession

. . . I'm excited to see God, the Father working in my heart and life. The most significant difference has been in my prayer life and my time in the Word. It feels fresh, more alive and very personal. – GS

God is here! ☺ *I'm more conscious of His presence. I'm eager to understand God's truths and put them to practice, and to learn to pray with more understanding.* – LK

Self-Help Books

There is a lot of very good material out there. Many of the self-help books, tapes and videos may be useful to us now since there has been resolution of the roots of the problem.

There seems to be something written on every kind of struggle we may encounter. Once the root has been resolved, there may now be a need for information, feeding and the exercise of new patterns and so on. There may be a need to learn better communication skills or to under-stand more clearly who we have been created to be or how to be better in tune with our own sexuality.

Satan would love to rob me of my freedom from my bondage. I know I am free but still struggled with this issue. Although I had asked my Father to break the bonds, I needed to relearn the area of healthy bonding.

We purchased a book entitled A Celebration of Sex by Douglas Rosenau . . . it has helped me to relearn and to establish a good foundation for intimacy with my husband. Our times together are now a joyous celebration of what God intended. – J R

Therapist

We might want to see a therapist or be in a support group to help us establish and strengthen our new healthier life patterns now that the negative power sources have been resolved.

After Resolution

On Wednesday evening, I saw my counselor, MT___. When he first came out he looked at me in an exaggerated way and tilted his head and said, "I'm trying to see if there is any kind of special glow coming off of you." Then we laughed. I smiled broadly and told him that I felt like I was glowing. He said, "Tell me all about it then." What he seemed the most interested in was how the prayers went. I was miraculously able to remember the structure of the prayer [and resolution] times and I went through them with him. He seemed to grasp right away what each statement meant or the purpose of the statement to God. When our time was almost up, he said that I had told him so much that he was not able to process it all, but that something had definitely changed in me and he was intrigued. He said that he was cautiously optimistic that I had indeed experienced emotional healing. I am going to go to two more counseling sessions, partly because he really did not want to let me go yet. I FELT that it was because he was very interested in prayer [and resolution] counseling and he wants to see for himself if it has really changed me in a permanent way. – NO

Sharing with Others

I see things different now. I see the WHYs of witnessing. One cannot witness as well out of obligation, but when it comes from a thankful heart, recognizing what God has done, it becomes 'natural' (due to supernatural)! – ES

Normally, we tell people not to share what God has done. Instead, we suggest that they to go home and live life. Let God bring someone into their lives that sees the difference in them and brings it up.

We will have the witness of our own spirit that God is continuing to do his work in us but how special it is when others notice the change. That is outside confirmation of our inward change.

On Wednesday morning, I went to prayer with the B__ women. Only one other woman was there but I was so excited because it was the other divorced woman who is searching for emotional healing just like I had been. Her name is, M___, the psychology professor/counselor. When we sat down she said, "We have been praying for you while you were gone, tell me all about it." I talked almost non-stop (because she kept encouraging me to tell her more) for 45 minutes. When her next client came she said, "N__, I want to go to Virginia and do prayer [and resolution] counseling with them. How much does it cost? How do I contact them?" I was amazed because when I started talking she made a couple of statements that showed she was skeptical. I think that was her psychologist voice speaking. When I was done she was relaxed, teary eyed and so soft and vulnerable. She asked me if you two were safe. I said, "YES!" – NO

God will continue to do his work from the inside out after we have finished our prayers. Our job is to let him get on with the process without our getting in the way.

A word of caution: when we explain what God has done in our lives we must guard what we do share. Once God has answered our prayers, we have no need to share the sordid details with others. Others include spouses, children, other family members, friends or strangers.

We can share the principles behind prayer and resolution counseling that brought healing to us but we do not share the garbage with others. *Especially, we do not share the garbage with our husband or wife.* If we do so, then we will give them a burden they cannot easily put down.

In Africa, we spent time with a woman in prayer and resolution counselling. She and her husband brought up her past—he only knew that she had previous relations before marriage. Before we asked her about her sexual encounters, we had her husband leave the room. He did not need to know how many and who these men were.

He was healthy enough not to *want* to know more. Another husband, upon hearing that the woman he married had had sexual relations before marriage, could not let it rest. He constantly brought up her past and wanted to know who the men were and the details. She rightfully refused to tell him.

It was only after prayer and resolution counselling that he stopped seeking the sordid details of her past life.

Being in Fellowship

We encourage people to seek the company of other Christians. *"Let us not give up meeting together, as some are in the habit of doing, but let us encourage one another – and all the more as you see the Day approaching"* (Hebrews 10: 25). They need to get together with other Christians for encouragement and uplifting. One is able to be stronger than the one when with others of like-mind.

People should have some spiritual disciplines: prayer, Bible reading, reaffirming the truths they have learned. Above all, people must claim their rightful places in the family of God and live and behave in keeping with their being sons or daughters of God.

Staying in Touch

We do encourage people to phone or write if they have questions or need encouragement. However, we are not the Holy Spirit, nor are we the standard by which they should live.

There is potential for an abuse of power and a temptation to take over people's live but we must reject this. This is why we have included a "prayer of release." People must learn to live their lives confidently in the abiding presence of God: Father, Son and Holy Spirit.

After Prayer and Resolution Counseling, life may get more complicated. When people have victories, they need to share these and the Prayer and Resolution Counseling team needs the encouragement!

After Prayer and Resolution Counseling, we want four things to happen:

1. The force and power of sin no longer dominates people's lives.

2. People walk away with a greater appreciation and acceptance of who they are as creations of God.

3. People walk away with a greater appreciation and acceptance of who they are as sons and daughters of God.

After Resolution

4. People walk away with the tools to deal with life and keep short accounts so they can continue to walk in freedom and righteousness.

It takes time to accept and let all these things happen but God will do his work within us and that will affect our attitudes and outward behaviour in often unconscious ways.

Here is one young woman's response to her time in Prayer and Resolution Counseling.:

How can I express my endless gratitude to you both for the joyous life you have given back to me? How can I thank the people who support you, enabling you to free me from the bonds of, and cleanse me from the defilement of, child-hood molestation, incest, rape, and fornication?

You have made it possible for me to call my God "my Heavenly Father" without mistrust and fear and pain. You have made it possible for me to see my Heavenly Father as the daddy I deserved to have.

Through you, my Father in Heaven has restored my mental and emotional stability and my sense of identity—unique and separate from anyone else. . . . – BR

22

Conclusion

I have presented an overview of Prayer and Resolution Counselling in this book. When someone comes for help, Connie and I usually start with a life history. From it, we, together with the hurting one and the Holy Spirit, determine the areas that we need to present to the heavenly Father.

No session is like another. Each person is unique. Each issue is different in its particular circumstances and development. An issue can affect one person very differently from another person and yet the sin and the circumstances can be similar. This means that there is no printed sheet to pull out when we address a particular sin.

There are certain aspects, however, that we must handle, depending on the category of sin: sexual sins have aspects that occult sins do not. Words of power and lies have their own considerations.

The character of God is unchanging. The more we learn as students of prayer and the more we utilize the system that God has put in place, the more fully we will see resolution and victory over sin and the forces of sin.

Normally we deal with sexual issues first. Ninety-nine point nine percent of the time, sexual sin is an issue.

Conclusion

Sexual sins are garbage that blurs the other issues of life and this tends to feed and create the ground for other unhealthy patterns. Also, people tend to experience release in a more powerful way that when we deal with other issues—except for the occult

From the beginning, the importance of forgiveness has been evident. Everyone says forgive but what does that really mean? I have two theology books in my office and neither one spends more than *a paragraph* on forgiveness. Neither defined forgiveness. When other books did not help me to handle the issues in practical ways then I have written my own. So I began with a booklet, *Forgiveness: An Act of Mercy and a Key to Answered Prayer*. Forgiveness is still as central as I first thought. Anytime people come to us with anger or hatred, pain or sorrow, forgiveness will be a consideration.

Later, I found more than forgiveness was needed to bring resolution and wrote: *Cleansing: Resolving the Consequences of Sexual Sin*. Rarely have we had someone come who has not had a sexual encounter, as a victim, partner or perpetrator. Sexual sin has many aspects that I am only beginning to understand. For example, when it comes to dealing with those under bondage to pornography, there are both sexual and occult implications.

People kept bring up situations where there were destructive words of power: hurtful words from a parent or authority, an unwise or unfulfilled vow, a wrong dedication. I found I needed to write, *Freedom from Words of Power: Breaking the Chains of Harmful Declarations, Vows and Lies* to help describe the steps to be taken in order to gain this freedom.

It seems like we always have to deal with some violation of authority. Resisting or cursing one's parents was a capital offence in the Old Testament. In the modern family parents do betray their children and the children do learn to distrust and rebel against their parents. We must deal with such sins to heal and restore the family relationships when possible.

This power and attitude, out of control, effects our submission to, and trust of, any authority—even God's.

Another area that is becoming an increasing problem centers on the occult. Satan will use whatever place or foothold we give him. As Satanism increases, as cults flourish, as missionaries continue to live in strange cultures unaware of the spiritual forces at work, there is a need to know how to deal with the occult, past and present. This demands an entirely different approach in prayer.

So now, I am writing a book on handling occult issues. I write a book when I find that other authors allude to resolution but do not show us how to do it. My emphasis has been on the practical and with details that other authors leave out. I am presenting this topic in more detail in a separate book in the future.[66]

This book has been more on the general theme of what Prayer and Resolution Counseling is all about. I have not gone into specific details on handling sexual sins, occult sins, rebellion, words of power or even forgiveness.

As people go further into Prayer and Resolution Counseling, they should read the other booklets and books. Prayer and Resolution Counseling is not easy but it is a blessing.

We must always remember that healing does not come through us; it comes from God. We are only channels—maybe facilitators is a better word—as we act in our priestly function. It is both a privilege and a responsibility.

---

[66] Possible title, *Resolving the Consequences of Occult Involvement*, by the author.

Conclusion

If God should bring someone into our lives to help in Prayer and Resolution Counseling, we should not be afraid. God has provided all we need for resolution in Christ's death and resurrection. When we approach God as our heavenly Father, we will see the issues more clearly.

Unfortunately, issues do not come in neat and tidy bunches but appear as a mess of tangled string: here some sexual sin; there some authority violation; over here some occult influence and there some unwise vows or words of power. And intermixed in the tangle are smaller strands that represent the accompanying sins of bitter-ness, anger, hatred and false guilt, just to name a few.

Scars are there in the knots of hurt and pain, sorrow and lies, and terror.

The tangled mess looks impossible to unravel, but when we believers are desperate enough to be honest with God and ourselves, then he will help us. There is a need for Safe Others to share our burdens for the time it takes to give these over into God's hands. With care and gentleness, the Holy Spirit really does direct, reveal and unravel. He shows us the first significant strand and we begin . . .

Bibliography

The bibliography does not necessarily reflect my approval of the authors' views. I believe that we must review, reaffirm and test what we have believed through the years. Too often, we have read familiar scriptures and not clearly considered what they said nor the implications.

I may not disagree with certain authors but feel that they have taken too much for granted. They have assumed that everyone knows, for example, what forgiveness is. They have assumed that God fills in the blanks in our prayers when I have seen otherwise.

Adams, Jay E. *Competent to Counsel*. Grand Rapids: Baker Book House, 1970.

Anderson, Neil T. *The Bondage Breaker*. Eugene, OR: Harvest House, 1990.

Augsburger, David. *Caring Enough to Forgive—Caring Enough Not to Forgive*. Ventura, CA: Regal Books, 1981.

Backus, William. *Telling Each Other the Truth*. Minneapolis, MN: Bethany House, 1985.

_____. *Telling the Truth to Troubled People*. Minneapolis, MN: Bethany House, 1985.

Bibliography

Backus, William & Marie Chapian. *Telling Yourself the Truth.* Minneapolis, MN: Bethany House, 1980.

Barclay, William. *The Ten Commandments for Today.* Grand Rapids: Wm. B. Eerdmans, 1973.

Bass, Ellen and Laura Davis. *The Courage to Heal.* New York: Harper & Row, 1988.

Beattie, Melody. *Co-dependent No More.* New York, NY: Harper-Hagelder, Harper & Row Publishers, 1987.

Bennett, Rita. *How to Pray for Inner Healing for Yourself and Others.* Old Tappan, NJ: Fleming H. Revell, 1984.

Black, Claudia. *It Will Never Happen To Me!* New York: Ballantine Books, 1981.

Blume, E. Sue. *Secret Survivors: Uncovering Incest and its Effects in Women.* New York: Ballantine Books, 1991.

Bobgan, Martin & Deidre Bobgan. *Psychoheresy: The Psychological Seduction of Christianity.* Santa Barbara, CA: Eastgate Publishers, 1987.

Brand, Paul, and Yancey, Paul. *Fearfully & Wonderfully Made.* Grand Rapids, MI: Zondervan, 1980.

_____. *In His Image.* Grand Rapids, MI. Zondervan, 1984.

Bubeck, Mark I. *The Adversary.* Chicago, IL: Moody Press, 1975.

Chapian, Marie. *Love and Be Loved.* Old Tappen, NJ: Fleming H. Revell, 1983.

Chaplin, James P. & T. S. Krawiec. *Systems and Theories of Psychology.* New York: Holt, Rinehart and Winston, 1960.

Crabb, Larry. *Effective Biblical Counseling.* Grand Rapids: Zondervan, 1977.

Collins, Gary. *Psychology and Theology: Prospects for Integration.* Nashville: Abingdon, 1981.

____. "Christian Counseling and the Church" in *Christian Counseling Today* (Vol 7, No. 2), 1999.

Cowan, Connell and Melvyn Kinder. *Smart Women Foolish Choices.* New York: New American Library, 1985.

Dalbey, Gordon. *Healing the Masculine Soul.* Dallas, TX: Word Publishing, 1988.

Day, Larry, G. *By Design and in God's Image.* PO Box 33024, Portland, OR 97233: MT Tabor Press, 1992.

Dickason, C. Fred. *Demon Possession and the Christian.* Chicago, IL: Moody Press, 1987.

Ellis, Albert and Catharine MacLaren. *Rational Emo-*

Bibliography

tive *Behavior Therapy: A Therapist's Guide* (Practical Therapist Series). Atascadero, CA: Impact Publishers, 1998.

Ellis, Henry, C. and R. Reed Hunt. *Fundamentals of Cognitive Psychology.* Dubuque, IA: Brown & Benchmark, 1993.

Ensign, Grayson H. and Edward Howe. *Bothered? Bewildered? Bewitched?* Cincinnati: Recovery, 1984.

Epstein, Robert. "Why Shrinks have so Many Problems," in *Psychology Today* (July/August), 1997.

Frank, Jan. "Rebuild Self-Image and Relationships" in *A Door of Hope.* San Bernardino, CA: Here's Life Publishers, 1987.

Freud, Sigmund. *A General Introduction to Psychoanalysis.* New York: Liveright, 1920.

_____. *About Behaviorism.* New York: Knopf, 1974.

Friesen, James G. *Uncovering the Mystery of MPD.* San Bernadino, CA: Here's Life Publishers, 1991.

Glasser, William. *Reality Therapy: A New Approach to Psychiatry.* New York: Harper and Row, 1965.

Glennon, Jim. *How Can I Find Healing?* London: Hodder and Stoughton, 1984.

Harris, Thomas A. *I'm Ok - You're Ok.* London: Pan Books, 1969.

Hawkins, Tom R. & Hawkins, Diane W. *Healing Process for DID*. Grottoes, VA: Restoration in Christ Ministries.

Howard, Grant, J. *The Trauma of Transparency*. Portland, OR: Multnomah Press, 1979.

Janov, Arthur. *The Primal Scream*. New York: Dell Publishing, 1970.

Johnson, David & Jeff VanVonderen. *The Subtle Power of Spiritual Abuse*. Minneapolis, MN: Bethany House, 1991.

Jung, Carl G. "Psychotherapists or the clergy," in *Modern Man in Search of a Soul*. New York: Harcourt, Brace, 1933.

_____. *Psychology and the Occult*, translated by R. F. C. Hull. Princeton: Princeton University Press, 1977.

Kelsey, Morton T. *Healing and Christianity*. New York: Harper & Row, 1973.

_____. *How to Forgive*. Glorieta, NM: Dove Leaflet # 75, 1995.

Lindsey, Hal. *Satan is Alive and Well on Planet Earth*. Grand Rapids, MI: Zondervan, 1972.

Maltz, Maxwell, M.D. *Psycho-Cybernetics*. New York: Pocket Books, 1969.

Bibliography

McCormick, Patrick. *Sin as Addiction.* New York, NY: Paulist Press, 1989.

McDowell, Josh. *His Image My Image.* San Bernardino, CA: Here's Life Publishers, 1984.

McGee, Robert, S. *The Search for Significance.* Houston, TX: Rapha, 1990.

McKay, Matthew & Patrick Fanning. *Self Esteem.* New York, NY: MJF Books, 1987.

Mowrer, Hobart O. *The Crisis in Psychiatry and Religion.* Princton: Van Nostrand, 1961.

Norwood, Robin. *Women Who Love Too Much.* New York: Pocket Books (Simon & Schuster), 1985.

Osborne, Cecil. *The Art of Understanding Yourself.* Grand Rapids, MI: Zondervan Books, 1967.

Payne, Leanne. *The Healing of the Homosexual.* Westchester IL: Crossway Books, 1984.

_____. *Crisis in Masculinity.* Westchester, IL: Crossway Books, 1985.

Peck, M., Scott. *People of the Lie: The Hope for Healing Human Evil.* New York: Simon & Simon, 1983.

_____. *The Road Less Traveled and Beyond: Spiritual Growth in the Age of Anxiety.* New York: Simon & Schuster, 1997.

Piper, John. *What's the Difference? Manhood and Womanhood Defined According to the Bible.* Wheaton, IL. Crossway Books, 1990.

Piper, John and Wayne Grudem. *Recovering Biblical Manhood and Womanhood.* Wheaton, IL. Crossway Books, 1991.

Price, Ron. "Mental Health Attitude," in *The Healthy Cell Concept.* Nampa, Idaho: AIM International, 1989.

Prince, Derek. *Blessing or Curse: Your Can Choose.* Grand Rapids, MI: Chosen Books, 1990.

Roberts, Ted. *Pure Desire.* Ventura, CA: Regal, a Division of Gospel Light, 1999.

Rogers, Carl R. *Client-centered Therapy: Its Current Practice, Implications, and Theory.* Boston: Houghton Mifflin, 1951.

Rosenau, Douglas E. *A Celebration of Sex.* Nashville, TN: Thomas Nelson, 1994.

Rubin, Theodore I. *The Angry Book.* New York, NY: Collier Books, 1969.

Sala, Darlene. *Created for a Purpose.* Uhrichsville, OH: Barbour Publishing, Inc., 1999.

Sala, Harold. *Coffee Cup Counseling.* Nashville, TN: Thomas Nelson Publishers, 1989.

Bibliography

Sandford, John L. *Why Some Christians Commit Adultery.* Tulsa, OK: Victory House, 1989.

Sandford, John & Paula. *Transformation of the Inner Man.* S. Plainsfield, NJ: Bridge Publishing, 1982.

_____. *Healing the Wounded Spirit.* S. Plainsfield, NJ: Bridge Publishing, 1985.

_____. *Restoring the Christian Family.* Tulsa, OK: Victory House, 1986.

Sandford, Paula. *Healing Victims of Sexual Abuse.* Tulsa, OK: Victory House, 1988.

Schaef, Anne Wilson. *Co-Dependence Misunderstood—Mistreated.* San Francisco, CA: Harper & Row, 1986.

Schlessinger, Laura and Rabbi Stewart Vogel. *The Ten Commandments: The Significance of God's Laws in Every-day Life.* New York, NY: First Cliff Street Books, 1998.

Shults, F. Leron & Steven J. Sandage. *The Faces of Forgiveness: Searching for Wholeness and salvation.* Grand Rapids, Baker Academic, 2003.

Seamands, David A. *Healing for Damaged Emotions.* Wheaton, IL: Victor Books, 1981.

_____. *Putting Away Childish Things*. Wheaton, IL: Victor Books, 1982.

_____. *Healing of Memories*. Wheaton, IL: Victor Books, 1985.

_____. *Healing Grace*. Wheaton, IL: Victor Books, 1988.

_____. *God's Blueprint for Living*. Bucks, England: Scripture Press, 1988

Shostrom, Everett, L. *Man, the Manipulator; the Inner Journey from Manipulation to Actualization*. Nashville, TN: Abingdon Press, 1967.

Skinner, B. F. *About Behaviorism*. New York: Knopf, 1974.

Smalley, Gary & John Trent. *The Blessing*. Nashville, TN: Thomas Nelson, 1986.

Smith, Richard D. *Forgiveness: An Act. of Mercy and a Key to Answered Prayer*. Bland VA: CM Publications, 1998.

_____. *Cleansing: Resolving the Consequences of Sexual Sin*. Laguna Niguel, CA: Cross Ministries, 1991.

_____. *Freedom from Words of Power: Breaking the Chains of Harmful Declarations, Vows and Lies*. Bland, VA: CM Publications, 2000.

Bibliography

Stapleton, Ruth Carter. *The Experience of Inner Healing*. New York: Bantam Books, 1977.

Stern, Paul J. *C.G. Jung, The Haunted Prophet*. New York: Dell, 1976.

Tapscott, Ruth. Set *Free through Inner Healing*. Kingwood, TX: Hunter Books, 1978.

Thorp, Louis P. & Barney Katz. *The Psychology of Abnormal Behavior: A Dynamic Approach*. New York: The Ronald Press, 1948.

Vredevelt, Pamela, & Rodriguez, Kathryn. *Surviving the Secret*. Grand Rapids, MI: Fleming H. Revell, 1992.

Walters, Richard P. *Forgive and Be Free*. Grand Rapids, MI: Zondervan, 1983.

Ward, Ruth McRoberts. *Self-Esteem: Gift from God*. Grand Rapids, MI: Baker Book House, 1984.

Watson, Thomas. The Ten Commandments. London: The Banner of Truth Trust, 1965.

Wegscheider-Cruse, Sharon. Learning to Love Yourself: Finding Your Self-Worth. Pompano Beach, FL: Health Communications, 1987.

Wertheimer, Max. *Productive Thinking*. New York: Harper & Row, 1959.

Whitfield, Charles L. *Healing the Child Within.* Deerfield Beach, FL: Health Communications, 1987.

Woititz, Janet Geringer. *Adult Children of Alcoholics.* Pompano Beach, FL: Health Communications, Inc., 1721 Blount Road, Suite 1.

Worthington, Everett, L. Jr. *Forgiving and Reconciling Bridges to Wholeness and Hope.* Downers Grove, IL: InterVarsity, 2003.